THE FIRE WE INHERIT

LARIC TOLLESON

AFTERFIRE BOOKS

For every kid (and kid at heart) who is stronger and more capable than they know.

Contents

1

FIRST DAY ON THE JOB

"Now that we know our kids will not succumb to the sickness as the rest of us have, many have wondered what their future holds once we are gone. Will they starve? Will they have to fight and kill for survival?

"I'm addressing every Las Vegas citizen here today to tell you—no, they will not. We have a plan! A plan that will ensure that the future of our kids is bright. But this plan will not work without every available hand helping prepare the way. And I mean every.

"We have less than three years—three years to create ranches and farms for sustainable food. Three years to convert all gas-powered machines to electric, so our kids won't be without power or transportation. Three years to build production, manufacturing, and storage facilities so our kids can create their own goods and be self-reliant. Many

of the casinos have agreed to fund this endeavor, since their fate is linked to ours.

"But who's going to run it all?... Our kids! We have three years to prepare them—to teach them the skills to keep everything functioning, to turn them into adults. They must be able to grow, produce, build, and sustain everything that will allow them to thrive—not simply survive. I will not allow this city that I love to turn into a pile of desolate ash. Our days are numbered, but we can ensure our kids' days are endless.

"But we need buy-in from every adult, because if we don't believe our kids can do it, our kids won't believe either. So, believe... Believe that this will be the greatest achievement known to mankind. Believe... that this will be our legacy."
— Mayor Cathleen Goodson, three years before the After

The After

Countless times I'd been in this fire house before. I'd sat in that chair across the table for Thanksgiving. I'd played cards with my dad right over there. I could practically hear his laughter echoing through the station.

Six years ago, he was exposed. Three years ago, his voice fell silent—just like every other adult's.

For a second, I was back in my childhood. Back in the Before. I shook my head, shoving aside the distant thoughts of the past to focus on the present, rolling my dad's old black silicone wrist band between my fingers. The red stripe down the middle was faded from years of use. It was one of the last things he ever gave me—right before our world changed. I swore then that I would never take it off. Now, it was all I had left of him, a daily reminder to follow in his enormous footsteps.

Today was the day I'd been preparing for the last few years. I was now a full-fledged firefighter assigned to Station 3. Though I had spent countless hours in this once-familiar place, I was now a stranger, the new guy. Everything looked the same, although the new "Station 3" sign hanging above the kitchen table reminded me that long gone were the three million citizens and the sixty fire stations from the Before.

Only six stations remained—six stations to serve the 300,000 kids who survived.

Standing where my dad once stood felt surreal, but the pressure weighed heavily on me. I had to make him proud. I stood tall in the corner of the room as the rest of the firefighters filed in for morning muster. Some brushed by me without a second glance, carrying on their conversations as if I weren't there. Others studied me, looking into my soul as if they were determining my worth. A couple looked my age, but some were obviously a little older.

I straightened up, hoping to appear confident despite my stomach's churning.

Captain Jefferson entered last, and the chatter died immediately. I snapped to attention, avoiding eye contact with everyone and staring at the wall. Even without his thick mustache—a rare sight in the After—this was the kind of man you listened to. If I hadn't known he couldn't possibly be more than two or three years older than me, his lightly salt-and-peppered hair would have convinced me he was much older. If ever there was someone who looked like a fire captain, it was him. His dark eyes, tired but kind, landed on me.

"Good morning, everyone," he said, his voice firm and raspy. "I'm sure you have spotted a new face with us today. Why don't you tell us about yourself, rookie?"

"Yes, sir."

My voice cracked through my tightening throat. The rehearsed speech I had practiced so many times for my sisters felt clumsy and disorganized. I took a deep breath, attempting to calm my nerves.

"My name is Aiden Brann. I was born and raised here in Las Vegas, like most of you. I have two sisters at home. Aubrey is the oldest, and she is a 911 dispatcher for us. I bet you would recognize her voice. My younger sister, Ally, is a massage therapist and works out of our house. My dad, Ashton Brann, was a Captain in the Before at this very station." I paused, shoving down the emotions that attempted to boil to the surface. "I'm excited to follow in his footsteps and ready to help people the best I can. I want to learn everything you all have to teach me. And... I just turned 14 yesterday."

A slow clap broke the silence. I met eyes with a gargantuan, freckled-faced, red-headed tank reclined in his chair. He leaned back, revealing his workout shorts, even though everyone else wore pants with their shirts tucked in. He continued to clap sarcastically, thoroughly unimpressed.

"Quite the moving speech," he said. "Must have taken you weeks to come up with it. Reed isn't buying it, though. You know this is the busiest station in the city, right? Reed has been here since day one and doesn't think you are ready."

I flinched. Who was he talking about? Oh, he meant himself.

"I think I..." I began, but Reed cut me off with a wave.

"You got any jokes, Rook?"

Jokes? Of all the things I trained for, this wasn't one of them. My hands began to sweat as I scrambled for something, anything, to say.

"Uh, why shouldn't you write with a broken pencil?" I asked with a pathetic attempt at a smile. "Because it would be pointless."

Dead silence. I scanned the room, looking for even the slightest smirk from anyone. But none came. No longer standing tall, my once-confident demeanor wavered as they stared at me with judgmental eyes.

Then I realized how dumb my joke was. We rarely used pencils anymore. There was barely even paper for us to write on. Even though the kids in the city produced all kinds of goods, paper products weren't among them. No trees in Vegas = no paper products.

In my distress, I attempted to explain the joke, as a bead of sweat ran down the side of my forehead.

"If you have to explain it, it isn't a very good one," the lone girl firefighter interrupted.

All of us were above-average size for our age, but this girl was tiny. However, her thick black ponytail, dark skin, and deep piercing eyes commanded just as much authority as Captain Jefferson.

"Besides, we get it. It's just terrible. Do you think we are stupid or something?"

"Uh, no, sir, I don't."

"Do I look like a sir to you?!" she shot back, standing up, though there wasn't much of a height difference between her standing and sitting.

"All right, everyone, that's enough," Captain Jefferson interrupted with a smirk. "Brann, why don't you go make sure you have your gear set up the way you want on the engine, in case we need to run a call. We'll come out and find you in a second to go over a few things."

Grateful, I silently thanked him for his mercy and hurried out. The station bay housed one fire engine and a rescue, basically an ambulance. The early morning light gleamed on her waxed frame and polished tires. She was beautiful.

I set up my turnouts, tools, and SCBA with military precision, peeking over my shoulder periodically to see if anyone was watching me. Everything needed to be perfect—I had to be perfect. My gear felt heavier than normal, as my own and others' expectations began to bog me down. But I knew I could do this. I excelled in my training.

Before I could finish, three sharp beeps blared through the station, making me jump. A robotic female voice crackled through the intercom.

"Engine 3, outside fire. Repeat. Engine 3, outside fire."

It was already happening! I was about to fight a fire, within minutes of arriving at work. The embarrassing morning would be erased once I showed them how good I was at firefighting. I was lucky to be able to prove myself so early.

I stepped into my turnout boots, nearly falling over as the rest of the crew sprinted out to join me. I threw on my jacket, which still felt unfamiliar against my skin despite all my training. Though the turnouts were remade for our smaller bodies, they were still thick, stiff, and heavy. Moving in them was awkward to me.

The SCBA wasn't much better. The large bottle weighed so much, I always felt like I could suddenly tip over backwards and become stuck like a flipped turtle. I'd learned to work through it though.

Captain Jefferson sat in the front seat, and another firefighter slid into the seat beside me in the back. The bay doors opened and we sped off with lights and sirens blaring. I was still fumbling with my gear, my hands shaking as I tried to fasten my straps. Another firefighter sat beside me, smiling as he pointed to the headset over his ears, reminding me I had forgotten to put mine on.

After frantically searching, I found them dangling from a hook on the ceiling. When I placed them over my head, Captain Jefferson was speaking to me.

"Can you hear me, Brann?"

"Yes, sir, I can," I replied, already out of breath.

"Do you have your radio and seatbelt on?"

"Uh, no sir, sorry sir, I'll put them on now."

I yanked at my seatbelt, feeling much more awkward than I'd hoped. I strapped in and beamed with a weird sense of pride in my accomplishment.

Now belted in, I only needed the radio. I located it clipped onto the inside of the door, barely within reach. I placed it in my front coat pocket, wrapped the spiraled lapel mic cord around the back of my neck, and clipped the mic to the other side of my jacket. I was ready.

I smiled, looking out the side window at the city speeding by in the background. Driving the streets, you would never know how different things really were. Vegas appeared much the same as the Before, minus the lack of heavy traffic.

Suddenly, the engine turned hard, tossing my head to the side. I grabbed my seat to steady myself, and peered towards the front windshield. The engineer, who was the driver, slammed the brakes, jerking me forward in my seat. We swerved around a slow-moving car that blocked our path, sending my helmet sliding onto the floor in front of me. Who the heck was driving this thing?

To my astonishment and terror, the tiny girl firefighter commanded the wheel. I instinctively grabbed my seatbelt with one hand and the bottom of my seat with the other. There was no way she was the Engineer. It wasn't possible.

The fact she was a girl had nothing to do with my fear. My sisters were decent enough drivers. I didn't understand how she could control such a massive vehicle at her height. How could she reach the pedals? Could she even see over the dashboard? I inspected a little closer and noticed a booster seat, which still didn't explain how she reached the pedals.

"Pull to the right, you idiots!" she screamed. "How can every single driver in the city be so stupid? These flashing lights mean get out of my way!"

No way we weren't going to crash. My body clenched, waiting for the inevitable impact as she weaved in and out of cars at dangerous speeds. Yet, despite her size, she navigated the long-bodied engine with impossible skill and precision.

"So, Cap," she said in a sweet, casual tone. "Did you see the new episode of *Loose Change* yesterday? It was hilarious. Me and my sister were dying laughing."

I wasn't laughing, but was convinced I would be dying. With one hand on the steering wheel, she continued this casual conversation with Cap, periodically yelling at anyone who dared get in her way. I remained glued to my seat, panicking and praying for us to arrive in one piece.

"There it is," Captain Jefferson said, pointing out the front windshield. "You ready, rookie?"

Thick black smoke rose above the nearby buildings. My heart began racing. This was the most smoke I'd ever seen. The fire must be enormous. When we turned into the parking lot, I was surprised to see only a dumpster with orange flames licking out the top, releasing a nauseating smell.

I frowned, but no matter the size, this was my moment! The engine stopped with a hiss as the air brake engaged.

My partner exited, and I attempted to do the same, but was pinned to my seat. I forgot to pull the tab to release my air pack.

I struggled to find the yellow pull string. After what felt like an eternity, I yanked it with all my might. The pack released, and I attempted to stand again, but got slammed back into the seat.

My seatbelt! I fumbled with the buckle, my stiff gloves proving impossible to manipulate. I grunted as I released the belt pinning me. Still stuck! Attempt after attempt, I ripped at everything in desperation to free myself. This couldn't be happening. I needed to prove I was a good firefighter, but they would never respect me if I couldn't even get out of here.

I was alone in the engine now, though it felt like a million eyes were watching and judging me. I found the last culprit, which was my radio and corded lapel mic. Too entangled to fix at the moment, I abandoned my radio in the knotted carnage.

Freed, I tumbled out of the engine and ran toward the dumpster fire, where a hose line had already been pulled. My partner waited with the hose in his hand, tapping his foot and pointing to his wrist. I reached for the hose, only for it to be yanked away at the last second.

"Beep," he said. "Times up."

He faced the fire and began spraying water, using a smaller booster line that was easily manageable by yourself. I paced behind him, desperately looking for something to do. I had been dreaming of this moment, this opportunity, for so long. This was my chance to show them what I was made of, and I blew it. My dream of an epic first impression was up in smoke, much like that fire I didn't get to extinguish. My dad would be so disappointed.

While I paced, a delivery driver, probably a year or two younger than me, drove by us slowly, hanging his head out the window.

"I hope the Children aren't becoming a problem," the young driver said, pointing to the wall behind the dumpster. "Thanks for what you do!"

I nodded, though I didn't feel deserving of his gratitude. I hadn't done anything. Behind the dumpster, some graffiti was scrawled on the brick wall—something that had been popping up around the city for the last month or so. The symbol of the Children: a small "T" sitting in the center of a larger "C."

A pit formed in my stomach, though I wasn't sure why. I wondered if they started this, which wasn't like them. They were known for being lazy and unwilling to work, not for being destructive—but I couldn't dwell on that now.

My partner finished putting the fire out and returned to me while removing his helmet. He was slightly shorter than me, with slicked black hair that somehow remained perfectly shaped despite his helmet. He was not your typical rugged firefighter. He appeared clean, crisp, and fresh even while wearing dirty turnouts, almost as if nothing could bother him.

"I'm Ryan Mitsuya, by the way," he said with a relaxed smile. "Most people just call me Mi, though. And yes, it's pronounced exactly like I said: 'me.' To remember, just think, you are you, and I am Mi! Anyway, I'm 15 and have been on the job for just over a year. It's probably a good idea for you to introduce yourself to everyone. Tradition matters around here, you see."

"Yes, sir, sorry sir," I muttered, still feeling puny. "I'm Aiden..."

"Yeah, I know your name. You told us this morning at muster."

Captain Jefferson left to speak to the building's owner to inform them what had happened, so I took Ryan's advice and introduced myself to the girl who had been driving like we were in a race car. She remained by the engine, wiping off a bit of smudge near the tires.

"Sorry I didn't introduce myself earlier," I said, extending my hand. "I'm Aiden Brann. Nice to meet you."

She stared at my hand as if I held something rotten, then shot me a piercing glare. She took another step closer to me, trying to get face to face, though she barely reached my chest. For a second, I thought she was going to punch me. Instead, her face broke into an uncontrollable grin.

"I can't do it anymore!" she blurted in tearful laughter.

Ryan jogged over, groaning. "Come on, Mum. You couldn't even make it through one call?"

"I tried my hardest," she gasped between laughs. "I promise. But I couldn't take it anymore. He looked so concerned, like a cute, confused little puppy. It was just too much."

Ryan shook his head. "You're gonna have to pay for Reed's chow now."

"I know! I knew I wasn't going to win." She returned her attention to me, wiping the tears from her eyes. "I'm sorry. I'm Wendy Fisk, but everyone calls me Mum. I'm 16 and have been driving this engine here since the start. It's nice to officially meet you, Aiden."

I grasped her outstretched hand hesitantly, still trying to process what had happened. Ryan was quick to explain.

"So, funny thing, Brann. Mum here is probably the nicest person on the entire planet, you see. Reed made a bet with her that she couldn't be mean to you all the way until dinner. Obviously, she lost."

"Um, okay," I said, still confused. "So, you have to pay for... chow? What's that?"

"Chow is our meals. We all pitch in money each shift and take turns cooking for each other. We call breakfast, lunch, and dinner 'chow.'"

"So... you were just pretending to be mean?" I asked, glancing back at Fisk. "When you were screaming at all the drivers, was that a part of it?"

"Oh no, no, no," Ryan answered, turning me away from Fisk. "Sorry, I should clarify. Mum is the nicest person unless she is driving. Then she becomes... well... you saw for yourself."

Before Fisk could defend herself, Captain Jefferson returned and looked over the scene.

"Fire's out? You guys ready to go?" he asked.

"Yup, just finished picking up," Fisk answered, hopping back into the driver's seat.

"Brann!" Captain Jefferson said. "Me and you are gonna have a little talk when we get back to the station. Understood?"

"Yes, sir," I replied, my stomach sinking.

As we climbed into the engine, Ryan quickly inspected my gear. His eyes widened when he saw the mess of tangled cords on my seat.

"Oh, man. You left your radio?"

"It got tangled up, so I left it behind, sir. Is that bad?"

Ryan smirked and shook his head in mock sympathy. "Nah. You're lucky. Looks like you'll get to meet Greta sooner than we thought. You're gonna love her."

I sank into my seat, dreading whatever Ryan found amusing. Whoever Greta was, I had a feeling I did not want to meet her.

2

MEET GRETA

"It's like I always tell my son, who is a little younger than you, just keep going!" — Captain Ashton Brann

"Brann, let's go to my office," Captain Jefferson said, calm but serious.

After resetting my gear, I stood outside the captain's office door, searching for the courage to enter. When I did, the rhythmic clicks of the keyboard Jefferson was typing on filled the otherwise silent room. Desks with four computers lined the walls, and I noticed the smell of stale coffee in the air.

"Close the door," he said without looking up. "Take a seat."

I sat at the table in the center of the room, pinning my shaking leg. Once I stopped shaking, my eyes began to wander at the photos that hung around the office. Some were from the Before and some from the After, but I wasn't close enough to see more than that. When Captain Jefferson finished typing, he rolled his chair to the table across from me.

He rubbed his eyes with a single hand and let out a sigh. "Tell me how that dumpster fire went," he said, locking eyes with me.

Though I wanted to break eye contact, I held firm and answered. "It didn't go well, sir."

"What didn't go well about it?"

I hesitated, choosing my words carefully, and began to make some poor excuse for my performance.

Captain Jefferson held up his hand, mid-sentence. "I'm gonna stop you right there, Brann. On my crew, we don't make excuses. We own our mistakes. So that is the last one you will make to me. Understood?"

"Yes sir, sorry sir."

He leaned back in his chair, eyes softening slightly. "I don't care that you got tangled up in your gear. It happens to every new rookie. Mistakes happen. It's how you handle those mistakes that matter to me. You panicked and left your radio behind. Do you know why that's an issue?"

He then explained why the radio was important to him. Besides being able to hear dispatch when they called, it was also our only lifeline to call for help if we found ourselves trapped in a fire or being threatened by someone danger-ous.

It seemed like a bit of a stretch to think I would find myself being threatened. Life in the After was safe and firefighters were well respected. He was probably just trying to be dramatic to drive home his point.

"I'm surprised I have to teach you these lessons," he continued. "Considering who taught them to me."

"Who taught them to you, sir?"

"Someone I respect incredibly. But don't think that you are going to simply get my respect just because you are his son. You're going to have to earn it."

My heart skipped a beat as I sat up straighter. I knew my dad trained one of the kids during the Preparation, but I never knew who. I was sitting across from the person who learned from the man I admired most.

"He did?" I asked, my voice unable to suppress my excitement. "Can you tell me about him? What kind of Captain was he? Did he talk about me at all? Did you two fight lots of fire together?"

Captain Jefferson let out a reserved smile but shook his head. "We can talk about him another time, Brann. We need to address your deliberate choice to leave your equipment behind. To help you understand how seriously I take this, I want you to meet Greta. Go find Mitsuya and tell him you owe me five Gretas. He will show you what to do."

"Yes, sir," I said with a gulp.

I left the office, ashamed of my mistakes, but hearing about my dad gave me a new sense of commitment.

As I wandered the station, searching for Ryan, I bumped into another crew member. A tall, lanky guy with dark skin and short hair with crisp, sharp lines. Music seeped out of the battered, black-and-teal headphones resting over his ears. He bobbed his head, mouthing the words to the song, unaware of my presence.

"Hello, sir. I'm Aiden Brann. Sorry, I didn't introduce myself earlier," I said, extending my hand.

"What was that?" he questioned, removing his headphones.

"I'm Aiden Brann, sir."

"Oh, gotcha. I'm Devin Hill. How was your first fire?"

I was sure he already knew. The whole department probably already knew what a colossal failure I was. I answered anyway. "Uh, not great, sir. I'm looking for Mitsuya. Captain Jefferson said I owe him five Gretas."

Hill let out a low whistle, snapping his fingers. "Five? Wow. Don't sweat it. No one nails their first fire. You'll be sweating plenty later." He grinned before placing his headphones back on. "Mi's in the kitchen. Good luck, man."

I thanked Hill as he disappeared into his dorm and made my way to the kitchen. Ryan chatted with Reed, the massive redhead who mocked me earlier. The moment he saw me, his expression hardened. He folded his arms and leaned back into his chair.

"Look who it is. The kid who can't even fight a simple dumpster fire," Reed sneered. "Reed heard you had Mi do all the work. Reed knew you didn't have what it takes. Maybe you should find an easier job. Maybe your sister needs an assistant. You can set appointments for her. In fact, I could use a massage myself. Maybe you can make me one."

Ryan quickly stepped between us, throwing his arm over my shoulder, and led me away. Reed continued chirping as we walked away.

"If you're gonna be so useless, you might as well go join the Children!" Reed called after us. "Reed thinks you'll fit in perfectly with them!"

"Don't worry about Reed," Ryan said as we walked down the hall. "He is a big ol' softy once you get to know him. He just likes to act tough, you see. You gotta butter him up a bit. Just ask him about the Raiders. He'll talk your ear off and be your best friend."

I nodded, grateful for his intervention. However, I was confused as to why the guy who had to do my work for me on the fire was now so friendly. I thanked him for his advice and explained to him what Captain Jefferson had asked of me.

Ryan stopped dead in his tracks, and his eyes filled with mocked horror. "Five Gretas? Dang, Cap's not playing around. Leaving your radio is his pet peeve, you see. But no worries. After you meet Greta, you'll never forget your radio again."

That did not sound good. I followed him outside to the parking lot. As we walked across the pavement, I scanned the area for Greta, uncertain what I was looking for. He led me to the curb's edge, where a giant tractor tire lay in the dirt, almost as tall as I was.

"This," Ryan announced proudly, "is Greta! Isn't she beautiful?"

"It's a tire?"

"Whoa, whoa, whoa," Ryan said, caressing the top of Greta. "She's not just a tire, you see. She is motivation, inspiration, determination. She is the reason we do our jobs right. Greta has been around longer than we've been alive. She has changed the lives of more firefighters than you could ever dream of. She probably helped your dad a time or two. So, show her some respect."

I nodded quickly. "Sorry, sir. What do I do with her?"

"You drag her, of course. To the fence and back is one Greta. You have five. Here's some free advice. Pull forward on the way there and backward on the way back. Works different muscles, you see. And you're gonna need it because your legs are gonna be smoked." Ryan turned away and sat in a nearby chair. "I'll be right over here watching. Enjoy!"

Greta was old and worn, with chunks of it missing. The smell of dirt and rubber overpowered my senses as I placed the rusted chain connected to the outer wall over my shoulder. An old fire hose covered the metal, adding an insignificant amount of padding.

I faced the fence, pulled the chain taut across my body, and took a deep breath. The fence was about 30 yards away, 60 in total for one single Greta. I couldn't fathom how this task was possible, but I refused to fail twice in one day.

I leaned forward and took a few steps. Discouragement rushed into my mind so quickly, it nearly shut down. Greta was heavy. I got lower to the ground, using all my weight to propel me forward. One foot in front of the other until I reached the fence. I inhaled deeply as I turned around to begin the journey back.

"One!" I yelled as I completed the first.

"Only four more," Ryan called as he munched on a bag of chips, one of the two kinds the city produced in the After.

I turned around, staring across the lot, which somehow seemed to have grown. I wasn't sure I could do this, but I had to try. I continued as gobs of sweat poured off my head and dripped onto the pavement below. My aching legs and heavy breathing reminded me of my racing days in the Before. The 400 meter was my specialty.

Before each race, my dad always asked me the same question. "What do you do when you get tired?" he would ask, with his hands on my shoulders.

"Just keep going," I would respond.

Every race, I could hear him yell, "Just keep going!" I wanted to hear those words desperately, now more than ever.

I touched the band on my wrist with my opposite hand for a couple of seconds. I said to myself, "Just keep going," trying to deepen my voice so that I sounded like him.

During the third stretch, my brain begged me to quit, practically refusing to let me move. Ryan yelled some words of encouragement, though even in my hypoxic state, I could hear his sarcastic tone. It didn't matter. His words fueled me.

By the time I started the fourth, I could barely stand. Ryan left his chair and wasn't watching me anymore. I almost stopped to rest, but thought it might be some integrity test. I had to keep going. My chest burned as I gasped for breath. My soaked shirt dripped like I had climbed out of a pool. Each step only brought me inches closer to my goal.

My dad would have been able to pull this tire. I bet it was easy for him. But I wasn't my dad. Not yet, at least. But he wouldn't quit, and neither would I.

"Just keep going," I yelled again as I started the last Greta.

Ryan had returned, along with the rest of the crew. All eyes were on me, not saying a word. Motivated by my dad's memory and the crew, I picked up the pace. One foot in front of the other, grunting with each step.

"Just keep going, Aiden," I whispered through gritted teeth. "Just keep going!"

With each step, Greta became heavier, but I wouldn't stop. With only a few steps left, I pushed with everything I had. My eyes filled with sweat and burned as I reached out toward the blurry finish.

I did it! I completed five Gretas. It probably wasn't good enough to make up for my stupid mistake, but maybe it was a start. Or maybe this should have been easier than it was for me, and all I did was prove to the crew that I was weak. I bet Reed could do ten of them.

After touching the finish, I stood up as straight as possible, which wasn't much, and stepped out of the chain. I turned to see the crew walk toward me, but the firehouse blurred and darkened behind them. My focus narrowed as I attempted to take another step.

Then—blackness.

Bang! The sound of the gun blast echoed through the stadium. The 400-meter race began. I took off like a jackrabbit in lane 4. Within the first 100 meters, me and the boy with the green headband and long hair separated from the rest of the pack.

I felt amazing. My legs no longer burned and moved faster than ever as I sliced through the wind. We remained neck and neck until the final turn. Then, as I started the final sprint, I heard a faint voice in the distance.

"Just keep going, buddy! Just keep going!"

Though it had been years since I heard my dad's voice, I knew it was him! I glanced up into the stands, but they were empty. Not a soul was watching. I looked back toward the finish line, and there he was! Exactly how I remembered him.

"Just keep going, buddy!" he said with outstretched arms.

Tears filled my eyes as I sprinted faster than I had ever done. I cruised past the boy on my right, and he disappeared from the race. I didn't care about winning anymore. I needed my dad. He kneeled at the finish line, still reaching his arms toward me.

Frantically and desperately wanting to reach him, I fell across the finish line to be caught by him, ready to feel the warmth of my dad's embrace again. But as I fell forward, he vanished.

I jolted awake, lying in the station bay with a pillow behind my head. The crew stood around me and had me hooked up to the monitor, an IV already in my arm. I surveyed my surroundings, trying to find my dad, but he wasn't there. I closed my eyes again, praying to fall back asleep just to hug my dad, but I couldn't.

"He's waking up," Fisk said with relief. "Aiden, can you hear me?"

"Yeah, yeah," I mumbled, still confused. "I'm fine. I'm sorry. I'm fine."

Utterly embarrassed, I tried to stand, but Reed nudged me back to the ground.

"Relax, brother. That was legit. Reed is impressed."

"What?" I asked, confused. "Why?"

"I didn't really mean for you to do all five at once," Captain Jefferson said, his expression lighter than before. "Didn't Mitsuya tell you that?"

"My bad, Cap," Ryan said, scratching the back of his neck. "I wanted to see how many he could do in a row, but he never stopped, you see. That's why I came to get you guys."

Exhausted and confused, I didn't know whether to feel proud or not. They seemed impressed, but it was hard to feel impressive lying on the ground after passing out.

The crew continued taking my vitals and administering fluids. Jefferson and Fisk were in the corner of the room, whispering amongst themselves, as if determining my fate.

I didn't like laying here, looking weak. I needed to prove to them I was okay.

"Hey, Reed," I said. "How are the Raiders looking this season?"

Reed immediately shot daggers from his eyes, not in my direction, but in Ryan's. He handed the bag of fluids he was holding to Hill and ran after Ryan like a bull. Ryan let out a high-pitched scream and attempted to flee, but Reed wrapped him in a bear hug. He lifted him off the ground, slinging him over his shoulder effortlessly, and stomped to a garbage can while Ryan kicked and swung his arms in vain.

Reed briefly held Ryan over the garbage can before dropping him in. Ryan folded in half as he landed in the trash, with only his arms and legs sticking out. He laughed as he wormed and kicked, struggling to free himself. Something told me that wasn't the first time he had been thrown away by Reed.

Reed trudged back over to me, and my smile faded. I hadn't kept up with the Raiders lately since I was preparing for this job, so I didn't know what the problem was.

"Reed has a little advice for ya, brother," Reed said as he placed his hand menacingly on my shoulder, sending shivers down my spine. "Don't listen to anything Mi tells you. He's always up to something. So, unless you want that chalk outline to become real, you just ignore him. Got it?"

Chalk outline? I nodded and looked out the open bay door, at where Reed pointed. Outside, there was an outline of a body where I had gone unconscious, with an inscription under it: "RIP Aiden Brann."

My face flushed as the crew peered at me with amusement. I smiled, trying to play it off, but it was just another reminder of what this day had been for me. A failure.

Captain Jefferson dismissed the rest of the crew, but had Fisk stay, so they could talk with me privately. Hill helped Ryan out of the trash as they laughed and exited the bay. Fisk grabbed a few chairs and set them up around us to sit on.

"How you feeling, Brann?" Fisk asked.

Her eyes seemed genuinely concerned for my well-being, and she was seeking an honest answer. I couldn't show any further weakness, though.

"I feel good. Sorry I passed out. It won't happen again."

"Nothing to be sorry about," Captain Jefferson said. "You showed us a lot of heart just now. That was no easy task, and neither is this job." He moved his chair closer, leaning in to drop some wisdom on me. "We have been called to do something extremely difficult. We see things no one ever should have to. People count on us during their worst days and no longer have the luxury of looking up to a hero like your dad. So, you have to be the hero."

Fisk leaned in now. "It may seem overwhelming, but you can do it. Cap here was one of the original Captains brought in during the Preparation six years ago. He was only 11 years old during the Preparation and was asked to learn how to not only take care of our community, but also all of us. Now that he is almost 17, he is still taking on that responsibility."

Jefferson interrupted. "Fisk likes to pretend she wasn't right there with me learning the job from the beginning, but she was."

"Driving is a little easier than being the captain. At least, I make it look that way."

I thought I had it rough, having to learn all I had so early. Even though literally every other kid was in the same boat. It was the older ones that really had to figure it out as quickly as possible. Even after the adults died, I still had three years to prepare for this. They were thrown right into the fire.

Captain Jefferson regained control of the conversation, obviously uncomfortable with the compliments. "If you handle each situation like you handled Greta, pushing through and never giving up till the task is done, you will be an excellent firefighter. So keep that drive, and you'll be fine."

"Thank you, sir."

Their words left me proud and more determined than ever to be a great firefighter. They were passionate about their job, and I wanted to be like them. Maybe I still had a shot at redeeming myself.

Captain Jefferson left, and Fisk disconnected me from the monitor and IV.

"You still feeling okay, Aiden?" Fisk asked. "Cap was talking about sending you home, but I said I would talk to you first."

"I feel good, I promise," I answered, dreading the idea of being sent home on my first day. "The IV helped."

"Perfect, we will try to take it easy on you the rest of the day."

"Engineer Fisk," I said cautiously. "Did I say something wrong to Reed?"

She chuckled to herself. "I'm guessing Ryan suggested you ask him about the Raiders?"

I nodded my head.

"Well," she continued. "Reed talks about being a football player all the time. He has always loved it, and playing for the Raiders is his dream. He is actually very good."

"Why doesn't he then?" I asked.

"He never seems to give us a straight answer when we ask him," she said as she bandaged my arm where my IV was. "Just know we are happy and lucky to have him here. And deep down, he loves it here, too."

"Well, you guys are brave for teasing him. He is a giant."

"Yes, he is," she chuckled. "A giant teddy bear."

3

THE NEIGHBOR

"I don't know why this is happening either, sweetie. I miss him, too. But I got you something to keep you company once we are gone. Well, three somethings, actually." — Tasha Hunt

I sighed as I pulled into my driveway, my legs barely able to press the brakes. It took all my strength to lift my finger to turn off the ignition. My bedroom window was visible though, and a wave of relief rushed over me. I groaned as I hobbled to the front door and stared at my keys, unable to even remember which one was the house key. I enjoyed my day, but the excitement had worn off, replaced by an urgent need to rest. I could practically hear my soft, warm bed calling out to me to crawl under my covers.

We'd lived here since the Before. Our house was a gray two-story with black-trimmed windows. Our neighbors' orange cat, Paddington, was currently walking across the peak. The yard had just enough space for a grassy area and a small basketball court. Many people chose to relocate to newer, nicer homes in the After. Ours wasn't overly flashy or even luxurious; it was just home—the only home I ever knew. Our height marks over the years were still etched into the side of the doorframe, including my parents'. I ran my hand by their names as I walked through.

Ally and I had rooms on the top floor, and Aubrey stayed downstairs because she wanted her own bathroom. We left my parents' room alone for the most part. However, I used my mom's tub when I felt sick, though my sisters used it much more than I did. She had a TV mounted above it to watch movies. It was my mom's favorite room.

I entered the front door and my sisters swarmed me the second I stepped inside.

"How did it go?" Aubrey, my 16-year-old sister, asked. "You were supposed to text us when you were on your way home."

Her dirty blonde hair was pulled neatly into a ponytail, like it always was, without a hair out of place. She looked most like me, paler skin with a few freckles on her nose. She immediately grabbed my bag and told me she would get my clothes into the laundry—then asked if I got the reminder on my calendar that Kim would be coming over later.

"Did you see anything crazy? Was everyone nice to you?" Ally chimed in. She was almost 13 and much shorter than either of us, with lighter hair that framed her face. She also had the ability to tan, a luxury neither Aubrey or I had. Despite her age and petite frame, she had a talent for deep-tissue massages that could rival a full-grown adult's, or so her clients claimed.

"You okay, Aiden?" she continued. "You look like you had a tough day. Did everything go okay?"

I was hoping Ally wouldn't be able to see how I was feeling, even though she always seemed to. I smiled and appreciated their enthusiasm, but my exhaustion quickly took over. I typically shared how my days had gone with my sisters, but this level of tired was new to me. We'd had a couple of calls at night, though they weren't particularly exciting. I wasn't accustomed to this kind of schedule yet.

"It was the worst and the best first day I could have had," I answered, rubbing my eyes. "I'll tell you about it later if that's okay. I've got to get some sleep."

I kicked off my shoes and trudged upstairs, wincing in pain with each step. My legs protested every movement, though I mostly used my arms and the handrail to pull myself up.

I eventually reached my room and stood at the end of my unmade bed. Too spent to do anything else, I collapsed onto the mattress, the stress of the day melting into it. Beyond comfortable, sleep pulled me under almost instantly.

When I woke a few hours later, I limped downstairs to make breakfast, although it was already lunchtime.

Kim, our neighbor, was sitting on the couch talking with Aubrey. Ally was putting the sheets from her massage table into the wash.

"Hey, Kim," I said groggily. "Just finished your massage?"

"Sure did. You know I can't survive without Ally's weekly massages. Plus, she lets me unload all my thoughts on her. It's like a therapy session for the body and mind all at once. The girl's got magic hands. She should be charging me double. But don't tell her that!"

Ally blushed at the compliment as she walked by with new linens for her table.

"How did your first day go?" Kim continued.

I shrugged, still embarrassed by my mistakes, but proud of my accomplishments. "It was... fine. I made some mistakes, but I did some good things, too. Is Paddington still on our roof? Did you bring Blazie over?"

"Paddington is napping in my tree. And no, I didn't bring Blazie. I'm sorry. I can go get her if you want?"

A large part of me wanted her to. Relaxing with her cat always seemed to make me feel better, but I didn't want to admit that.

"That's okay. I need to eat and start studying some more anyway."

"Well, lucky you. I brought over a breakfast quiche. We saved some for you in the fridge if you want."

"Sweet! Thanks!"

Kim was only 10 years old. She had short, curly hair and freckles dotting her face. She was probably one of the most intelligent, well-put-together people I knew. She lived next door by herself. In the Before, she had both her parents and a baby brother. Kim was old enough to survive the sickness. Sadly, her brother was so young when the exposure happened that he passed away within a few weeks. Her parents, like the rest of the adults, survived the typical three years post-exposure—give or take a few months—that anyone beyond puberty survived.

When her parents died and she was left alone, Kim was only 7 years old. We offered to let her stay with us, but she politely declined since she was truthfully more self-sufficient than we were anyway. She excelled during the Preparation and was training to become one of our government officials.

Her three cats, Blazie, Harvey, and Paddington—whom she referred to as her 'kiddos'— were her pride and joy. Blazie was my favorite. She was chill, black with little hints of orange. Kim usually brought her over for me when she came to visit.

My stomach growled when I saw the fluffy egg quiche with sausage, bacon, and peppers. Food in the After was in abundance, although we did lack the wide variety of processed foods we'd had in the Before. We had a handful of those options: chips, sodas, a few candies, but for the most part, we ate rather clean. Anything we could raise or grow was at our disposal. Large ranches, farming areas, and green houses were converted for us to maintain and cultivate. And the kids who managed them were obviously doing a great job.

After warming the quiche in the microwave, I sat on the couch, desperate to eat, only to be interrupted by cramps in both legs.

"Ahhh!" I screamed, collapsing to the floor.

"What is going on?" Aubrey asked.

"I'm cramping! Ow, ow, ow."

Ally rushed to me, grabbing my legs and stretching them out.

"You really should let me give you a massage," she said. "It'll help with the cramps. I can fit you in today."

She attempted to rub my calves to release the tension, but I pushed her off, still sprawling in pain. "Stop! I don't know how many times I have to tell you. I don't want to ever get a massage from my sister. Gross."

Ally rolled her eyes. "It's not gross. I'm a professional, and I'm trying to help you, you whiny baby."

I stubbornly refused again, pushing myself off the ground and gingerly returning to my plate. The cramps subsided as I ate. Kim was an excellent cook, and this breakfast really hit the spot.

Suddenly, a faint sound caught my attention amid the girls' conversation.

I held up my hand, shushing them. "Do you guys hear that?"

We went silent, moving toward the windows. The noise grew louder, and moments later, two police cars sped down the street in a blur, sirens blaring.

"Whoa, that's rare," Ally said, her face pressed against the glass.

"It still surprises me that we even need cops," Kim said. "Everyone has more than we need. Even those who just get the monthly stipend have enough for all the necessities. What's the point of committing any crime?"

"Is there that much crime out there?" I asked. "I thought it's always been pretty peaceful."

"It has been," Aubrey said. "But it's getting a little worse out there. The Children seem to be causing more problems lately, even though they still get their stipends without working."

My blood boiled just thinking about them—the Children. Their claim was that they should get to be "kids." I even heard that some thought we were being lied to, and that we'd die once we hit puberty. Why would the adults set us up to survive, just for us to die within a few years? I didn't understand why they thought we were lied to—none of us kids had died from the sickness, proving we had been told the truth.

I couldn't comprehend how someone could be so selfish and childish at such an important time. Besides being a good, helpful citizen, who wouldn't want a little extra spending money for tickets to games, movies, or anything nonessential?

"What do you think is going on?" I asked.

"I don't know," Kim answered. "I don't like seeing cops flying through our neighborhood like that. I've heard that the Children might have a new leader. Someone's telling them what to do now. Directing the directionless."

"They've been more active lately," Aubrey added. "I've been getting more 911 calls about them. I even got a weird call from someone saying 'a Children' was after them. But they got disconnected. I figured it was a prank call, but maybe not."

I frowned and shook my head in disappointment. "Why can't they just help like the rest of us? We are all doing our part. What's their problem? Are they really that lazy?"

"I don't know, buddy," Aubrey replied. "It's best you find out now, though. It's only a matter of time until you run these calls, too."

Kim nodded in agreement. "I just wish people would follow the plan we were prepared for. It's like President Keres always says, *'This is our home. Together we live. Together we thrive.'* I'm glad I was lucky to have you guys as my neighbors."

We had heard that phrase from the President countless times. It was engrained in us since even before the last adult died. It was a phrase we had grown to trust and rely on. It may have taken a little while, but it was something almost everyone whole-heartedly believed, including me.

Kim walked toward the door, opened it slightly, and scanned the area. "Those sirens probably scared my kiddos. I better go check on them."

We told her goodbye and to be careful. She slowly stepped outside, then sprinted home as soon as she shut the door. Aubrey sat beside me on the couch, seeing my unease.

Up until now, the Children, though lazy, were mainly harmless and kept to themselves. They were more of a nuisance than a danger.

"Are things really getting worse out there?" I asked.

Aubrey wrapped her arm around me. "I'm afraid so, buddy. We used to get calls for minor things like sick people and some accidental fires here and there. But lately, calls have been getting worse. Violent crimes, intentional fires, fighting. Something out there is changing. I just don't know what."

I could feel the worry and stress tightening in my chest, though Aubrey's presence quickly calmed me down.

"Don't worry, buddy," Aubrey said, reassuringly squeezing me. "You have a solid crew and a great captain. Plus, you're gonna be amazing too, I know it. Besides, I'll be on the other side of the radio, listening in on you. In fact, I think I know how to let you know I'm listening—a way for me to say 'hi' to you. When I talk to your unit, I'm gonna say engine NUMBER 3 or rescue NUMBER 3."

I grinned. "I like that."

The secret code was simple, but knowing Aubrey would be watching out for me brought a small amount of comfort in this uncertain time.

4

TREATS AND TRAUMA

"Don't let what's happening take away your entire child-hood, buddy. Living is only worth doing if you have some fun along the way." — Ashlynn Brann

I walked briskly, a pep in my step, toward the station for my next shift. Despite the exhaustion from the first day, I had high hopes, perhaps delusional confidence, and was ready to prove myself again. Each day off, I dreamt about fighting my first house fire. It felt strange to want something so terrible and destructive—but that was the job, and I wanted to do it.

"You're on the rescue with Mitsuya today, Brann," Captain Jefferson called out as I gathered my gear.

"Yes, sir."

I tried to hide my disappointment. Fighting a house fire would not be a dream that would come true today. Medical calls would be the theme of the day. Still, this would allow me to test my paramedic skills on something other than a training dummy. This thought brought back my excitement, and Ryan seemed like a solid partner who would be fun to work with.

As I put my gear on the rescue and went through inventory, Ryan popped his head into the back. "Looks like it's you and me today, Aiden. Let's try not to kill more than two people. Sound good?"

"Uh, yes, sir."

"Nope—no 'sir' calling on my rescue. I like to keep things light, you see. That's your only warning. You call me 'sir' again, and you'll be hanging out with Greta all day. Got it?"

I chuckled nervously. "Yes, si... I mean, Ryan."

He grinned. "Much better. For today, I want you to focus on the inventory. You've got to know exactly where everything is, both in the back and in all these bags, you see."

"Absolutely, I'm on it."

Ryan left, and I remained in the back, meticulously studying each compartment and its contents. I pulled items out of the cabinets one by one. Most I recognized, but with others, I struggled to recall their purpose. How could I memorize everything when I wasn't even sure what some of them were?

I decided to start smaller and grabbed our approach bag—a backpack as big as me. It seemed as if every piece of equipment we had in the back of the rescue was crammed into it. This would not be an easy task.

Morning muster was called, and we gathered in the kitchen. I stood in my corner, hoping to blend in. But of course, Reed wouldn't allow that.

"You got a better joke for us today?" he asked, smirking.

This time, I was prepared. "Yes, sir. What do cops and firefighters have in common?"

The crew stared at me, waiting.

"They both wanted to be firefighters!"

Dead silence. A cricket literally chirped from under the sink. I chuckled awkwardly to myself, wondering if they had any sense of humor at all.

Thankfully, two tones blared throughout the station, just in time to save me from further embarrassment.

"Rescue 3, delta chest pain. Repeat, Rescue 3, delta chest pain."

I shot out of the room, grateful for the bailout. Ryan followed, and we climbed into the rescue. I immediately started running through scenarios in my head as to why someone would have chest pain. Heart attacks weren't likely. Kids our age didn't tend to have heart issues. They could be having trouble breathing, which could be causing the pain. Maybe they had been sick and coughing for days, which could be uncomfortable. Or it could be something simpler, like heartburn.

Those scenarios vanished as soon as I put the rescue into drive, and were replaced with a rush of adrenaline. Driving lights and sirens while cars moved out of your way, and you ran red lights on the wrong side of traffic, was every kid's dream. I was going to fulfill that right now. I gripped the steering wheel tightly, shaking with anticipation as I pulled out of the station. I tried to hold back my grin as I drove down the street, sirens blaring.

"Uh, Aiden," Ryan said, leaning back casually in his seat. "If you aren't going to go any faster, would you let me out here so I can walk? One of us needs to make it to the patient sometime today, you see."

I glanced at the speedometer. Twenty-five miles per hour! I wasn't even driving the speed limit. I knew I wasn't moving nearly as quickly as Fisk, but I didn't think I was going that slow. My face flushed with embarrassment as I cautiously pressed on the accelerator. After reaching a more suitable velocity, I approached the first vehicle. Surprisingly, they did not move, and I had to slam on the brakes. I muttered under my breath. Why weren't they moving?

"You're gonna learn real quick that no one seems to know what to do when we get behind them," Ryan said, shaking his head. "It's like they forgot to teach that in Driver Ed during the Preparation."

I remembered taking Driver Ed years ago. They definitely taught what to do when emergency vehicles were behind you. Maybe it stood out to me because I knew that's what I would be doing, though.

Whatever the reason, most people didn't do what they were supposed to when I got behind them. My knuckles were white from the stress of driving such a large vehicle, and now I had to avoid more in the street than I anticipated. It gave me a new appreciation for how Fisk handled the much bigger engine. I couldn't imagine ever being able to drive like her.

We finally arrived at the provided address, approached the front door, and knocked loudly. Someone yelled for us to come inside. We did so and found a boy, maybe 10 or 11, sitting in his living room. He did not appear to be in any immediate distress.

"Hi there," Ryan began. "This is my partner, Aiden, and I'm Mi."

The boy looked at Ryan, puzzled. So did I. Ryan wore a smug grin, clearly enjoying the confusion.

"What's going on today?" Ryan continued, moving closer.

"Don't get any closer!" the boy yelled, covering his mouth.

Ryan stopped in his tracks. "What? Why not?"

I stepped back, instinctively covering my mouth and nose with my shirt. Did he have something dangerously contagious? Tuberculosis? Meningitis? Something worse?

"I had a friend over yesterday, and we were watching *hiccup* movies and eating pizza. Randomly, my friend got the hiccups. I didn't think anything *hiccup* of it. But today, *hiccup* I got the hiccups too. I don't want *hiccup* you to get them. I didn't know they were *hiccup* so con-tagious."

Without hesitation, Ryan winked at me and slowly backed away from the boy, keeping his face serious. I wasn't sure what to do, so I followed his lead and hid behind him, keeping my face covered.

"Your friend gave you the hiccups, huh?" he asked. "I thought you called for chest pain."

"Well, it hurts when I hiccup. You guys *hiccup* got to help me. What do I do?"

"You just stay right there," Ryan answered. "Don't move. I'm gonna get something to help you. My partner here will stay with you until I come back. Okay?"

I shot a questioning glance at Ryan, but he smirked and bolted out the front door. I remained inside with the monitor in my hand. I felt I should take his vital signs, but the kid didn't want me to get closer.

"Have you tried drinking milk?" I asked. "That helps me sometimes."

"No. Do you *hiccup* think I should?"

"Yeah, might as well give it a shot."

The boy walked over to the nearby kitchen, holding his hand over his mouth. He soon returned, holding a large glass filled to the brim with milk. With each hiccup, he spilled more and more onto the tile until he sat down.

Moments later, Ryan appeared in my view, sneaking through the backyard. He motioned to me to stay quiet. He wasn't doing what I thought he was, was he?

I continued talking to the boy, attempting to distract him as he sipped his drink. Ryan tip-toed his way closer to the window directly behind him. Once in position, Ryan gave me a nod and a thumbs up. I rolled my eyes, then contorted my face to appear scared.

"What's that!" I screamed, pointing behind him.

The boy turned around to Ryan, yelling and smacking the window. He fell backward off the couch, spilling the milk all over himself as he landed on the floor.

Ryan strolled back in through the sliding back door.

"What did you do that for?!" the boy yelled, drenched with milk. "What is wrong with you? You're supposed to help people, not give me a heart attack. Who is going to clean this up?"

Ryan stood calmly, a shameless grin on his face. "You still got the hiccups?"

The boy blinked and patted his chest, before joyfully looking up at Ryan. "No way! They're gone! Thank you, thank you! You guys are amazing."

"Just doing our job," Ryan said with an animated thumbs up.

We got a quick signature from him for our report and returned to our rescue. I sat in the driver's seat but didn't start the ignition.

"What just happened back there?" I questioned.

"I know, right! I can't believe that actually worked."

"You've never done that before?"

"Have I ever had someone call 911 for the hiccups and then scare them as my treatment? No, I haven't. We get called for some ridiculous things, you see, but this was a new one for me. You gotta enjoy these ones when they come along. They aren't all like this. You were perfect, by the way. How you hid behind me! Genius!"

Ryan insisted we get celebratory treats and directed me to a small coffee shop called Holly Gals. We drove down the street for a bit, laughing periodically as we brought up another aspect of the bizarre call we'd just run. When we entered the shop, Ryan was practically vibrating with excitement.

I looked at Ryan curiously. "A coffee? That's the treat you want?"

"Not just any coffee. The best coffee! They have a million different flavors you can add, you see. You're telling me you've never been here?"

"I've never had coffee," I said as I scanned the menu. "My dad never drank it either. Said you don't need it until you start drinking it."

Ryan shrugged. "That's weird. I thought every firefighter drank it. Crazy nights and little sleep drive you to it. Plus, we gotta enjoy it while we can. The stockpile the adults from the Before saved for us won't last forever. It's not like we can grow our own coffee beans here in the Vegas desert."

I continued scanning the menu, which was on a tablet, until I found chocolate milk toward the bottom.

I loved chocolate milk. My parents would usually buy me one after any of my track meets. They said it was good for recovery. I didn't care about the recovery portion, though. I just loved the taste. I could put in any flavor I wanted here, which I had never done before.

I ordered a caramel banana chocolate milk, much to Ryan's amusement. He ordered a wild-sounding drink that I couldn't even attempt to repeat. We waited near the entrance of the building as they completed our order.

"Hiccup," Ryan mimicked.

Tears filled my eyes as I laughed along with him. I hadn't laughed like this in a long time. Everything for me had been so serious. I enjoyed my time with my friends and family, but in the back of my head, I always thought about preparing for this job. Even in our short time together, Ryan had a way of making me feel comfortable, as if we were old friends.

Feeling at ease, I decided to tell him what happened at our house the other day.

"So, a couple cops went speeding by my house on Tuesday. Looked like they were going to something serious. Probably those lazy Children."

Ryan tensed for a moment, squeezing the tablet in his hand, before relaxing again. "Oh yeah? Looks like our drinks are about ready."

As someone who seemed to love to talk, it was curious that he didn't engage in a topic so interesting as the Children. But I didn't give it much further thought. Our drinks arrived, and we returned to our rescue.

"That actually looks really good," Ryan said, eyeballing my drink.

"I guess you should have ordered it then," I replied, holding it away from his prying hands.

"Come on, let me have a sip."

I conceded and handed him my plastic cup. He took a small sip and swished it around his mouth, properly analyzing the beverage. Then he took a much larger swig.

"Whoa!" I said, snatching the cup from him. "You said a sip!"

I took a drink, and it was delicious. Cold, thick, creamy, and perfect. I hadn't had a drink this good in ages.

As we drove off, the radio crackled to life. "Rescue NUMBER 3, copy a vehicle accident."

I smiled to myself. The dispatcher was Aubrey and she remembered to use our secret code. It was almost enough to distract me from the stress of responding to my first car accident.

Ryan gave me the cross streets, and I flipped on the lights and sirens, still driving cautiously, gripping the steering wheel tightly. Our MCT notes indicated a vehicle had been t-boned, and that we had one person trapped.

"Get ready to do some work," Ryan said. "Looks like we are gonna beat the engine in. When we get there, I'll grab the gurney, and I want you to go check on the person still trapped. See how they are doing."

As we got closer, a black cloud of smoke appeared.

Aubrey radioed us again. "Engine 3 and rescue NUMBER 3. We are getting reports a car is now on fire, and someone is still inside."

I tried to slow my breathing. I wasn't in the right mind-set to respond to a fire. I thought it would be all medical calls today. Ryan advised me to throw on my turnout jacket before going to the trapped victim. I was lucky to hear him. Everything seemed so loud between the sirens and my own intrusive thoughts. Someone needed rescued. I hoped I was ready for this. Did I know what needed to be done? My dad would know.

We arrived before the engine and parked in a way that blocked traffic. As reported, the front portion of the vehicle was on fire and spreading toward the driver's compartment.

As I put on my jacket, the most awful, soul-piercing scream cut through the air, paralyzing me. My heart sank. I had to get her out fast.

I sprinted to the crushed driver's side door of the car. The door wouldn't budge, and smoke continued to fill the compartment. I could barely see inside, but there was the outline of a person. She wasn't screaming anymore.

I pulled at the door several times, foolishly expecting a new outcome. My mind raced as I tried to think of a solution. I continued pulling at the door, unable to focus. How would my dad handle this situation? Finally, the most obvious one came into my head—the passenger-side door!

I ran to the opposite side, tripping under my frantic feet. The door was undamaged and opened easily. Smoke poured out the top and I could see her face slumped over the center console. The fire had reached her and covered most of her body, especially her lower half, charring her clothes.

For a split second, I froze. This felt surreal, like a fever dream. Shaking my brain back into reality, I held my breath while I unbuckled her seatbelt. The radiant heat pounded against my skin. My gloved hands slipped from her arm as I pulled with all my might. Her skin sloughed off, revealing a shiny layer of skin underneath. I fell backward, though I don't know if it was because I slipped, or from the horrific sight. But there was no time to dwell on it.

She was pinned under the steering wheel. Was I going to have to watch her burn? The engine wasn't there, so we could not extinguish the fire. We didn't have the tools to extricate her, which would take too long anyway.

Ryan came up next to me with the gurney. He didn't take long, though it felt like an eternity.

"She's stuck! I can't get her out," I said, my voice cracking.

Ryan jumped right in with a solution. "Grab an arm. We'll pull together."

I did as he said, ensuring I got a good grip on her wrist.

"One, two, three," Ryan yelled.

On three, we pulled, and she freed from her fiery seat. We lifted her onto the gurney and moved away from the burning car. Most of her body was burnt beyond recognition, and her clothes melted into her skin. Yet, her face mainly seemed untouched. She was maybe 15. I couldn't avert my gaze from her lifeless, empty eyes, feeling a hollow pit in my stomach.

"Is she... dead, Ryan?"

"I don't know, but we have to work her."

The engine arrived as I loaded her into the rescue. Ryan told Cap he needed Reed and Hill to ride with us to the hospital. Cap and Fisk remained on scene to extinguish the car fire and to check on the other driver, who was out and walking around. Reed jumped in the driver's seat, and the rest of us got in the back.

I began tearing through our medical compartments, grabbing IV bags, burn sheets, and non-rebreather masks. Anything and everything I could get my hands on.

"Aiden," Ryan said, his voice calm. "What do we do first?"

Whether I didn't hear him or couldn't slow down enough to stop myself, I don't know. I continued rummaging through our supplies.

"Aiden!" Ryan said again, sterner. "Stop. Take a breath."

He sat at the patient's head, looking at me. I did as he said and took a deep breath.

"Now tell me," he continued. "What do we do first? Think of the basics."

Getting my thoughts to slow down was no easy task. With an unconscious person, I should use the CAB acronym: circulation, airway, and breathing.

"Circulation," I answered.

"Good. Check for a pulse."

I felt for a carotid pulse near her throat, hopeful that I would find a sign of life. But none was there. "I don't feel anything, Ryan."

"Okay, then let's do compressions," he responded.

With both hands in the center of her chest, I began pushing hard and fast, her ribs cracking beneath my hands. It was a sickening feeling.

"I think I broke her ribs, Ryan."

"Probably," he answered, unsurprised. "Keep going. What do we do next?"

"Uh, airway. We need to breathe for her."

"Yes, I'll work on that. What can Hill be doing?"

I looked up at Hill, still too panicky to think straight. He held a sealed bag, discreetly flashing it to me to give me a hint.

I examined the bag from a distance. "Oh, we need to put her on the defibrillator pads in case we need to shock her."

"Perfect," Ryan said. "Hill will put her on the pads. I'm breathing for her, and you keep doing compressions."

As I continued compressions, I noticed we were moving. Each time Reed took a turn, I struggled to keep my balance. He wasn't driving fast, but any slight movement seemed amplified to me, standing in the back of the rescue.

"All right, Aiden," Ryan continued. "Hill has the pads on, so now what?"

"A rhythm check?" I said, questioning, even though I knew that I knew the answer.

"Yup, and while we check that, what else needs to get done?"

Hill held up a box of medication I recognized as epinephrine.

"We need to give her Epi," I said confidently. "So, we'll need IV access. Or, even better, an IO, but her legs are pretty burned."

"Then do a humoral IO," Ryan suggested. "After the rhythm check, Hill will take over compressions, and you can work on the IO."

I stopped compression and intently watched the monitor. Flatline, asystole. Unlike some movies, you don't shock a flat line. Hill continued compressions, and I worked on setting up the IO.

I pulled out a small drill and attached an almost two-inch, large-bore needle. After moving the girl's arm into position, I felt for the location to drill into, which was at the head of the humeral bone on her shoulder.

I pointed to the location and looked up at Hill, who gave me a confirming nod. My hands shook as I punctured the needle through her skin until I felt it rest against the bone. Then, pulled the trigger. The needle spun like a drill and bored itself into the bone.

I did it! I was in. Relieved, I nearly forgot what was happening in front of me. Ryan tapped me on the shoulder with the Epi syringe, and I delivered the medication through the IO.

Ryan was on the radio explaining to the hospital what we were coming in with. Hill was sweating profusely, obviously getting tired from doing compressions.

We performed another rhythm check, but she still had no heartbeat. I switched positions with Hill and began compressions again. Her chest was even more pliable than before. I didn't like the feeling. Luckily, Reed announced that we were arriving at the ER.

I had never been to the hospital yet in the After. I had only visited my little sister once in the Before when she got sick. It seemed so big and was mostly empty.

After wheeling the girl into the hospital and transferring her to an ER bed, I stayed close, hoping to see the patient's outcome. The doctors worked on her for about 20 minutes. I remained hopeful they would be able to save her. They were trying so hard, and we had done so much.

I kept that optimism and was positive the doctors would save her. My heart soared when they stopped doing compressions. Did they finally get a heartbeat?

Ryan turned away, patting me on the shoulder as he walked by.

The doctor covered her with a sheet, and checked his watch. "Time of death. 8:37."

5

ACCEPTING DEATH

"Those boys you end up working with will act tough, but deep down, they will be desperate for a mom. They may even turn to you." — Engineer Lucille Fisk

D ead.

The word echoed in my mind, consuming every thought. The girl we pulled from the burning car. The girl we worked so hard to keep alive was dead. How could she be? We did everything we were supposed to do. We followed every step and every protocol. Our job was to save people, and we failed. I failed.

I sat on the nearest bench, staring at the floor as questions swarmed my mind. What more could we have done?

Did we forget to do something? Did I do something wrong? Was my CPR not good enough? What if we had not gone to Holly Gals? Would we have been able to get to her sooner? I should have driven faster. I should have gone to the passenger door first!

I squeezed my wristband so tight, my nails dug into my skin. My shirt felt suffocating. My head spiraled with self-doubt. The girl's lifeless eyes and charred, peeling skin were vividly present in my mind's eye. I should have saved her.

"Aiden," a soft voice broke through the paralyzing thoughts.

I picked my head up and saw Fisk before me, her eyes filled with empathy. They'd come to pick up Reed and Hill.

"I need your help outside," Fisk said, gently grabbing me by the arm.

She led me outside to the parking lot and walked me behind the engine, away from prying eyes.

Then, without warning, she wrapped her arms around me. Surprised, I almost pulled away, but instead stood stiff. My arms dangled awkwardly by my side, but she only squeezed tighter. Slowly my shoulders sagged, my body giving in to her all-encompassing hug. Despite her tiny frame, she seemed to surround me like a warm blanket. I could feel her warmth seeping through me and smell the wisp of smoke on her, lingering from the car fire.

Though I resisted for a moment, something inside of me broke. I felt ashamed. Firefighters weren't supposed to cry, but the tears came anyway. Slowly, I let myself succumb to her embrace, my body trembling as I tried to hold back the sobs. I had never felt so small, so inadequate.

After a couple of minutes, Fisk pulled back, placing her arms on my shoulders. Her eyes were wet too, though she had a gentle smile. "You did nothing wrong, Aiden."

I shook my head, wiping the tears with the back of my hand. "Yes, I did! I could have gotten her out sooner, but I messed up. I let her die in there."

"You did nothing wrong," she repeated.

I covered my face, knowing she was wrong. "Someone else could have saved her. I should have driven fast like you. I should have gone to the right door. It's only my second day, and I've already let someone die. Maybe I can't do this. Maybe I can't be as good as my dad was."

"Aiden, you did nothing wrong," she said firmly. "Sometimes... sometimes there is nothing we can do. Even if we do everything perfectly, it still might not be enough. We can't save everyone, and that's the hardest part of the job. Not even our parents could save everyone. We are still just kids. We can't expect everything to go perfectly."

Her words lingered with me for a moment. I wasn't sure I believed her. I had made mistakes—I knew it—and maybe those mistakes cost someone their life. At the end of the day, I wasn't fast like her, I wasn't experienced enough like everyone else, and I wasn't my dad.

Seeing I was still doubting her counsel, she continued. "I had a call just like yours. Different situation, but the same outcome. For months I replayed the call in my head, trying to fix it. I felt like it was all my fault, and the truth is, the memory of this person is going to stick with you for the rest of your life. You're going to remember her face, just like I remember the one from my call. But it wasn't my fault, and it's not yours."

"How do you handle seeing this stuff all the time then?" I whispered. "How do you deal with... this?"

Fisk sighed, contemplating her answer. "What works for me probably doesn't work for you. Everyone has their own process for handling it. You'll have to find yours. What you can't do is let it fester, Aiden. If you hold it in, it'll tear you apart. Do you understand?"

I nodded, "Yes, Mum, I mean... Engineer Fisk."

She hugged me again.

"It's okay, Aiden. You can call me Mum if you want to." She pulled back and smiled at me. "Oh, and for the record, no one drives faster than me."

She winked and walked back inside. I returned the gurney to the rescue, feeling a little lighter, though the guilt of failure still clung to me. As I cleaned, I thought about what Mum had said and tried to think of something I could do to feel better, something that would bring back some joy.

Then, it dawned on me. My chocolate milk! My drink was still in the front, ready for me to finish. That would surely do the trick. I slid into the driver's seat and grabbed my cup with both hands, excited for the sweet, comforting taste.

But when I lifted it, something was wrong. The cup was almost empty.

"What the...?"

Before I could process what happened, Reed swaggered by, grinning like a kid up to no good.

"Thanks for the drink, brother! Reed loves chocolate milk!" he called out, giving me a mock salute before returning to the engine.

My head fell forward against the steering wheel. I probably didn't deserve any joy this last sip would bring anyway. I let someone die. Desperate for relief, I tried to take a swig but spat the milk out the window. It had gone sour, sitting in the warm Vegas sun. I was crushed beyond words. What little comfort I had hoped for was gone.

Soon after, Ryan entered the passenger seat, spilling an armful of goodies onto the dashboard. "I brought you some snacks, Aiden."

"Where did you get those?" I asked, though I was too drained to care.

"The EMS room," Ryan said, stuffing a cookie into his mouth. "Every hospital has a room for us to write reports and grab a drink and snacks. I grabbed some extra for you if you want. Someone made cookies and they are pretty decent."

I couldn't imagine eating treats at a time like this. Ryan started typing out his report, and I wasn't sure if I should start driving, so I waited for instructions.

After a few minutes of silence, Ryan looked up with an odd expression. "She kinda looked like a Barbie doll, huh?"

I blinked. "What?"

"The girl. When her skin peeled off... it looked plasticky, like a doll. Don't you think?"

I stared at him, unsure how to respond to such a bizarre comment. How could he say that? She wasn't a toy. She was a person. A person with a name. A life.

Ryan didn't notice my discomfort and continued, oblivious, "Oh, and how about her clothes melting into her? If I wanted permanent clothes, I would have chosen something nicer to wear. Right?"

"How can you say that?"

Ryan shrugged. "You'll understand one day."

Before I could ask a follow-up, Captain Jefferson approached my window, his face serious. "Hey, guys. Sorry to do this, but I have a job for you two. The hospital found the girl in the registry. Her name is Jennifer, and she has a younger brother named Chris at home. It's our job to inform him of what happened and set him up with the Hotel if he needs it."

My stomach dropped. This day couldn't get any worse. "You want us to tell him?"

"Unfortunately, yes," Cap said. "It's a good learning opportunity for you. Here is the address. Remember to be patient and understanding. He might not take the news well. A police officer will also meet you over there to help out. Any questions?"

"No sir," Ryan answered. "We can handle it."

We began the long drive out toward Henderson, where Chris lived. My mind raced the whole time.

"How come firefighters break the news to family now?" I asked. "I don't remember my dad ever talking about doing that."

"Yeah, it started in the After, you see. I honestly don't know why, though. We have just taken on a few more roles. By the way," Ryan continued, munching on another cookie, "you're gonna be the one to tell him. That's the benefit of seniority."

Now I was stressed about what I would say to this poor kid. What could you say when you are going to destroy their whole world?

I thought about the Hotel and how they could help. I had visited it before, since it was near some of the old casinos where we took our Preparation classes. I used to visit my old friend Jaxton, who decided to live there after his parents died. The Hotel was the biggest repurposed casino; they created it for kids who were too young or having trouble living independently. It was a place where everyone could live together, and some older kids ensured they had what they needed and made it to their Preparation classes. From what I saw, it was an extremely nice, well-run place.

We arrived at a well-kept, larger-than-average beige home with a half-circle driveway, which was atypical for Vegas. After knocking on the door, my face went flush. I forgot everything I planned to say, and my mind became blank.

A young boy, about eight or nine years old, answered the door. This had to be Chris. He wore shorts and a dark grey hoodie. His messy brown hair fell over his eyes, and he looked up curiously.

"Is my house on fire?" Chris asked.

"No, buddy," I replied, my voice shaky. "My name is Aiden, and this is my partner, Ryan. What's your name?"

"Chris."

I swallowed hard, searching for the right words. But nothing came. I glanced at Ryan, silently pleading for help, but he shook his head.

"Chris," I continued. "It's hard to tell you this, but your sister Jennifer was in a car crash."

"What?" he asked, removing his hood. "Is she okay?"

"No, buddy. The car started on fire, and she got burned really bad."

"But you put out the fire, right?" he said. "Did you take her to the hospital?"

I hesitated. "Um, yes, we put out the fire, and yes, we took her to the hospital, but she didn't make it."

His face turned confused. "Didn't make it? So where did you take her?"

"No," I said, flustered. "We took her to the hospital. The doctors tried to help her, but she passed and is in a better place now."

"Like a better hospital or something?" Chris frowned.

"No, uh. Not another hospital..."

"Chris," Ryan interjected, his voice blunt. "Jennifer died. She was in a car crash. The car was on fire, and we tried our hardest to save her, but she died. I'm very sorry."

Chris stared back at us, remaining motionless before dropping to his knees. I attempted to console him by putting my hand on his shoulder, but he pulled away. He took a step back into the house, muttering to himself. He pulled at his hair, taking another step in.

We followed Chris in as he stopped in the living room, going motionless. Suddenly, he grabbed a lamp and threw it across the room into the TV. They both shattered and crashed to the floor.

I flinched at the sound of exploding glass, half-expecting the wrath of an adult to come raining down on us, but of course nothing came.

He flipped over the loveseat, tossed chairs across the room, and tore through the dishes in the kitchen, plates and glass shattering in every direction. A part of me wanted to join him. Another part wanted to grab him and tell him everything would be okay, but I knew it wasn't. And maybe it never would be.

After breaking nearly everything in sight, he finally collapsed onto the couch, sobbing into the cushions. My heart broke for him.

"What am I supposed to do now?" Chris whimpered. "Jenny took care of me. I can't do this alone."

"That's why we are here, Chris," Ryan said, kneeling beside him. "I'm sure you know about the Hotel where kids who need help can stay. They will give you a place to live, food to eat, and help you keep preparing for your career. I know it's sudden, but it's a nice place, and there will be a lot of kids your age."

A knock at the door interrupted us, and I answered to find a police officer. She was an average-height girl, probably 15, with glossy black hair pulled so tightly into a bun that it appeared painful. She was a beautiful girl and her dark brown eyes were calming.

Chris fidgeted, uneasy at the sight of her. But without prompting, she went to him and bent down to eye level.

"Hi, I'm Officer Keller," she said, touching his shoulder. "I heard about what happened, and I'm so sorry. This must be a hard time for you. I'm here to help you in any way I can. Will you let me do that?"

Chris nodded, relaxing a bit, and Officer Keller suggested he head to his room while she spoke to us.

Ryan had an awkward look in his eye as he stared at Officer Keller. When Chris left the room, she walked over to us.

"I'm Kaylyn," she said with a smile. "Looks like he didn't take the news too well. Poor guy."

Ryan stepped forward, outstretching his hand. "Hi, I'm Mi, I mean, my last name is Mi. Well, actually, that's not true. It's Mitsuya. They say Mi, but I'm Mi Ryan, you see. I mean, Ryan Mi... Mitsuya."

I chuckled to myself as they shook hands. It was strange seeing Ryan, who always spoke clearly and purposefully, struggle to introduce himself.

Ryan could not seem to release the officer's hand, so I stepped in. "I'm Aiden Brann. Thanks for coming. Yeah, he took it hard but calmed down right before you got here."

"Is he planning on going to the Hotel then?"

"Yes," Ryan said. "I mean. I think so. We told him about it, you see. He hasn't answered. I think yes, maybe."

Kaylyn grinned, seeing his struggles. "Well, thanks for getting things going. That's great work you did."

Ryan shuffled to the corner of the room with his head bowed while Kaylyn and I went to find Chris in his room. His room was set up with multiple computers on desks along the walls. The floor was tile, with a single rolling chair. It was an elaborate setup.

"You a gamer, Chris?" I asked.

"No, not really. I like to build computers and work on them. Stuff like that."

"Really?" Kaylyn asked. "What did your testing show for your career choice?"

"Computer programming was the top choice, but I can do a lot more with computers than that."

Kaylyn walked further into the room, admiring the set up. "Like what?"

"Most of the stuff you see on those TV shows, I can do."

Most kids completed the testing processes the adults had set up, which were simple enough. There were written portions, physical tests, and problem-solving skills. After the Preparation, most kids took the tests to determine their career options. Kids my age and older had the option to test, or to follow the career path of one of their parents. I never took the test myself.

"Well, that's a unique skill," Kaylyn said. "I'm terrible with computers. Maybe you can teach me a thing or two.

But right now, we need to talk about what you would like to do. I know it's a hard decision to make so suddenly, but I would like to offer you a place at the Hotel. I think it would be a wonderful spot for you."

"Okay," Chris said, his head lowered. "I don't want to be alone, but I don't want to leave my computers either."

"I'll make sure they get you everything you need. It's a good place, and they will help you until you are ready to be on your own. Sound good?"

Chris nodded.

"I can help you pack up your things," Kaylyn offered. "Would you like to ride with me to the Hotel, or do you want to go with the firefighters? I'll let you play with the sirens if you want."

Chris pointed to Kaylyn. She asked him to start packing and led me out of the room to find Ryan.

"I think I got it from here, guys," Kaylyn said. "Thanks for your help."

"You sure we can't do anything else?" I asked.

"I'm okay. I'm sure you have stuff to do. It doesn't look like he has a ton to pack. I'll take him and get him situated. They make the process super simple. Thanks again."

We said bye to Chris as he packed and returned to our rescue.

Before driving away, I stared over at Ryan, batting my eyes. "So, do you want to talk about Officer Kayl..."

"Nope! Take us home!"

6

THE END OF THE BEFORE

I tapped my pencil absentmindedly against my note-book, my mind far from the math lesson being taught, when I felt a light poke on my shoulder. Startled, I turned to see my friend, Jaxton, grinning at me.

"Mrs. G is asking you a question," he whispered.

I whipped my head forward to see Mrs. G staring daggers at me, lips pursed, foot tapping impatiently. Years of unappreciated, thankless teaching were evident in her greying hair, tired eyes, and wrinkly skin. She didn't say anything, only pointed to the whiteboard, where a math problem was scribbled.

"Uh, sorry… I couldn't hear you," I stammered, trying to save face.

"No, Aiden," Mrs. G said, her voice annoyed. "You're not listening. I asked if you would come up here and solve this math problem for us."

Though a daydreamer, I wasn't a troublemaker, and did as asked. I reluctantly walked to the front of the class, taking her dry-erase marker. I examined the written problem, which looked simple enough, but embarrassment wouldn't allow me to think straight. I could hear a few snickers from my classmates behind me.

Suddenly, the sound of static crackled through the room.

Saved by the bell, I thought, as the principal's voice came over the PA system.

"I need all teachers to report to my office immediately. All staff, to the principal's office now. Students will remain in their seats!"

I exchanged a curious glance with Jaxton as I hurried back to my seat. "That was lucky!"

"Yeah, it was," he whispered back, grinning.

It was strange, though. I had never seen all the teachers get called out of class at the same time. Something about it made me uneasy, but I brushed it off. Whatever it was, it couldn't be worse than having a brain fart in front of the whole class.

"Hey, do you want to come over and play after school?" I asked Jaxton.

"Can't," he groaned. "My mom says I'm grounded this week because she thinks my room is dirty. It's not even that bad. I don't have any old food under my bed anymore."

"Lame. My mom made me clean the whole upstairs yesterday, even though Ally was the one who made most of the mess. She barely helped."

"Glad I don't have a dumb little sister," Jaxton snickered.

"Yeah, you're lucky. Sisters are dumb."

A few minutes later, Mrs. G burst into the classroom. She leaned heavily against the door, clutching the handle as if that was all that kept her upright. Her face was paler than normal as she attempted to catch her breath. Without waiting for anyone to settle down, she started speaking rapidly.

"Everyone needs to gather all their things. Grab your lunches, backpacks, and everything from your desk. You're going home early."

Whoops and cheers echoed in the class, but Mrs. G didn't smile. We never got to go home early! Were we having a snow day or something? Though, a heat day would make more sense, but it wasn't any hotter than usual.

We lined up single file and marched to the gymnasium, where it seemed all the students were being funneled. They instructed us to remain inside until our parents came to retrieve us.

Once inside the gym, I immediately began looking for Ally. Since Ally was in 2nd grade and I was already in 3rd, Mom said she was my responsibility. My job was to ensure she made it to class and the bus after school. There wasn't a lot I took seriously, but this job I did.

I found her sitting on the bleachers, clutching her lunch box. Her eyes darted around as she scanned the hundreds of kids, looking for me.

"Ally!" I called, running toward her. "I'm here. You okay?"

She nodded and gave me a hug. I gently pushed her away, not wanting to be seen hugging my little sister.

"Let's go find Aubrey," I said, leading her by the arm.

We found her quickly. Aubrey seemed more concerned than most kids. That should have made me nervous, because Aubrey always seemed to know when something was off. I couldn't care less, however. All I knew was I got to leave early, which was great.

Soon, parents began entering, calling out for their children within the sea of students. After about 30 minutes, though it felt like forever, we heard our mom shouting our names. She rushed over, grabbed our hands, and escorted us to the van.

Aubrey kept asking questions the whole drive home, but Mom didn't answer. Her knuckles were white, gripping the steering wheel. Her eyes shifted nervously up, down, and around as she drove. The music on the radio cut off and a voice began to speak, but Mom immediately turned it off.

When we arrived home, she ushered us inside. "Up to your rooms," she finally said. "You can play on your tablets if you want."

My eyes widened in surprise. We never got to use our tablets unless we were on long road trips. This was turning out to be a weird but amazing day. I hoped it meant we'd have ice cream for dinner.

"Where's Dad?" Aubrey asked before closing the door to her room.

"Dad got called into work," Mom answered. "Stay in your rooms till I come get you."

It was weird Dad wasn't home. If he was home when I went to school, he was always there when I returned. I never remember him getting called into work in the middle of the day.

We stayed in our rooms for what seemed like hours. At first, I didn't mind. Extra screen time was always fun, but even this was too much. I didn't like feeling trapped, either. I needed to stretch out. I headed to the bathroom, but as I passed the top of the stairs, I heard my mom talking in a hushed tone.

"I don't understand what is happening, Ashton," she said. "Why would they call you in? And why aren't they telling you anything? It's scaring me."

I leaned over the stairs, trying to hear my dad's response, but it was muffled. Mom's voice grew louder as she got closer, and I knew I would get in trouble if I was caught eavesdropping. I quickly slipped back into my room.

I looked out my window, hoping to see my neighbor Jaxton in his room. The light in his room was on, so I tossed a bouncy ball across the twenty-foot gap between our houses and hit his window. Dozens of balls lay under each of our windows from previous throws. We gathered them back up every couple of months.

To my delight, Jaxton heard it and opened his window.

"You finally cleaning your room?" I asked.

"Nah. My mom just told me to stay in here for some reason."

"Me too. What do you think is going on?"

Jaxton shrugged, and before we could keep talking, his mother barged into his room. She yelled for him to get away from the window, told me to do the same, and apologized as she slammed his window shut and closed the blinds.

Jaxton's mom had never before had a problem with us talking like that. In fact, she always seemed happy to see me when she walked in on Jaxton and me talking. The adults were acting strangely today.

After another hour, I couldn't take it anymore and snuck into Aubrey's room, where Ally was already curled up on the bed next to her.

"What's going on?" I asked.

Aubrey shook her head. "I don't know. But it's not good if they brought Dad back to work and canceled school."

Ally sat up in the bed. "Is there a big fire?"

"I didn't see any smoke on the way home, Sis," Aubrey answered, trying to sound calm. "Some people at school said we were under attack. But we would have heard or felt something, right?"

"I'm scared, Aubrey," Ally said, burying her head into Aubrey's chest.

"It's gonna be okay, Sis. Dad is out there fixing things, and Mom will keep us safe here."

We stayed in Aubrey's room, playing board games to pass the time. I would leave the room occasionally to see if I could overhear something. Mom was always talking to someone, but I could only hear fragments of the conversations, and nothing made sense.

By the time dinner rolled around, we were finally called downstairs. Mom sat at the table, her eyes red and puffy. She barely looked at us as she served us our plates of frozen lasagna. We ate in silence for most of the meal.

Aubrey couldn't take it anymore, though. "Mom, what's happening? You need to tell us. Ally is scared, and so am I."

Mom raised her head slowly. "I'm sorry. I know you are, but I don't have many answers. Dad got called into work and is helping block streets with the fire engines. They aren't letting anyone in or out of the city. I don't know anything else, though."

We weren't happy with the answer, but we finished our meal in silence. Mom offered to let us have a movie night and ice cream before bed to lighten the mood. This didn't sound as wonderful now as it had earlier today. After dinner, we watched a movie quietly. I barely ate any of my ice cream, which had never happened before.

Mom tried to put us to bed, but I think she could tell from our faces that we were too scared to sleep alone. So, she brought us all into hers, which never happened unless we were extremely sick. We all snuggled up together, and Mom turned on the TV to help distract us until we fell asleep, and slept through the night.

The next morning, we were awoken by the creak of the front door. I raced downstairs with Aubrey and Ally right behind me. Dad was home!

He looked exhausted, his eyes bloodshot, with dark bags beneath them. He hugged and kissed us all before embracing Mom. A few tears rolled down her cheek as she kissed him repeatedly.

"What's going on, babe?" Mom asked, pulling back to look at him. "Did you find out anything?"

Dad sighed, rubbing his hand through his hair. "Let's sit down. I'll tell you what I know."

We gathered in the living room. My parents sat on the couch and we sat on the floor near their feet. I held my breath as Dad started to speak.

"Okay," he began. "I don't know everything, but here's what I know. The city is on lockdown. All planes are grounded. They were using us to help block the highways so no one could travel."

"What's lockdown?" Ally asked.

"It's where no one is allowed to leave the city, Sis," Mom answered.

"Or come in," Dad continued. "Luckily, we have the Air Force base in town, so they were able to help get it all set up properly, and we got to go home. Everyone is quarantined, though."

"Quarantined?" Mom questioned. "From what?"

"That I don't know. There were no bombs, smoke, fires, nothing. They sealed off the entire Valley, though. Vegas,

Henderson, North Town, everywhere. And they are stopping traffic 30 miles outside of town in every direction."

Dad thanked us for being good so far and asked us to remain brave for a bit longer. We nodded in agreement. It scared me to think that Dad didn't know the answer to something. I literally thought he knew everything.

That afternoon, Dad turned on the news, hoping for answers. Cameras showed both major highways completely lined with cars, none of them moving. At one of the blockades, hundreds of people were lined up against military personnel.

"You can't keep us from our families!" one person shouted. "You have to let me out to be with them."

The screen cut to a news anchor. "Authorities are still blocking all exits. They are warning anyone trying to enter or exit that they will be turned around, forcefully if necessary. They are asking everyone to return to their homes and await further instruction."

I'd never liked watching the news before, but I really didn't like it now.

For the next week, we remained quarantined in the house. No school, no practices, no friends. We would get updates every few days, but no answers. Dad was one of the few who still went to work because they said he was essential. Every time we watched him walk out the door, my mom's face grew more worried.

We spent most of the days in the backyard in the sunlight, or inventing new games to pass the time. Our absolute favorite became scavenger hunts, with clues marked by a special family logo we'd designed.

The logo was so simple that even I, with no artistic skill, could draw it—but it was still unique enough to make it our very own. Since all our families' initials were "A.B.," our symbol was the @ sign with a lowercase b attached on the right side, drawn in one fluid motion.

I won the first hunt that my dad made. After dozens of clues, I found myself in the garage.

"Found it!" I exclaimed, holding up a bag of cookies. Ally was behind me, bouncing on her toes.

"Great job, buddy," Mom said.

"I'm gonna have to make the next ones a little harder," my dad added with a smile. "You blew through that too fast."

The hunts became more creative and cleverer as the week went on. At the end of each, we would find small prizes or treats. The actual clue-following was the fun part, though. This game became the family favorite.

By the end of the second week, the news station announced we would finally be addressed by the President of the United States. They advised us to watch our televisions at 5:00 p.m. Thankfully, Dad was home that night.

At 5:00, the President began his announcement, his face somber. "Good evening. I want to start by thanking everyone for their patience and compliance in what is a difficult time, especially for our fellow Americans in Las Vegas and surrounding areas. I sincerely apologize for the delay in providing answers. Rest assured, we have been fighting tirelessly to obtain them."

My stomach churned, and my family fell silent as the President explained that the city was quarantined due to a catastrophic failure at an illegal experimental facility. This had released an unknown substance into the air. The Valley was completely sealed off to prevent the spread, while they determined the potential effects.

"We will continue to ensure your safety," the President continued. "We will provide aid and resources for everyone in the Valley. We have a hotline to call for those needing help or have parents or guardians outside the quarantine zone. Please know this is for everyone's safety, inside and out. Do not attempt to leave or enter Las Vegas. You will not be allowed to do so, no matter the circumstances."

I had hoped the President would give us some good news. But this couldn't have been worse. Could they really trap us all in here? Could they keep everyone out?

The President continued. "Lastly, we ask that you cooperate with any physical testing that needs to be performed. We have a lot of people working on finding answers, and the more compliant everyone is, the sooner we will have those answers. May God bless and watch over you."

Dad tried to reassure us that all the smartest people were working on a solution, and that everything would be okay. I wanted to believe him, but something inside me told me this was only the beginning of something much worse.

7

OPENING NIGHT

"Places to live won't be the issue. They won't have the means to import materials, so anything gasoline-related will need to be converted to electricity. Since the Hoover Dam and solar fields are within the quarantine zone, we will have to turn them over to the kids, which will give them more than enough power and water. We will need to figure out a way to continue distributing those resources to the surrounding states outside of the quarantine." —
Lonnie Creamer, City Manager

"D̲o you want to go to the movie premiere with us tonight?" Aubrey asked, leaning against my doorway.

I hesitated. Even though I showered, I couldn't get the smell of smoke off me, a haunting reminder of Jenny's burned body. Chris now didn't have a sister to go to the movies with him anymore. I should have gotten to her sooner.

"Aiden?" she prompted again.

I forced a smile. "Yeah, sounds fun." Any other answer would have been a red flag. "Do you care if I ask a buddy from work to come?"

"Of course not."

I called Ryan, and he agreed to come with us. First, I would need a nap. The new firefighting schedule was brutal, and I was having a hard time falling asleep at work because I was so worried about screwing up the next call. After a couple hours of restless sleep, filled with images of burned bodies and piercing screams, I woke up to Ally sitting on the edge of my bed, startling me.

"Ally! What are you doing? You scared me!"

"I think you need to let me give you a massage, Aiden."

I rolled my eyes. "What are you talking about? Why do you have to be so weird all the time?"

"I'm serious," she insisted. "I really think you need one. I promise it won't be weird. Just try it once, please."

I gagged, "Nope! Can't do it. It's gross. I don't understand why you want to give me one."

"I just think it can help you."

"With what?" I asked, offended, though I wondered if she somehow knew what was in my head. "I'm fine."

"I don't know. I just want to help."

"Well, I don't need help."

Ally walked toward the doorway, looking hurt, but she didn't push the issue.

"You coming to the movies tonight?" I asked, trying to soften the tension.

"Duh! I'm not missing a night out."

Later that evening, we drove to pick up Ryan from his place. I had never been to his home before. He didn't live too far away. Of course, no one really lived that far away, traveling by car. Getting anywhere in town was quick. The Valley was built to support over 3 million people, and now only sustained 300,000. Cars, which were all electric now, were usually on the roads, but never enough to cause any real traffic.

When we arrived, I had to double-check the address. The house was huge. I didn't know the name for a house bigger than a mansion, but this was it. The driveway led to a seven-car detached garage bigger than my entire house. The home itself was massive, with huge windows, steep-pitched roofs, and a custom cobblestone driveway.

"Welcome to my humble home," Ryan said, grinning, as he opened the enormous front doors.

"This is really where you live?" I asked, in awe. "Who else is here with you?"

"It's just me. I like having some room to stretch out, you see. I hate feeling crowded. You guys want a quick tour?"

Before Ryan could finish, Ally was rushing through the doors. "Yes!"

"That's my sister Ally," I laughed. "I guess she wants a tour. This is my older sister Aubrey, the dispatcher."

"Hi, I'm Ryan. I'm kinda in charge of your baby brother at the station. I have to teach him everything I know, you see."

"I do see," Aubrey responded. "Your house is beautiful. Is this where you lived in the Before?"

"I recognize your voice!" Ryan exclaimed. "You're probably my favorite dispatcher. Something about your voice just calms me down. And no, I didn't live here. My place in the Before wasn't quite this size. I found this after the Preparation. Decided to claim it for myself."

I couldn't help but wonder if we made a mistake not moving to a house like this. I didn't think I'd ever seen a cooler house. I wasn't sure I would want to live alone in something so big, though. I would probably never be able to find my sisters. Even though I liked the thought of this house, I liked where I was. Luxurious or not, it was home.

Ryan led us inside. The elegant chandelier hanging above cast a warm glow over the living room. Everything was sparkling white, with an electric fireplace on the far wall, which seemed out of place in Vegas. The kitchen was equally impressive, with commercial appliances that looked like they belonged in a restaurant.

"Where is your fridge, Ryan?" I asked, glancing around the spotless kitchen.

Ryan smirked, strutted to a portion of the cabinets, and grabbed a handle. He pulled it open to reveal a massive hidden refrigerator.

"A hidden fridge?" Ally said, shocked. "That's so cool."

"It's pretty immaculate in here," Aubrey pointed out, running her finger over the counter top. "No way you are keeping this clean all by yourself."

"Of course I do," Ryan answered with a sly grin. "All right, you got me. I use that cleaning company called *The 3 Broom Chicks*. They come by twice a month. But I am actually pretty clean on my own, you see."

We continued the tour, moving to the back of the house. A glass wall folded open, revealing an extravagant backyard with a pool, a water slide, and a lazy river. To the side of the pool was yet another building.

"What's that?" I asked, pointing to the structure.

Ryan casually leaned against the wall. "Indoor basketball court," he said with a grin.

"Are you kidding me? This place is insane!"

We headed back inside, and Ryan led us to the final stop. Once inside the dark room, he closed the door behind us, leaving us in pitch black. I couldn't see my sisters even though they stood right next to me.

"Aiden?" Ally whispered, her voice trembling.

Ryan laughed. "Sorry, guys. This is my favorite room, and I have to show it properly, you see."

"No, we don't see," Aubrey answered, grasping Ryan's arm.

Ryan flipped a light switch, and the room glowed with soft accent lighting. The ceiling twinkled with tiny lights edging it, and rows of recliner seats filled the sloped floor. Fluffy beanbags sat invitingly in the center of the purple-walled room, in front of a projector screen covering the entire wall. It was a theater room.

"This is it, guys," Ryan said. "This is my sanctuary. Movies here are a million times better, and don't even get me started on video games. I have a huge collection of movies and games that you guys can borrow or come watch whenever."

"That sounds so fun," Aubrey said. "I mean... for you, Aiden."

I sighed, wishing we could stay here and watch a real movie instead of whatever "masterpiece" they'd be showing at the theater tonight.

We drove to the theater, and I couldn't help but groan once we parked. "Do we have to watch the new one? It's gonna be so crowded on opening night. Can't we watch one they are playing from the Before?"

We still had access to movies from the Before. I loved them. Good acting, graphics, storylines. The new films kids were making? Terrible. But somehow everyone ate them up.

"No way," Ryan contested. "Why would we watch some old crappy movie?"

I scoffed. "Not you too, Ryan? You guys are delusional!"

We purchased tickets to *The Tunnel,* a movie about a group of kids who go on a treasure hunt and stumble upon a tunnel that leads to a land of monsters and riches. It sounded fine on paper, but I knew better.

After grabbing our food, which Ryan had paid for since we had given him a ride, we found our seats. It was already almost full, but we found enough seats for all of us toward the back. I sat between Ally and Ryan.

Ryan leaned back casually, grabbing handfuls of popcorn while he attempted to explain why these new movies were superior, and why he always tried to make it to opening nights.

His eyes suddenly fixed on the entrance, his hand freezing over the bucket I was holding. His whole body tensed, then he dropped to the ground, spilling most of the popcorn.

"It's her," he whispered.

"Her who?"

"The cop. Kaylyn."

Ryan had caused enough commotion that the kids in front of us turned and shot us curious looks.

"What are you two doing?" Aubrey asked. "You okay, Ryan?"

Ryan ducked his head further down. "I'm fine, it's nothing."

"Why are you kneeling on the ground then?" Ally asked.

I laughed before explaining, "Ryan saw someone walk in that makes him nervous."

"Nervous?" Ally asked. "Like a bully? You need me to take care of him for you?"

"Oh, it's no bully," I said.

"I'm not nervous!" Ryan said. "It's none of your business, you see."

"Oh..." Aubrey mocked. "I do see. It's a girl, isn't it?"

Ryan sat back in his seat but tucked his head between his knees. I wanted to tell my sisters how we met Kaylyn, but I wasn't sure how to explain it without having to mention all the traumatic events beforehand. However, I came up with a better story and shared it in my best narrator's voice.

"So, there we were, fire all around us! I already had a kid in each arm and one on my back. Ryan could only carry one. We made it to the front door but were still in danger because the house was about to collapse. Suddenly, someone appeared in front of us."

I paused to add to the suspense as Ryan covered his face with his hands.

"It was the girl," I continued. "Ryan took one look at her and dropped the kid at the door. His mouth wide open, with drool coming out. I had to grab the 4th kid with my teeth and carry it like a kitten until we made it to safety. Ryan stayed in the doorway, with smoke blowing out behind him. The cop tried to help him, but he was unable to move. Finally, he did, but only to lift his arm, point directly at her, and yell, 'Girl!'"

"Liar!" Ryan yelled loud enough that even more people turned around to glare at us. "That's not what happened."

Ally stood up to walk down to Kaylyn to ask her to come sit with us, but Ryan grabbed Ally and pulled her back, then hid behind the seats again. It was weird seeing Ryan like this. He seemed so confident and sure of himself. After some careful persuasion, Ally agreed to stay put.

But it didn't matter. Kaylyn had already spotted us.

"Hey!" Kaylyn said. "Ryan and Aiden, right? You guys remember me? Did you lose something?"

Ryan scrambled to his feet. "Uh, yes, I mean, no. I thought I lost something, but I found it, you see, and no, I remember you."

I introduced my sisters to Kaylyn. Ally asked her to sit with us. Kaylyn said her friend was supposed to meet her here but had to cancel at the last minute, so she agreed.

Ryan blushed and sat stiffly in his seat, trying not to fidget, even though Kaylyn sat at the end by Aubrey. Soon after Kaylyn joined us, the lights dimmed, and the movie began.

The movie was exactly how I expected. Sub-par acting, poor writing, and awful graphics. I was more entertained by watching the reactions of the people around me. Everyone seemed brainwashed and mesmerized, wholly invested in what I thought was a train wreck of a movie.

At around the halfway point, our popcorn buckets were nearly empty. As the only one who wasn't delusional about the movie, I volunteered to refill them.

Kaylyn stopped me. "Let me do it. You guys were nice enough to share with me. I can refill them. I need to use the bathroom anyway."

"I'll help," Ryan said awkwardly. "With the popcorn, I mean."

Still watching the moviegoers, I noticed a couple kids in the front row all pull hoodies over their heads at the same time. I frowned. *Weird.* Then, they stood in unison and walked toward the hallway exit. After a minute or two, I smelled something strange, but I couldn't see anything.

"Do you smell that, Aubrey?" I asked.

She raised an eyebrow and looked at me in disgust. "Did you fart or something?"

"No, I'm serious," I said, now sniffing the air more intently. "It smells like smoke."

Before she could respond, multiple red traffic flares flew from the entrance, landing on the floor in front of the room. The red glow filled the theater, as did the screams of the moviegoers.

People scrambled from their seats as even more fiery flares rained down upon them. I watched in disbelief from the back. As the small fires began, I wondered with dread if I would see another person burn. I was frozen, the screams piercing my soul, bringing me right back to Jenny's car fire.

Ryan must have heard the commotion because he entered from the opposite entrance, immediately taking charge of the chaotic scene unfolding. "Everyone, stay calm! Slowly exit the theater."

His demeanor commanded respect, and most of the kids obeyed his orders. He continued his orders by telling Aubrey to make sure Ally and everyone else got out.

"Aiden!" Ryan's voice snapped me back. "You work on these fires."

I shook my head, forcing my legs to move. I couldn't fail again. I wouldn't be able to live with myself.

We all separated to work on our assignments. I ran to the chair on fire, which wasn't out of control yet, and smothered it with my jacket. Ryan and I then moved on to the rest of the flares, stomping each one out.

"Ryan, Aiden," Aubrey yelled. "I got someone hurt up here."

With the flares out, we ran to Aubrey to find a young girl crying on the ground at the end of a row. Ryan and I grabbed her and carried her out. She had twisted her ankle and was frozen in fear, but was okay.

Outside, the lobby was in a panic, with people crying and arguing. Many were upset with the theater workers, as if they were at fault. We continued checking people for injuries when Kaylyn walked out of the bathroom.

"What is going on?" Kaylyn asked.

"I don't know," Ryan answered. "I saw some kids sprint out of the theater after you went into the bathroom, and then I heard screaming. Someone threw a bunch of road flares in there."

"Did you see what they looked like?"

Ryan shook his head. "No, they were wearing hoodies and had their faces covered."

A couple of minutes later, Engine 2 arrived. I met them at the door to explain what happened. The first crew member who arrived at the door was a short guy who walked tall and with purpose. He had a water extinguisher in his hand, similar to your typical extinguisher, but one that only sprayed water.

"Hi, I'm Aiden Brann," I said to the firefighter. "I'm a rookie at station 3. There was a small fire in Theater

Number 1, but I put it out with my jacket. We evacuated everyone already. There are lots of flares that I only..."

The firefighter scoffed and looked at me like I insulted him. "A rookie? You're a brand-new rookie, and think you completely put out a fire with your jacket? Did you make sure it was fully out? No, you didn't! Now get out of my way and let a real fireman handle this."

He bumped me with his shoulder as he walked past and into the theater room. The rest of his crew followed in soon after, but I didn't dare talk to them, fearing I'd receive the same treatment. Ryan, however, saw them and went to speak with them.

"Mi!" the captain said. "What are you doing here?"

Ryan greeted them and explained what happened. He also introduced me to them.

The captain extended his hand to me. "So, you're the new rookie. Brann, right? Captain Jefferson has already told me a little about you. I'm Grant Reynolds, out of station 2."

"Nice to meet you, sir."

Reynolds looked around, shaking his head. "Now, where did Brett run off to? I can never keep track of that kid. He is always running off without thinking, trying to handle everything himself."

Brett soon returned, chest puffed, beaming with pride. "You're lucky I went in and checked on the fire you supposedly put out, rookie! Captain Reynolds, I wet down the seat that was on fire, as well as all the seats in the same row. Then I threw the flares into the trash. We are good to go!"

Reynolds raised an eyebrow. "You threw the flares in the trash?"

"Yup!" Brett answered with a grin.

"So, you thought throwing hot flares into a trash filled with paper garbage would be a good idea?"

The other firefighter, who appeared much more competent, rolled his eyes, grabbed Brett's extinguisher, and returned to the theater. I got the impression this wasn't the first time he had to clean up one of his messes. Brett no longer stood so proudly.

Reynolds stepped closer to Brett. "You need to stop freelancing. We work together as a crew. Got it?"

No sooner had Reynolds finished that sentence, than the other firefighter came running out of the theater, holding a trash can at arm's length, struggling to keep his face from the flames shooting out of the can.

"He used all the water!" he yelled.

He continued out the front door, leaving a small trail of smoke in his wake. The rest of the crew followed him outside as Captain Reynolds smacked Brett on the helmet. I couldn't help but grin, seeing such swift karma.

"That guy is always screwing up," Ryan said. "But he seems completely unaware and never learns, you see. What do you think the flares were about, Aiden?"

I shrugged. "It's gotta be the Children, right? Aubrey said they have been causing more problems lately."

Ryan shrugged, but before he could respond, his phone buzzed. He studied the screen intently, his demeanor turning serious. Then quickly returned it to his pocket without touching it further.

"Hey, sorry, Aiden," Ryan said. "I have to go. I'll find my own way home. Thanks for the ride. I'll see you at work."

"Wait. What?"

He didn't even say goodbye to my sisters or Kaylyn. He briskly walked away from the building and down the street, disappearing into the darkness.

Something was gnawing at my gut. Ryan was hiding a secret.

8

PILES OF FIRES

"I'll only be gone for a little while, and then I'll be back for you... someday." — Kodi Mitsuya

I was anxious to return to work today. After the strange way Ryan left the movie theater, I had some questions I wanted answered. I couldn't shake the feeling that something about it was off.

I arrived at the station, hoping to corner him before the others showed up, but he walked in much later than he typically would.

"Ryan," I called out, stepping in front of him as he entered. "Where did you go the other night? How come you haven't been answering my texts?"

He barely slowed down, brushing past me. "It's nothing. Just forgot something I had to do, you see. Don't worry about it."

I frowned. "Well, what was it? I could have given you a ride. Was something wrong?"

Ryan's shoulders tensed. He turned just enough to meet my eyes. "Seriously, drop it."

His voice was sharp. Sharper than I'd ever heard it. He left the bay, leaving his gear by the engine without even checking it.

Mum, who was sitting in the front seat, raised an eyebrow.

"That's not like him. What was that about?" she asked.

"I don't know," I said, shaking my head. "We had a crazy night. I'm sure you heard about the incident at the theater. Well, we were there. We helped put out the fire and got everyone out. Ryan basically handled everything, and then he just left. Didn't even say goodbye. I think he got a text or something. Whatever it was, it seemed serious."

"That is weird. But, just give him some time. I'm sure Ryan has a good reason for doing whatever it is he is doing."

Ryan's unusual silence continued through morning muster. His eyes were worn and bloodshot. There were plenty of chances for him to crack a joke or two, but he barely spoke. Even Cap gave him a few curious glances when he expected a quick-witted response, but he didn't push the issue. Reed, however, wasn't about to let it go.

"It sure is quiet today," Reed said with a sly grin as he nudged Ryan. "Reed loves the quiet. Don't you think it's quiet, Mi? Reed wonders why it's so quiet. Don't you wonder, Mi?"

Ryan didn't bite, and Reed's grin faded. Even Reed knew when to back off. The crew was dismissed. I began my morning details of cleaning bathrooms and mopping floors, when four bells sounded!

"Engine 3, building fire. Repeat, Engine 3, building fire."

I dropped the mop and sprinted into the bay to don my turnouts. Cap, Mum, and Ryan ran out soon after me. Although I moved quickly, I took extra precautions to not get tangled up again. I couldn't afford another rookie mistake.

We barreled out of the station, Mum driving like a speed demon. Flying down the freeway, I maintained a death grip on my seat. Mum's foot was pressed to the floor as she reached the engine's maximum speed.

"These stupid safety features!" she yelled as the engine refused to go any faster. "What idiot had the bright idea to put a governor in an emergency vehicle? Don't they know I got places to be?"

Cap chuckled in the front seat. It was one of the few times I saw him smile like a little kid. He seemed to relish in Mum's road-raging maneuvers.

"Let's go, Fisk," Cap said, egging her on. "This fire isn't gonna put itself out."

"All incoming units, be advised, we are getting multiple calls," the dispatcher crackled over the radio.

Caps' tone changed, his voice becoming serious again. "Be ready, guys," he said. "Looks like we are gonna be first in."

I leaned forward to look out the windshield as we approached. Thick, black smoke rose in a column straight ahead of us. We turned sharply onto a residential street, the engine leaning hard and my pulse racing.

We pulled up in front of a single-story house, where flames licked out of the window on the Bravo side. The engine's air brake hissed as we stopped, and I quickly unbuckled my seat belt and stood with no resistance. I wasn't tangled this time, and clapped my hands together. "Yes!" Getting out was only the first step, though.

After grabbing my axe, I climbed up the side of the engine, where Mum met me to help pull the hose line. These hoses were so heavy that it took a lot of effort for us kids to pull them off and get them flaked out. We managed to do so, and I kneeled at the front door as Mum charged the line.

"Let's get that door open!" Cap said as he approached.

Ryan was already at the front door, a Halligan tool in hand, which was excellent for prying.

"Set the Halligan Ryan," I said. "I'll drive it in."

Ryan glanced back at me, shaking his head slightly before reaching for the door handle. It opened easily.

"Come on, Brann. You can't forget the basics," Cap said. "Try before you pry. Now, lead us in."

Smoke billowed out the front door in turbulent, rolling waves. I connected my regulator to my mask, which was already on, and felt the cool rush of air fill my mask. I crawled in, dragging the unyielding hose along. Each step was a battle.

Visibility dropped quickly. The blackness swallowed everything. The movies always made it look easy, with perfect visibility and no masks. But here? Without our masks, we'd be dead in seconds. I couldn't even see my hand in front of my face.

My turnouts filled with sweat, the heat pushing me lower to the ground. I couldn't see the fire, though.

"Keep moving, Brann," Cap yelled from the rear. "Just past the table and to the left."

I didn't realize I'd stopped moving. And what table? I continued forward, ramming my head into a solid object. Oh, that table. First my ears were burning, and now my whole body. I couldn't stop again, though.

A sudden wave of fire rolled across the ceiling, directly over my head, like a monstrous spider. I aimed the nozzle upward and pulled open the bail. The force nearly ripped it from my hands. I gritted my teeth, fighting for control. The stream hit the ceiling, hissing violently as it turned to steam. I pushed forward, the scalding water dripping into the small gaps in my gear.

The glow above me disappeared, and I directed the nozzle to a now prominent larger glow ahead, which I assumed was a bedroom. I sprayed all over the room, from side to side and top to bottom, until the orange vanished and the temperature cooled. I could still barely see.

Engine 1 arrived shortly after and set up ventilation. As the smoke cleared out, we finally saw the source of the fire: a large pile of random objects, mattresses, clothes, chairs, and decorations stacked in the center of the room. This was no accident.

We searched the rest of the house. Dishes were in the sink, and groceries were in the fridge and pantry. Someone was living here.

After ensuring the fire was completely out, Cap, Ryan, and I joined Mum outside to clean up. As I removed my air pack, Mum pointed at my helmet.

"Whoa, was it that hot in there?"

I took my helmet off to inspect it. The leather E3 identifier on the front was charred and shriveled beyond recognition. My yellow helmet was now almost completely black.

"Wow," Cap said, noticing it as well. "I guess it was a lot hotter for you upfront than it was in the back. I was wondering why you kept stopping. You good?"

"Yes, sir," I said, though my whole body ached.

"Well, solid work. That was a hot one."

The fire was out, and the rest of the crews were released. We reloaded our hoses and put away our tools. As I returned my air pack to its bracket, equipped with a fresh bottle, a dispatcher crackled over the radio again.

"Engine NUMBER 3, copy another building fire."

Another fire? I put on my turnouts, which were less inviting than usual. My feet sloshed as I stepped into the wet boots. The cold, bogged-down turnouts sent a shiver down my spine.

We drove off again and arrived first at an apartment complex. It was safe to assume this place was vacant. Few people, if anyone, lived in these older types of apartments. There were plenty of houses to choose from, so these became obsolete.

Fire was shooting out of a window on the 2nd floor on the Delta side. Mum helped Ryan get the hose off the engine, but I assisted with getting it up the stairs. We stumbled multiple times as we climbed. Each step felt like climbing a mountain. With the heavy, wet turnouts and the fact that we were already tired, this was a taxing operation.

Cap met up with us soon after arriving at the entry door. "Here, Brann. You hold this, this time."

He handed me a thermal imaging camera, called a TIC, which was how he was able to see during the last fire. A TIC displayed the heat signatures it was pointing at. I should have known Cap used one when he guided me so efficiently through the darkness.

We entered a living room and soon encountered conditions similar to those we'd seen earlier. Heavy smoke, low visibility. Except for this time, I was able to see—the TIC's screen outlined Ryan, who was in front of me. Even the stream when he sprayed water was visible. I guided him through the living room and down a hall to our right.

When we reached the fire and extinguished it, we quickly noticed it was from another pile of objects stacked in the center of the room. Someone was out setting fires.

Cap had me take the TIC and search the rest of the apartment while Ryan extinguished the blaze. I entered through a closed door into a bedroom across the hall. After quickly scanning the room, I opened the closet and nearly fell backward.

A girl was sitting inside, clutching a backpack.

"Are you okay?" I asked, my voice muffled through my mask.

She nodded but didn't speak. I radioed Cap, informing him we had a victim. He and Ryan rushed in. We waited in the clear-air room until another crew could get the rest of the smoke out of the building.

"What are you doing here?" Ryan asked.

She lowered her head and didn't answer.

"Are you living here?" Ryan continued.

She nodded.

"Where do you work?"

I was confused by that question. It didn't seem very pertinent to the situation. She didn't answer and turned her head away from Ryan.

He got closer, kneeling at eye level with her. "It's okay. I am, too. I can help you."

She locked eyes with him, and tears welled, squeezing her backpack tighter. Cap was relaying information to crews on the radio and wasn't listening to this conversation. Ryan gave her a reassuring smile and placed his hand on her shoulder.

Finally, she spoke, in a low whisper. "They found where I was hiding. I came home and saw the fire but had to get my pack. By the time I grabbed it, it was too hot to leave the room."

This was all very cryptic. Why would anyone need to be hiding? It didn't make sense, so I was certain I misheard most of what they said. It was hard to hear with all this gear on and crews working just outside the door.

Once the smoke cleared out, we escorted her downstairs and toward the rescue. Ryan quickly grabbed a piece of paper and scribbled something on it, handing it to the girl before she entered the rescue. As soon as he turned away from her, she jumped out and disappeared down the street.

Thoroughly confused, I confronted Ryan. "Why did she run off like that? What's going on?"

Ryan shrugged. "I don't know. Must be scared of ambulances."

"You wrote something to her. Did you tell her to leave? She needed medical attention."

I asked a few more questions, but Ryan denied everything and seemed to have an answer for everything. I knew something was up, though.

Reed and Hill took the rescue and drove around looking for the girl, but could not find her. Even Cap and Mum interrogated Ryan, but he dodged each question like a politician from the Before.

Once we finished with the fire scene, Cap pulled me aside.

"Keep an eye on Mitsuya for me. Something about him and that girl was weird."

I nodded my head and we returned to the station.

We all moved much more slowly than normal, exhausted and worn from back-to-back fires. My calves cramped hard, locking up as I tried to walk. I groaned as I stretched them out and attempted to clean and reset our equipment. My main priority was to switch out my waterlogged turnouts for fresh, dry ones.

Mum went into the kitchen after she finished her assignments and returned to us soon after. An intoxicating smell wafted in after her.

"Bless that Devin Hill!" Mum said, raising her hands above her head. "He cooked us something for lunch since we were gone so long!"

Mum licked her lips and looked overly excited about the meal. I was hungry, too, but this seemed excessive.

"Is Hill a good cook or something?" I asked Ryan.

"Probably one of the best, and I don't even mean just among firefighters. He's funny, though, because he claims he has no idea what he is doing, you see. But every meal he touches is fantastic."

At least Ryan answered that question.

Hill made Philly cheesesteaks. They looked appetizing, but I didn't understand the big fuss. A cheesesteak didn't seem all that impressive. My opinion changed when I took the first bite.

A perfectly cheesy sandwich with just the right amount of peppers and onions, seasoned with something I had never tasted before. Each bite melted in my mouth, and my eyes rolled into the back of my head.

"Hill," I said, mouth full. "This is amazing."

"Thanks," he answered, removing his apron. "Sorry, it isn't anything special. I just had to throw something together."

"Hey, Brann," Reed interjected. "That was your first house fire, right? You know what that means!"

I shook my head, my cheeks too stuffed to speak.

"Pies!" Everyone yelled in unison.

I tilted my head.

"It means you get us pies," Reed explained. "It's a little tradition to celebrate your first fire and to reward us for putting up with you."

I smiled. "Oh! Yeah, I can do that."

I shoved the last bite of the sandwich into my mouth. With the combination of fatigue and a full belly, I couldn't possibly move. But then, four bells went off again!

"What is happening?!" Mum yelled as she shoved in one more bite.

I attempted to run through the station, moaning and limping my way to the engine. I got ready, relieved I'd switched out my turnouts and got to wear warm, dry ones again. It was a strangely satisfying feeling. However, climbing into the engine was more challenging than it should have been, with my legs cramping in objection, but I had to get in. We began the drive, and Mum cursed the drivers even more than usual.

"Cap," Ryan said, "I don't know if I've got anything left in me. I can't move."

Cap let out a heavy sigh, obviously as tired as the rest of us. "This is the job. We gotta figure it out."

We arrived at an old abandoned warehouse with industrial roll-up doors. A small amount of grey smoke seeped through the creases. Ryan and Mum pulled the hose, and I followed them.

Mum stopped me once she flaked out the line. "Stop for a second and look. What are you going to need besides water, for this fire?"

I surveyed the property, trying to evaluate the situation better.

"How are you going to get inside?" she asked.

She was right. We needed to get inside, and these roll-up doors would not simply open for us, and we wouldn't be able to force them with our hand tools.

"The K-12!" I exclaimed.

I ran back to the engine, fighting off my cramping legs as I did. The K-12 was a heavy circular saw that was great for cutting through metal. I carried it across the lot to the roll-up door, where Ryan waited with the hose.

The blade spun rapidly as I turned on the electric saw. Lifting it high above my head, I began my first down-cut. Beautiful, bright embers shot off the end of the blade like a thousand sparklers. The sight was mesmerizing, and I forgot how tired I was until I had to make the next cut.

The second cut was across the top. It took a few tries to lift the saw above my head, but with a loud grunt, I was able to do it. My arms shook from both fatigue and the vibrations as I pulled the saw across the door. I was so tired, but I refused to drop it, knowing I would not be able to get it back up.

The last down-cut was more manageable, and when I finished, I pushed the door inward. It crashed to the floor with a resounding thud, sending a cloud of dust into the air.

Another pile of junk was stacked in the center. Luckily, the warehouse was wide open and had tall ceilings. Nothing besides the pile was on fire. I sighed in relief, knowing none of us had the energy to handle anything more extensive.

Ryan put out the fire, and Cap and I began searching the building. We started on opposite sides, planning to meet in the middle. However, I didn't make it there. My flashlight flickered over the warehouse wall. At first, I thought it was just random graffiti, maybe from the Before. Then I read the message:

Vegas will fall and your perfect world will end!

A chill ran through my body, the hairs on my arms standing on end. Below the words, drawn in a dark, red paint, was a symbol that everyone was beginning to know all too well. A simple "T" inside of a larger "C."

The symbol of the Children.

The message was clear. They were no longer simply going to be lazy kids sitting idly by. They were declaring war against the city. My city.

9

THE PRESIDENT

Within minutes of Cap informing our Chief about the Children's ominous writing on the wall, Officer Kaylyn Keller arrived in her police cruiser. She was soon followed by our Chief, more police officers, a news team, city officials—and, to my surprise, President Paislee Keres.

The moment the President stepped out of her vehicle, I felt like I was in the presence of a celebrity. I had only seen her on TV, giving speeches in formal, neatly pressed suits. Today, she looked completely different: tall, with long, brunette hair pulled into a ponytail and a backward trucker hat, dressed in jeans. It threw me off. It didn't seem very presidential, but I couldn't stop staring. She carried herself with confidence, the kind that came from being in charge of an entire city.

Within minutes, a perimeter had been set up around the warehouse with portable barriers and caution tape. The area buzzed with activity as officials, officers, and reporters swarmed in. This was more than just a fire. This was a threat.

President Keres approached us, and shook hands with Cap and the rest of the crew. When she got to me, I froze for a moment, glad I'd managed to outstretch my hand.

"Thank you for your service," she said, her grip firm yet soft. "I'm Paislee Keres. I've heard you've been dealing with these fires all day."

"Yes. That's correct, President Keres," Cap answered.

"Call me Paislee. President makes me sound like an old lady," she said with a chuckle. She turned to Ryan and me, studying us for a moment. "Are you the two that helped with the theater fire?"

"Yes, we did," Ryan answered, standing a little straighter. "I'm Ryan Mi, Mitsuya. This is Aiden Brann. How did you know it was us?"

"Well, Ryan and Aiden. It's my job to know and your efforts haven't gone unnoticed. You've both been invaluable to us in the Valley. If more people were as dedicated as you two, our city would be in even better shape. I just wish these 'Children' would realize they could be a part of something historic instead of causing us all these headaches."

She moved on to speak with a group of police officers gathered with Kaylyn. Ryan shifted uncomfortably next to me. His usual humor was still missing and he was unable to stand still.

"You good, man?" I asked.

He didn't answer, but continued fidgeting with his gloves. President Keres made her way to a podium set up in front of the graffiti. We were shuffled in behind her, making a backdrop. Multiple cameras aimed directly at us. I had never been on TV before. Ryan stood next to me, sweating and shifting uneasily.

"Do you think this is going to be broadcast to everyone?" he whispered to me.

"Of course. It's the President. This is pretty exciting, huh?"

Ryan stiffened, his gaze fixed like a deer in the headlights. His breathing turned shallow, then erratic. A slight tremble ran through his hands.

"Ryan?" I whispered.

No response. I nudged him, saying his name again, but he barely blinked.

"Ryan?" I said again. "You with us?"

Still nothing. Then he gasped, like he couldn't get enough air, tugging at the collar of his shirt. Without acknowledging me, he leaned over to Cap. "Can I go, Cap? Please."

Cap nodded and Ryan turned on his heel and hustled to the engine, looking around as if he was being hunted. I was worried about him. What could have him so spooked? I wanted to follow him, but one of the President's aides informed us the speech was about to begin.

President Keres stood at the podium, took off her hat, fluffed out her hair, and effortlessly transformed into the poised leader we always saw on TV. She approached the microphone, adjusting it slightly before looking directly into the camera.

"No more!" she began. "For too long we've given these 'Children' a chance to do the right thing. We've let them take advantage of our generosity. We gave them the opportunity to build a future with us. These brave firefighters have put a stop to their destruction for today, but even they can only hold off the Children for so long. And now we know. Now we know that the Children intend to tear down this beautiful city."

She stepped to the side, motioning to the Children's written threat, which loomed behind her with a menacing energy. "Vegas will fall." She turned back to the camera, her voice hard as steel. "I promise you—Vegas will not fall! This valley is our home. Together we live. Together we thrive!"

The crowd erupted in support of the President's rally cry, chanting in unison for the downfall of the Children.

Feeling the magnitude of what I was standing in the middle of, I rocked nervously, looking over the crowd, hoping to catch a glimpse of Ryan near the engine. As soon as the speech ended, I slipped away to check on him, and found him sitting in the engine with his head between his knees. He flinched when I opened the door.

"Hey, what's going on?" I asked.

He tried to play it off, but I could see the fear in his eyes. "Nothing. I'm fine. I'm just tired."

"You don't look fine. Why are you so jumpy?"

"I'm not jumpy. I told you. It's nothing. I'm not used to fighting so many fires, and I'm exhausted, all right? Not all of us can pull five Gretas straight."

I ignored his small outburst and continued to push. "If we are gonna be friends and partners, we need to be able to talk to each other."

"Aiden, I'm asking you to leave it alone. Please. For your own good."

"If you don't want to talk to me, that's okay. Talk to Mum or Cap. I know something is up, though."

Ryan lowered his head to the ground, covering his face. I moved to the seat across from him and waited, giving him a chance to speak. After a few moments of silence, he finally made eye contact with me.

"Fine, listen," he said, his voice barely above a whisper. "I have never told anybody this before, you see, and you can't tell anyone. Not Mum, not Cap, not your sisters. No one."

I wondered what secret could possibly be so important that he had never told anyone. Did I even want to know that kind of secret? Though our friendship felt old, it was still very new.

"Yeah, of course," I said, leaning in. "I promise."

Ryan took a deep breath, running his hand through his hair. "I used to be one of them."

I blinked. "One of what?"

"The Children," he whispered. "I was a part of them."

It hit me like a gut punch. This was my partner. My friend. Or so I thought. I'd never met an actual member of the Children before. I rubbed my forehead, trying to process it. Was I friends with a criminal? The Children were now actively trying to tear our city down. Could I trust someone who used to be a part of that? How could I be sure he still wasn't? Maybe that was why he had been acting so weird.

"What do you mean?" I asked, hoping for some reasonable answer.

He glanced out the window, exhaling like years of pressure were being lifted from his chest. "We were just kids. Orphans. We were alone long before the sickness. No parents. No future. No one cared about us." His hands clenched to fists. "They failed us. So, when the adults died, we decided we wouldn't ever be a part of something they created."

Ryan's voice filled with a bitterness and sorrow I had never heard from him before. "We did our own thing for a while, and it was fine. But then I started to feel like I wanted to do more. I wanted to help people who were alone, like I was in the Before."

"So, you became a firefighter," I said, putting the pieces together.

"Yeah," Ryan nodded. "I turned in my Preparation test to the city and finished my training. But most of my old friends never forgave me. We weren't violent before, though, and I don't know why they are getting violent now. That was never part of the plan."

I let out a slow breath, trying to take it all in. The Children were getting violent now. I wasn't sure if I believed him at first, but his eyes were sincere. He was genuinely devastated.

"Ryan, that's a lot. Sorry you had to go through all that. But you did the right thing. You chose to help people."

Ryan looked at me, his eyes filled with gratitude. "Thanks, Aiden. I just get nervous when people talk about the Children because I know them. I used to be one of them, and I don't really like people knowing that."

Even after he told me the truth, I could see in his eyes that he was leaving something out. He still had more secrets, but I didn't want to push for more now.

Before I could respond, Mum appeared at the door, motioning for us to join her outside. "You guys okay? The President wants to thank us again before she leaves."

We walked back toward the podium, where President Keres spoke to a group of police officers. Kaylyn stopped us, smiling at Ryan on the way there.

"Hey guys," she said. "You all look like you've been hit by a train."

"Yeah," Ryan replied with a sheepish grin. "We were. Well, not really. We had lots of trains today. I mean, we fought lots of trains. Fires! We fought fire today. Lots of it, you see."

I chuckled to myself. Ryan stumbling through a conversation with Kaylyn was a welcome sight.

"Right," Kaylyn said with a raised eyebrow. "Sounds intense. Well, maybe you guys need to get back to your warm, comfy beds and get some sleep. You know, since you get paid to sleep while we are out here working."

Kaylyn smirked, obviously proud of her little jab, but Ryan had no response. I bailed him out by excusing us and leading him toward the President. When she saw us, she smiled warmly.

"I just wanted to personally thank you again for all your hard work," she said. "I know today was rough. So, as a small token of our appreciation, we've got tickets for you all to attend the Raiders' opening night tomorrow. Take a day to enjoy yourselves. You've earned it. Oh... and go, Raiders!"

10

THE FOOTBALL GAME

"Football is not a real career. I doubt anyone is going to have time to be messing around with games in your future. Do something that will actually contribute to society." —
Rusty Patton

The President had given us seven tickets to the Las Vegas Raiders' season opener against the North Town Thunderbirds. Reed and Hill claimed two tickets since they were a part of the crew. Ryan convinced everyone to invite Kaylyn, saying she deserved it since she had been the first cop on scene during the warehouse fire.

Games were well-attended and always packed; it was one of the few times when the roads were congested. We decided to carpool to ease the parking issues, but Ryan soon regretted this. Once we all piled into Mum's vehicle, the teasing began.

"So, Ryan," Mum said with a mischievous smirk. "Tell us about this Officer Kaylyn Keller."

Ryan sighed. "There is nothing to tell. She helped me and Aiden on a call and was quick to the warehouse fire. I figured she deserved to come, you see. That's all!"

Mum smirked. "So, do you think she's cute?"

Ryan nearly choked on his water. "What?! Why would you ask that? No!"

"So, you think she is ugly?" Reed chimed in. "That's messed up, man. Reed didn't think she was ugly."

"That's not what I meant. I just didn't notice or anything."

Cap turned in his seat. "That worries me, Ryan. I expect my firefighters to be observant. If you can't even notice a pretty girl, how can I trust you to notice hidden dangers?"

Even Hill, the quiet one, spoke. "It's too bad you don't like her. She was asking about you."

Ryan literally jumped. "She did!?"

Laughter exploded in the car.

Hill calmly placed his headphones back over his ears. "Nah. I wasn't even there."

"All right guys," I said, calming down the ruckus. "Go easy on him. You'll see once we meet up with her. Ryan will act completely normal. He won't even forget how to speak."

Ryan's face turned a shade of red I didn't think was possible. When we reached the stadium, Ryan sprinted out of the car, eager to escape the relentless teasing.

I had been to multiple games in the After but still couldn't help but marvel at the sheer size of the structure. The black and silver building was flat-out cool. A massive screen on the outside displayed the top players for each team.

I wondered if the threat of the Children would deter people from coming to the game, but any doubt I had vanished once we tried to park. It was going to be a packed house as always. There was significantly more security and a larger police presence than normal. Probably smart. I was glad to see that the city wasn't so easily scared.

The tickets President Keres had given us were incredible. They were right on the 50-yard line, and would put me closer to the field than I'd ever been. I proudly wore my North Town Thunderbirds jersey, though they were the clear underdogs, while most of the crew was decked out in black and silver for the Raiders.

Four professional teams remained in the After: the Las Vegas Raiders, the Summerlin Elite, the Henderson Hustlers, and the North Town Thunderbirds.

Ryan wore gold and silver for the Elite, even though they weren't playing. Most people wore the colors of whatever team they supported, whether they were playing or not. Mum sported a Hustlers green and black T-shirt with their logo, which had a deck of cards in the center.

As we approached the entrance, we spotted Kaylyn waiting for us. Much to my delight, she was wearing Thunderbird colors.

"The Summerlin Elite, huh, Ryan?" she teased, eyeing his jersey. "You must think you're better than everyone else."

Ryan fumbled for a response, his cheeks reddening. "Uh... no. I just live there, so I'm elite. I mean, I support the Elite, you see. Not that I'm elite. You're elite."

Mum leaned over to me and whispered, "I see what you mean about forgetting how to talk."

The crew laughed, and Ryan lowered his hat, wanting to disappear. But as we took our seats, the energy in the stadium seemed to lift his spirits. The view was spectacular. The excitement in the air was contagious, and I stood in awe at how massive some of the players looked up close.

After a while, the teams formed along the sideline for the singing of the Vegas Anthem. The stadium erupted when they announced Misty, one of the most famous singers in the After, would be performing it.

She walked out of the tunnel, waving as she went to center field. Her long black dress, adorned with silver rhinestones, glimmered as the spotlights hit her.

We stood and placed our hands over our hearts as she began singing. She was a beautiful girl, but her voice was even more so. She sang the song a capella, and it was one of the most inspiring renditions I had ever heard.

Hill removed his headphones and listened intently, almost reverently. Watching Hill, I decided to pay closer attention to the lyrics. Soon after the adults passed, someone rewrote our version of the National Anthem. We were no longer truly part of the USA. Walled off from the world, we were our own city, state, and country, so it made sense. The song was sung to the original tune, however:

"Oh, say, can you see
How our Valley's still lit.
Battle born were we raised
Proudly, we are enduring.
From the red rocks to lake
We will never submit
Families, we won't forget
As we start our new beginning.
And united, we'll stand
As we work hand in hand.
Together, we will commit
To make this valley grand.
We see how our Valley still lights the night sky
In our land that we love, our hope will not die."

The crowd went wild as Misty hit the last high note, holding it out for longer than I could hold my breath. The applause, whistles, and stomping were so loud you couldn't hear anything else, and the floor beneath us shook from the vibrations.

The game kicked off, and the Raiders scored after only a few short plays. Their running back, much smaller than most of them but very fast, broke a tackle and bolted into the end-zone. Cap, Reed, and Hill cheered, high-fiving each other while I groaned.

"Just wait," I muttered. "You won't be able to stop our QB."

T.J. Griffin, the Thunderbirds' star quarterback, was the most well-known athlete in the Valley. He was the only athlete who played multiple sports year-round instead of returning to their jobs in the offseason. He was also widely considered the best player in each one. I had high hopes he would turn the Thunderbirds' luck around this year. But on the first play, the receiver dropped a perfect pass from Griffin.

"Noooo!" I shouted. "Come on."

Cap laughed. "Doesn't matter how good your QB is if his teammates can't do their job. You need a whole team to work together to win."

The game continued through halftime in a back-and-forth fashion, with Griffin scoring on his own at times to keep the Thunderbirds in the game. Ryan, surprisingly, wasn't as awkward as I feared he would be around Kaylyn, and was even starting to open up. He managed a few short conversations that didn't end in disaster.

During the second-half kickoff, a Thunderbird player was hit so hard he flipped backward and landed awkwardly on his arm. From our seats, we could see the gruesome injury perfectly, and the sound of his scream echoed across the field.

The EMS crew assigned to the game rushed onto the field, stabilized his arm and loaded him into an ambulance. The crowd applauded as the player gave a thumbs-up before they closed the ambulance doors.

The game took a small break, so I decided to grab a snack. Making my way up the stairs, I scanned the crowd and, to my surprise, saw Chris, the boy whose sister Jenny had died in the car accident. He was sitting with a laptop. For a second, I thought I saw Jenny sitting next to him. I rubbed my eyes and she disappeared, replaced by a stranger.

"Chris?" I called out. "Hi. Do you remember me?"

He looked up, startled, and studied my face momentarily. "Oh yeah, the firefighter, right? Aiden?"

"Yeah. How are you doing? How's the Hotel?"

"The Hotel," he muttered. "Yeah, it's good. The Hotel is good."

I pointed to the kids next to him. "These your friends?"

A group of two boys and a girl sat next to him. One of the boys had a somewhat large bandage between his elbow and bicep. I could see redness around the edges, where the bandage didn't cover the skin. They didn't introduce themselves, and turned away slightly to continue their own conversation.

"Uh, yeah, I made some friends at the Hotel. They wanted me to come today."

I sat down on the armrest of his seat and glanced at his screen. It was filled with what looked like random numbers and symbols, and nothing I saw made any sense to me.

"What are you working on?" I asked. "Never seen anybody work on a computer at a football game before."

Chris shrugged and closed the laptop. "It's nothing, just some coding."

"Coding? That's cool. Can you show me?"

Chris hesitated, glancing at his friends, who suddenly went quiet. "Um, okay." He reopened the laptop. "This is actually pretty cool. You see the big screen on the other side of the field? Watch."

I followed his gaze to the jumbotron. It displayed stats, scores, and player info. Chris's fingers moved fast. Too fast. Then, the screen flickered. First red, green, then yellow, before returning to normal.

My jaw dropped. "Wait... did you just?"

Chris grinned, folding his arms smugly after closing the laptop.

I laughed and shoved him playfully. "Wow! You're a real-life hacker, huh?"

Chris shrugged. "Nah. I'm just messing around."

"Well, I think it's amazing. I've never met anyone who has that skill. I just hope you are using your superpowers for good!"

He smiled faintly but didn't respond, only looking at his friends, who were now whispering amongst themselves.

We said our goodbyes and I continued up the stairs, wondering why Chris would want to be friends with such strange, distant characters. He probably just didn't want to be alone.

I got in line at the concessions behind three people, minding my business while admiring the sprinkler systems running the corridor. I followed the pipes with my eyes, attempting to locate the fire department hookups. A fire in here would be insane. But I needed to know what I would do in this situation, so I played out the scenarios in my head.

Someone behind me said something to me, though I didn't quite hear them. I turned and froze, caught off guard by how striking this girl was. A beautiful girl, with slightly curly blonde hair intertwined with red and blue ribbons, stood smiling. I was instantly lost in her sparkling emerald eyes. She was shorter than me, wore a jean jacket with the Thunderbird logo on the back, and large, dangling earrings.

"I'm sorry, did you say something?" I asked.

She repeated herself, stepping closer. "I said, that was pretty gruesome, huh?"

I didn't answer and was also thrown off by her accent, which was not strong but unique enough to notice. I stared at her awkwardly.

"The football player's arm," she repeated. "That was gross, huh?"

I escaped my daze. "Yeah, that was a nasty break. It happened right in front of our seats."

"Really?" Her eyes widened as she held her stomach. "I only saw it on the jumbotron, and that made me queasy. I came up here to buy a ginger ale or something to help. You feeling sick, too?"

Her accent made every word sound like the most intriguing song.

"Nah," I said, trying to sound cool. "I've seen a lot worse than that."

"Worse than that?"

"Yeah, I'm a firefighter. When I was younger, though, I used to pass out from the sight of blood. Somehow, I grew out of it, and it doesn't bother me at all anymore." I paused, covering my face with one hand. "I'm sorry. I don't know why I told you that. That was super random."

She chuckled. "Your weakness became your strength. I love that."

I quickly changed the subject. "Where's your accent from?"

She lowered her head and smiled. "You noticed that, huh? I've been slowly losing it over the years, but it still slips out. I'm from Australia."

My brow furrowed, trying to comprehend how that was possible. I must have looked confused because she continued explaining.

"I was lucky enough to be visiting Vegas with my parents when it got locked down."

"I'm sorry," I answered. "That must have been hard."

She nodded, twisting one of the ribbons in her hair. "It was at first, but I'm trying my best to make this home now."

I'd never really thought of people getting stuck in Vegas during the quarantine, which is silly because I knew of plenty who were outside of it at the time and never got to come back.

I was about to ask her name when the person behind us cleared their throat and pointed to the concession counter. I moved to the register and ordered a hot dog for myself and a ginger ale for the girl.

I turned and handed her the soda. "Here, I hope this helps."

She graciously accepted it with both hands, slightly touching my own, sending a shockwave through my arm. "Thank you. You didn't have to do that."

I let out a strange giggle, then darted away, red-faced. It wasn't until I reached the top of our seating section that I realized how stupid I had been. I didn't ask her name! I doubled back, sprinting through the corridor to where I left her, but she was nowhere to be found.

How could I have let this happen? Between studying and preparing to be a firefighter, I hadn't had time to think twice about girls in the After. I wouldn't have been so upset, but something about her seemed different. I couldn't shake the feeling that I had just made the biggest mistake of my life.

After returning to my seat, Ryan immediately asked me if something was wrong. I played it off and continued watching the game, though I was no longer invested in it. Instead, I scanned the crowds, looking for this girl, but no matter how methodically I searched, I could not find her.

Suddenly, a collective gasp brought me out of my hunt, followed by a resounding silence. A player on the field lay motionless as coaches and teammates ran to his side. We knew something was wrong even before they frantically waved for help, but the ambulance was no longer there.

The PA system crackled, "If there are any doctors or medics present, we need your help on the field, please."

Cap stood up. "Let's go, guys. This is the last time we go anywhere with Brann! He is a special kind of black cloud."

Black cloud? I didn't have time to figure out what that meant. We vaulted the railing and ran onto the field. The turf felt surreal, like I was moving through a dream. As did the thousands of eyes watching me. I wondered if the girl's were among them. I tried my best to remain calm, at least on the outside.

Reed shoved through the panicked players. "Move!"

Mum dropped to her knees and checked for a pulse and breathing. "I got nothing," she said.

"Start compressions," Cap ordered.

"Did he get hit, or just collapse?" Ryan asked.

"He just fell," Hill responded. "No one touched him. I saw it."

Ryan unclipped the player's helmet. "Okay, get his helmet and pads off."

Luckly, I had a pair of multi-use shears in my pocket and used them to cut off his jersey and pads. By this time, I had forgotten that everyone was watching me. As far as I could tell, it was just me, my crew, and the patient. I began chest compression, and workers from the stadium brought us the minimal medical supplies they had, which included an AED and an O2 tank with a non-rebreather mask. Mum placed the mask on his face, and Hill applied the AED pads to his chest. I stopped compression to allow the AED to analyze the player.

"Analyzing heart rhythm, do not touch the patient," the AED said in a robotic woman's voice. "Shock advised. Charging. Do not touch the patient."

"Everyone clear?" Cap asked.

"Everyone's clear," Ryan answered. "Shocking now."

Ryan pressed the red shock button, and the player's body jolted violently.

The AED spoke again. "Shock delivered. Resume CPR."

We quickly checked for a pulse but felt none, so I began compressions again for another two minutes until the AED prompted us to stop for another rhythm check. "Analyzing heart rhythm, do not touch the patient."

We cleared again, and the AED advised us to shock him a second time. It charged, and Ryan delivered another shock, jolting the player again.

"I have a pulse!" I exclaimed.

He still wasn't breathing on his own and did not wake up. This was another thing different from the movies. Patients typically did not magically wake up after being in cardiac arrest. Although I wished he would.

We continued supplementing his breathing until another ambulance crew arrived along with engine 2, the same crew who'd come to the theater.

"You again?" Captain Reynolds said, looking at me. "You are a dark, dark black cloud, my friend."

I still didn't know what that meant, but we helped them load the player into the ambulance. Once they left, I felt the eyes of the city on me again. If he didn't make it, everyone was going to blame me. I was the one doing CPR. I hoped it was good enough this time.

We walked back to our seats as onlookers applauded our efforts. They didn't finish the rest of the game, not that it mattered. I checked the scoreboard, and to my surprise, the Raiders were up multiple touchdowns, with only a few minutes left. I hadn't realized how much they scored in the second half.

We started exiting the stadium along with everyone else, but I still had something I needed to figure out. "What's a black cloud, Ryan?"

Ryan laughed. "You are! All the terrible calls happen around you. Black clouds are the busiest and get the craziest calls. There are white clouds, too, which is the opposite. Reed is a white cloud. Usually, the black cloud curse stays at work, though. Yours seems to follow you everywhere."

Was he right? Was I cursed to have all the worst things happen around me? I couldn't help but imagine all the worst possible scenarios that could play out in my future.

Ryan put his arm around my shoulder as we walked. "I'm gonna have to keep my guard up when I'm around you from now on. Who knows what's going to happen to us next."

I forced a laugh. But deep down, I wasn't sure I could take much more.

11
Gifts in Various Wrappings

"There's a reason firefighting is one of the few jobs that continued during the lockdown. It is essential. You are essential and will be even more so because you will have to lead and guide your crew members. This is more than a job. It's a calling. We do the right thing on and off duty."
— Battalion Chief Rod Jefferson

Ryan and I barely had time to load our gear onto the rescue before the tones blared.

"Rescue 3, traumatic injury. Rescue 3, traumatic injury."

We sped to the address, arriving at a rundown house. As I knocked on the sun-bleached front door, I kicked at the weeds overrunning the walkway by the door. It was opened by a boy, probably my age. The smell of stale take-out and dirty laundry practically slapped me in the face. The place looked like it hadn't seen a broom or vacuum in years.

Inside, the only furniture was a few sets of mismatched futons surrounded by piles of moldy fast-food containers. Multiple gaming consoles lined the walls, each with its own dedicated TV set.

I introduced myself with a smile, trying my best to be professional. "Hey guys, I'm Aiden, and this is Mi. What's going on today?"

The kid who opened the door looked confused for a second, processing my introduction. Ryan, behind me, stifled a laugh. Though he used the same "me" joke countless times, I caught him off guard by using it myself. The other boy sitting on the couch eventually found his words.

"A few days ago, my stomach started hurting really bad," he began. "And I was trying to figure out why."

"Could it be all the take-out?" I interrupted, motioning to the stacks of to-go containers.

"No, that's not it," he replied. "I eat out all the time. The pain got really bad, and my stomach got really hard. So yesterday I went to the doctor. They asked when was the last time I... uh... pooped, and I realized it had been over two weeks. But all they gave me was a dumb piece of paper and sent me home."

"Where's the paper at?" I asked.

The kid rummaged through the stacks of garbage before eventually finding a crumpled piece of blue paper under a pizza box. I glanced at it, trying not to laugh as I showed it to Ryan. It was a prescription for a stool softener.

"This is for a medicine that will help you... go," I said carefully.

"Help me go where?" he asked.

Ryan spun away, clawing at his own hair. He seemed mostly back to normal after his confession to me, but maybe something still bothered him. I took a breath, keeping a calm and professional tone. "It's to help you poop."

He raised an eyebrow, looking even more confused. "I already pooped."

Ryan stepped forward, his frustration boiling over. Something was definitely still bugging him. "Then why are we here? You said your stomach hurts because you couldn't go, but now you have! What's the problem?"

The boy looked from Ryan to me, clearly not understanding our frustration. "Well, it was... huge."

Ryan clenched his fists, exhaling and biting his tongue. The kid continued his explanation.

"I've never seen a poop so big in my life. I didn't think it was normal. And it kinda hurt, so I thought something might be wrong. If you don't believe me, I saved it for you."

Too stunned to answer, the kid who'd opened the door walked over to us, holding a plastic grocery bag in front of him like it was a priceless artifact.

"We put it in here," he said proudly. "We figured you'd need to see it."

I raised my hand, shaking my head. "No! Nope. Stop. We don't need to see it."

"But... poops aren't supposed to be this big. Don't you think something is wrong with him?"

Ryan rolled his eyes. "Oh, something is definitely wrong with him."

With every ounce of courtesy I had, I began to explain in the simplest terms possible. "Look, you didn't poop for two weeks. So, all that poop just stays in your stomach. That's why it hurt and got hard. The medicine would have made it softer and not hurt so much, but by that time, you'd built up a lot of poo, which is why it was so huge. But either way, you've pooped now. So, you are fine. You should start pooping normal-sized again."

The boy looked at me with a raised eyebrow, "I don't know... I think I should still go to the hospital and see a doctor, just to make sure."

"You serious?" Ryan groaned.

"Uh, yeah. I called 911, so you have to take me, right?"

"Whatever," Ryan muttered. "Let's go! But leave the poop. I'm not putting that in my rescue, you see."

The boy seemed hesitant. "But what if the doctors need to see it?"

"They don't," I assured him.

Still unconvinced, he pulled out his phone. "I'm gonna take a picture then to show them."

Ryan rolled his eyes and stormed out the front door. I gathered our things as the boys arranged the photo, angling the bag perfectly and placing his hand next to it for scale. I sighed in disbelief and led them out.

Ryan waited in the back of the rescue, obviously annoyed and preparing an IV. As I secured the boy to the gurney, Ryan explained our procedure.

"We are going to start an IV on you and put some stickers on your chest to take a picture of your heart," he said, not bothering to hide his irritation.

The boy winced. "Do you have to poke me with a needle? They had a hard time getting one when they did our blood tests during the Preparation."

"Yup. You want to get transported to the ER, so we have to do the full workup."

Ryan placed a rubber tourniquet on the boy's left arm and struggled to find a vein, muttering under his breath. Unable to find a suitable site, he threw his arms up and told me to check.

I switched places with Ryan and found a small vein in an awkward position on the back of his forearm. I had the kid bend his arm toward him, and I stood up to get a better angle. Ryan watched me with amusement.

Using a gentle touch, I slid the needle in. A flash of blood confirmed I'd hit the vein, and I secured the catheter before attaching the saline flush.

"Have you missed an IV yet?" Ryan asked, his tone softening a little.

"Not yet. I practiced IVs a ton with my dad."

With the boy all hooked up, I offered to stay in the back while Ryan drove us. When he got in the driver's seat, I poked my head through the section connecting the rear to the passenger area.

"Hey. You all right, man?" I asked.

"I'm fine. Just kinda wish all these kids would grow up, you see."

During the drive to the ER, I only spoke to the boy occasionally to obtain the necessary information. We left him with the nurses—who looked as unimpressed as Ryan—and then began our drive back to the station.

Before we made it too far, I noticed light puffs of smoke drifting up from a few blocks away on the street we were driving down. We decided to investigate, even though we assumed it was just a BBQ or something of that nature.

We pulled up to an abandoned grocery store that hadn't been used since the After. A thin trail of white smoke rose from what looked like the center of the roof.

"Is there a fire in there?" I asked.

"Not sure," Ryan answered. "That's not a lot of smoke for a big building like this, you see. Just grab the extinguisher and let's check it out."

I grabbed my radio and the extinguisher from the side compartment and headed toward the front of the building. Some of the older stores from the Before were rarely used anymore and were mostly left alone since we used the newer stores. The last time I was in one like this was to play capture the flag with friends, which many kids did, probably two years ago.

As soon as we stepped through the front door, Ryan grabbed me and yanked me down, holding his index finger to his lips.

There were voices.

We could see where the puffs of smoke were coming from now. It drifted up through a broken skylight above in the center of the building.

We crept forward, trying to get a closer look at whoever was inside and what they were up to. In the center of the store, standing between two aisles, were four kids with their backs toward us. They were gathered around a small fire they were trying to start on one of the shelves, which was filled with random objects. The fire wasn't growing well, if at all.

"This is taking too long," one of them said. "For our plan to work, this whole store needs to go up in flames fast. There can't be time for anyone to undo what we start."

"It's the Children," Ryan whispered.

I nodded, my breathing halting as my heart rate increased.

"What do we do?" I asked.

Ryan motioned for us to sneak back out, but before we could, our radios crackled.

"Rescue 3 from dispatch. Status check."

We quickly turned the volumes down, but it was too late.

"Someone's here!" one of them said. "Masks on!"

Ryan and I sprang to our feet and sprinted toward the exit. I keyed up my radio as I ran, telling dispatch we needed PD at our location immediately. I didn't dare look back, but I could hear footsteps chasing us.

The door was in sight—until a huge boy, even bigger than Reed, stepped in front of it with his arms crossed. He wore a white mask with a red Children's symbol in the center.

This was new. As far as I knew, no one had ever seen the Children wearing masks. New or not, I knew it wasn't good.

The four chasing us stopped behind us, forming a circle. All of them wore the same mask. One stepped forward slightly—the leader of the group.

"What do we have here?" he said, his voice unnaturally deep, as if he were purposely distorting it. "A couple of firefighters, huh? Come to save the day?"

"Let us out," Ryan demanded. "What do you want?"

"Oh, you'll know soon enough." The leader tilted his head. "But right now, I'm a little upset you ruined the surprise. Our mask reveal wasn't supposed to happen quite yet. But hey—since you're here, I'd love your opinion. Do you like them?"

We didn't answer. He began circling us, evaluating us. When he got within inches of Ryan's face, Ryan shoved him hard. The other Children stepped forward, but the leader raised a hand for them to stand down.

"Nice to see you have a little fight in you," the leader said. "I'm surprised you still know how to fight for anything."

"What's that supposed to mean?" Ryan asked.

Before he could answer, dispatch came over the radio, informing us the police were just a couple minutes out.

"You called the police?" the leader said. "You really shouldn't have done that."

They all stepped closer. Ryan and I were not in a good situation. The biggest one was now only a few feet away. With nowhere to go, we had few options.

So, I did the only thing that popped into my mind.

I ripped the pin from the extinguisher and blasted it straight into the Children's faces. Through the thick fog, Ryan and I bolted through the gap and raced for the door.

Just as we made it outside, one of the Children hooked Ryan's foot and sent him crashing to the pavement. The big one pounced instantly, pinning him on his back and pulling back a fist to knock him out.

Before he could swing, I slammed the extinguisher into the side of his head, knocking his mask off. He toppled off Ryan, screaming and clutching his face.

But before we could run again, the others surrounded us. Sirens wailed in the distance—luckily.

"We gotta get out of here, KID," one of the masked boys said.

"I'll be seeing you again real soon... Ryan," the leader added.

Ryan's shock matched my own. I shouldn't have been surprised, given his history with them. Then again, I supposed Ryan shouldn't be either.

The group grabbed the injured boy, still holding his face, and disappeared around the corner before two police cars pulled in. One was Kaylyn, who sped off after the Children, while the other officer stayed with us. We checked the inside of the store and completely extinguished the small fire, which was already dying down on its own.

E3 arrived soon after, having been informed by dispatch of our call for help. Hill bent down near the entrance and picked up one of the Children's masks, which had been left on the pavement. A small chip had broken off the side.

"What's this?" Hill asked.

"It's the Children," I answered. "They are planning something. Something big."

"What should we do with it?" Hill asked, holding the mask toward Ryan.

Ryan shook his head. "I don't want that thing."

Reed snatched it from Hill and immediately placed it over his own face. "This is coming to the station! Reed is gonna hang it on the wall somewhere."

We stayed long enough to give reports to the police and to see Kaylyn return empty-handed. To my surprise, the police let us keep the mask, saying they weren't going to do anything with it.

Back at the station, Cap gathered us around the kitchen table.

"First off," he began, "I'm glad you guys are okay. I'm glad you had your radios on you. With everything going on with these Children, we need to stay alert and smart."

"We don't want anyone to ever get hurt," Mum added. "You're all too important."

Cap nodded. "We have to be on our 'A' game at all times. Speaking of... I have some good news. Chance Jones, the football player we helped, is doing well. Turned out he had an undiagnosed heart defect, but thanks to you guys, he's going to survive."

We cheered and high-fived each other. It felt incredible to finally hear that someone I'd tried to help was doing well. For once, I felt like I'd done something right.

"I want to tell every one of you how proud I am to be a part of this crew," Cap continued, his voice thick with emotion. "You guys stepped up and performed on literally the biggest stage we have, which is no easy task. You have made me and the entire city proud. With these Children causing so many problems now, we are going to need to keep performing. And since you have all been so awesome lately, we are going to Lovies for ice cream tonight. My treat."

Ice cream that evening was fantastic. Even though I was still the new guy, I was starting to feel a part of the crew. The ice cream was great, but the time we spent eating on the bumper of the engine in the parking lot was the best. We joked, laughed, and told stories from past calls—both intense and funny. These guys had so many fantastic stories, and I wanted nothing more than to make some of my own.

Later, when it was finally time for bed, I went into my dorm, where the lights were already dimmed. My meticulously made bed looked more inviting than ever. I grabbed the top sheet and flung it back... and screamed as I launched myself backward.

Ryan, Reed, and Hill doubled over laughing around the corner.

"Did you find Reed's gift, Brann?" Reed asked as they all stepped in.

"Yeah," I said. "Thank you so much. Very thoughtful."

Once I regained my composure, I approached the thing on my pillow that had scared me so badly. The Children's mask stared menacingly up at me with its empty eyes.

Reed snatched it from my hands. "You don't get to keep it. Reed has to find a place to hang it now. Probably in the day room above the TV."

And with that, the three left my dorm, laughing. Once I finally laid my head down, I couldn't help but smile.

I really was becoming a part of this crew.

12

THE BANQUET

"I think the best thing we can do is handpick the kids who will form the government. Voting can be implemented later once they are ready." — Mayor Cathleen Goodson

After some busy days at work, I was ready to do nothing and unwind. I plopped onto the couch and turned on my gaming console. Within seconds of the game loading, the doorbell rang. With a reluctant groan, I headed for the door, colliding with Ally in the hallway.

Kim stood on the porch with her cat, Blazie, lazily curled up in her arms. Barely acknowledging Kim, I reached for Blazie, snatching her away as she stepped inside. Harvey, one of her other cats, lurked on the porch with a dead bird clamped in his jaws, under his two-toned face that split perfectly down the center.

"What's Harvey got there?" I asked.

Kim rolled her eyes. "Oh, just ignore him. He's been trying to 'gift' me that dumb bird all morning. He's so proud of his kills. It's disgusting."

"Gross," Ally said, locking Harvey outside.

Kim settled into the living room, scanning the room. "Where's Aubrey? I've got some exciting news."

"She's in her room. I'll get her," I said, handing Blazie to Ally.

I peeked inside Aubrey's always immaculate room. She was rocking out to music through her headphones, lost in her own world as she danced and vacuumed away. Passionately singing into the cleaner's handle, she didn't notice me leaning against the doorway, trying not to laugh. When she finally spotted me, she jumped.

"Ah! What are you doing in my room?"

"Calm down, twinkle toes. Kim is here with some news."

Aubrey chucked a pillow at me, then followed me into the living room. Kim was pacing with a slight skip in her step. I reclaimed Blazie, and as Aubrey sat down, Kim blurted, "They called me!"

"Who called you?" Aubrey asked.

"The city," she replied. "They want me to fill the North Las Vegas Senator vacancy. They said the spot opened unexpectedly, and even though they were planning on me taking a position in a few years, they decided I was the one most ready now. They invited me to a banquet tomorrow night to honor Jennifer Goodson, who passed away a couple weeks ago. She was in a car accident. They want me to come so I can start meeting everyone."

My breath stopped in my chest. The room seemed to shrink, the sound of Kim's voice dulling behind the memory of that name. Jenny. The memory surged to the forefront of my mind—the thick smoke, the burning flames, the sickening sight of her peeling skin. I forced my expression to remain unchanged, but my fingers squeezed each other hard, cracking my knuckles.

Kim kept talking, oblivious to the way my pulse echoed in my ears.

"I want you guys to come to the banquet with me. They said I can bring some family and you guys are my family. Please come."

Aubrey answered first. "Of course. We will be there."

"Thank you!" Kim looked at me up and down, motioning to my outfit. "Maybe help Aiden find something nice to wear so he doesn't show up looking like this."

She eyed me, laughing, and headed for the door with Blazie.

"Well, that was uncalled for," I joked.

"She's not wrong," Ally replied, smirking. "We need to get you a nice suit or something."

The next evening, we arrived at a downtown building, repurposed from the Before. Large pillars lined the entrance, and a gleaming gold statue of a woman holding a scale crowned the top. The building read "Supreme Court of Nevada," but now served as a gathering place for the government.

I scanned the building, locating the fire control room and the Knox box location, contemplating how I would approach a fire inside this building. Aubrey bumped me, since I was frozen on the sidewalk.

I coughed and ripped at my stiff collar, uncomfortable in the rented black tuxedo. Aubrey and Ally, however, both looked stunning. Aubrey's red gown skimmed the ground with her high heels, while Ally's purple dress flared out to her mid-calf.

Kim greeted us at the steps, practically shining in a floor-length silver dress that sparkled under the lights. "You made it! And look at you, Aiden. Don't you clean up nicely."

"I can't breathe in this thing," I grumbled, tugging at my collar.

"You'll survive. Now, come on, they have a table reserved for us inside."

I spotted a familiar face as we followed her through the marble-lined halls. "Kaylyn! I mean, Officer Keller. You on duty tonight?"

She grinned. "Hey, Aiden. Yeah, they assigned me security for the event. I'm just here to keep an eye on all these important people." She gave me a once-over. "Speaking of which..."

"Hey, now! I happen to be very important, thank you very much."

Kim patted me on the shoulder with a smirk. "Yes, very important."

"Well, you guys have fun being important. Tell Ryan I said hi."

As we walked away to find our table, Aubrey nudged me. "That's the girl Ryan likes, right?"

"Yeah, but he hasn't admitted it."

Aubrey glanced back at her. "I haven't seen her in uniform before. She looks much more intense but still pretty."

I shrugged. "I guess."

Inside, rows of white-clothed tables filled the ballroom, with a small podium and projector screen at the front. Chandeliers hung overhead, casting a soft glow over the banquet below. Kim led us to a table where three people sat, formally dressed and chatting quietly. They were probably Aubrey's age, maybe even a year older. Kim was easily the youngest at the table, if not at the whole event.

Kim introduced us. "Everyone, this is Trey Creamer, the Senator of Las Vegas. Britney Savage, the Senator for Henderson. And Lizzy Brentwood, the Senator for Summerlin."

We exchanged handshakes and introduced ourselves as well before sitting down. Trey turned to us, smiling but serious. "So, Kim's friends. What do you all do?"

Ally answered first, explaining how she does massage out of the home.

"She is the greatest," Kim interrupted. "I get one from her every week. I can't live without them."

"I'm going to need your number, Ally," Britney Savage said, beaming. "I've been meaning to find one, and now you have fallen into my lap!"

Trey pointed to Aubrey, "And how about you? What do you do?"

"I'm a 911 dispatcher."

"Wow, that must be a tough job," Lizzy nodded. "I'm sure you've handled all kinds of terrible calls. Thank you for your service."

Aubrey smiled, a flicker of pride in her eyes when she thanked them.

Trey's gaze shifted to me. "And you?"

"I'm a firefighter at station 3. I started not too long ago."

"Another first responder, huh?" Trey grinned. "That's wonderful. You guys seem like a tremendous family. We love to see families like yours contributing like they should. You weren't working on the day of Jennifer's accident, were you?"

My heart sank instantly. I hesitated, feeling my sisters' eyes on me. I didn't want my sisters or Kim to know about it, but I didn't want to lie. "Uh, yeah, I was. My crew responded to it."

Aubrey and Ally exchanged glances, both looking a lot like my mom. Before the job, I had never kept anything from them.

"That must have been terrible," Lizzy said. "We thought these electric cars were a little safer. It's scary."

I nodded, forcing myself to look strong, at least on the exterior. "It was... hard. We tried our best, but we couldn't save her. I couldn't save her."

The table fell silent, the bleakness of my words settling in. Images of Jennifer's burned body flooded my brain again as my sisters stared at me sympathetically. Everyone's eyes felt suffocating. The silence was deafening, and my vision began to narrow. I could feel my sister's unwanted sympathy drowning me.

Thankfully, Trey shifted the conversation, allowing me to catch my breath and regain focus. He asked Kim if she'd met President Keres yet.

"Only in passing," Kim replied. "I'm sure I'll see a lot of her now, though."

"Well, she is incredible," Trey said, his eyes lighting up. "She is wonderful to work with and incredibly smart. She knows how to get things done and is probably the most important person in the After. Without her, we would be living like animals."

Lizzy interjected, placing her hand on Trey's knee. "I would say you also have a lot to do with our success. She has great ideas, but you are the one who carries them out. I would say that's pretty important, too."

Trey shrugged and pointed across the room to where the President stood. "Maybe, but just look at her. She is simply wonderful."

Soon, servers began delivering meals to each table. Bacon-wrapped steak, buttered baby potatoes, fresh salad, and warm bread. As we ate, various people spoke about Jennifer and her life in the Before and the After. She had accomplished so much in such little time.

Jennifer's brother, Chris, was then called up to accept a lifetime achievement award on her behalf.

"I've met him," I whispered to Ally. "That's Chris, Jenny's brother."

Chris passively approached the microphone with red, puffy eyes, accepting the plaque from the girl on stage. He remained motionless, gripping the plaque tightly to his chest and staring into the crowd before finally speaking. "Thank you... I miss her."

He looked like he wanted to say more, but couldn't. His words hung in the air as he returned to his seat. I excused myself and walked over to where he sat. Kaylyn was with him, offering some words of support.

"Hey guys," I said, keeping my voice low. "It's good to see you again, Chris. Your sister sounds like she was an amazing person."

He looked down, not meeting my eyes. "Yeah, she was. I wish she was still here."

"I'm sorry, buddy," I said gently. "She'd be proud of you, though. How have things been? The Hotel still treating you right? Are they teaching you any new computer skills?"

He raised his head. "Actually, I'm the one teaching them... at the Hotel."

"I've heard Chris is quite the wizard with computers," Kaylyn said.

The chandeliers flickered once, and I glanced around curiously. I tried to continue our conversation, but they flickered again. Suddenly, complete darkness enveloped the room. Gasps and whispers rippled through the banquet hall. The clank of silverware ceased. Someone knocked over a glass, the sharp crash breaking the eerie silence, followed by a girl's lone scream.

Then, the projector screen flashed to life, covering the room in a cold glow. The slideshow of Jenny vanished, replaced by something far worse. An unmistakable symbol.

The Children.

"Stay here!" Kaylyn said, as she ran off to investigate with the several other officers in attendance.

Three masked figures stepped into view on the screen. The red Children's emblem stood out, stark against their white masks. One stood in the center, stepped forward, and spoke with a distorted voice.

"Good evening, Las Vegas. Do you know who I am?" He paused, tilting his head slightly, like he was waiting for a response. "No? That's okay. Soon everyone will know me. I am KID."

A hush fell over the room as KID continued. Everyone was frozen to their seats, unable to look away, me included.

"We are the Children and will no longer be sitting idly by in the shadows. We refuse to live in the fake paradise you've created here. This world is built on lies and corruption, just like the Before. And we are going to tear it down, piece by piece."

He stepped forward, bringing his masked face right into the camera.

"We have no demands because you have nothing we want. Just know that we are coming for you. And to those who betrayed us, you cannot hide. The traitors will be the first to fall. Then the rest of you. The Children are coming."

The screen faded to black, and the room was silent for a few tense seconds. The lights brightened again, revealing the crowd's expressions of shock, confusion, and fear. Senator Lizzy clung to Trey, fighting back tears.

President Keres strolled to the front, her expression determined and her voice firm. She was always so poised.

"Everyone, stay calm. We are safe. This appears to be a recorded message, and there is no danger here. It is a travesty that such a beautiful and inspiring event has now been tarnished by such reckless and disrespectful behavior. I have tolerated these Children for far too long. Well, no more! No more will I sit by as they attempt to destroy our glorious valley. No more will we allow these Children not to work and still benefit from our generosity. No more!"

The crowd erupted in applause, chanting in unison, "No more! No more!" The energy in the room transformed, fear giving way to resolve as President Keres continued.

"First thing tomorrow, we will create a task force to oversee the best way to handle this. I ask all of you for your support as we implement these new ways to protect our city. We will not allow them to disrupt the peace we have worked so hard for. This valley is our home. Together we live. Together we thrive!"

As I watched, my mind reeled. The Children had declared war, not just on the city, but on so called "traitors" like Ryan. And for the first time, I understood how real the danger was.

13
My Mom in the Before

"How was school today, buddy?" my mom asked as I climbed into the car.

I didn't answer. I buckled my seatbelt, my head bowed. She allowed me to sit silently for a while as we drove to pick up Aubrey from her preparation assignment. But it wasn't long before she pressed me gently, sensing something was wrong.

"Is everything okay? What did you do in class today?"

"We practiced intubations," I replied, still avoiding eye contact.

"Is that where you shove tubes down people's throats?" she asked, making a gagging sound. "I don't know how you and your dad can do that stuff. I'd never be able to."

I didn't react. Her attempt to lighten the mood fell flat.

"Did it not go well, Aiden?" she asked. "I'm sure it takes some practice to get good at. Keep trying, and you'll be great."

"No, I did fine. Better than most, actually."

"So, what's wrong?"

I couldn't hold it in any longer. The words burst out in a rush. "They had us do the intubations on real dead bodies! Our instructor said we needed to practice on them while we had the chance. He said it would help us when we need to do it on someone still living."

Mom immediately pulled the car to the side of the road, put it in park, and turned to face me fully, her eyes filled with sympathy.

"I'm sorry, buddy. That must have been hard to see, but your instructor is probably right. It'll be helpful."

"I don't want you to die, Mom!" I blurted out, my voice breaking as tears welled in my eyes.

"What?" she asked, startled. "I thought we were talking about intubations?"

"The grownups are starting to die. That's why they had bodies for us to practice on. You and Dad aren't going to, though, right? They can still find a cure, right?"

"Oh, buddy…" Her voice trembled.

She climbed over the center console and slid into the backseat with me. Wrapping me in her arms, she held me tightly.

"I wish I could tell you we were going to be fine," she said softly. "But I don't think they'll find a cure in time. You need to prepare yourself for that."

I cried harder, gripping her shirt. "No! You're not going to die! You can't!"

Her hand rested gently on the back of my head, soothing me as she spoke. "This is hard to say out loud, but I think Dad and I are going to die, just like every other adult. And it's okay to be sad. I'm sad, too. I'm sad I won't get to see you and your sisters grow up. I'm sad I won't get to see you turn into the wonderful man I know you will become. I'm sad you had to grow up so fast."

She pulled back slightly, cupping my face with her hands. "But I'm so happy I got to be your mom and that you are my boy. Even though it wasn't as long as we'd hoped, I wouldn't change our time for anything."

"But what if I can't do this without you?" I whimpered.

Her forehead rested against mine, her eyes fierce yet full of love. "You can. And you will because you're my son. My son is no quitter. My son takes care of others, especially his sisters. My son is the best son I have!"

I managed a weak smile. "I'm the only son you have."

"And I'm so glad you are," she said, laughing softly as she climbed back into the driver's seat. "Now, let's go get your sister."

My parents and the government had been telling us for almost three years now that adults and teenagers who were further into puberty at the time of exposure were going to die. Still, I think a part of me never believed it. Reality started to set in, though. Adults were suddenly dying in their sleep in enormous numbers. Even some of Aubrey's friends, who were a little older than her, had already passed. The times for which we'd been preparing in the last couple of years arrived.

After getting Aubrey, we got home just in time for Ally to be dropped off by the school bus. Ally was still young and in preparation school. She was learning all the basic adult-like skills we all learned. However, she would get to spend more time than I would in those classes.

Aubrey got even less than me. The kids Aubrey's age had to learn their professions in a hurry. They would be the ones who would continue teaching once the adults died. The oldest kids received a crash course in basic life skills, but were soon transferred to focus solely on their professions.

I still had adults teaching me the paramedic curriculum. Still, I knew I would be learning the firefighter aspect from an older kid when the time came.

That evening, dinner was quiet—just Mom, my sisters, and me. Dad was on shift, like so many days before. We went through the usual routine, sharing what we'd learned during the day. I talked about practicing intubations but left out the part about the bodies. Ally had been learning to cook and claimed she could make excellent omelets. Aubrey said she'd taken more 911 calls, needing help only a few times. She said she even got to talk to Dad and the boy he was training on the radio.

After dinner, we were exhausted, as usual, from our Preparation assignments. Mom sat in the hallway outside our bedrooms, reading stories and singing songs until we fell asleep, a ritual she'd started when the Preparation began. I loved it because it was one of the few times we got to feel like normal kids again. Tonight, though, I couldn't sleep. Every time I peeked out, Mom was still there, watching over us. She always seemed to be there, somehow knowing when we fell asleep. By morning, she would be in her own bed.

"Go to sleep, buddy," she whispered each time I looked over, her voice calming and reassuring.

After hours, I eventually drifted off, Mom remaining steadfast in the hallway until I did.

When my alarm blared in the morning, I checked the hallway for her, but she had already returned to her bed, just like every other morning.

Downstairs, Ally was in the kitchen, eager to make breakfast for us. "I'm gonna make you guys omelets," she declared proudly.

Aubrey and I exchanged glances but let her do her thing while we studied on the couch. My stomach grumbled, sick of waiting for Ally to finish.

"Are we ever going to eat?" I asked. "I'm starving over here!"

"Yeah," Aubrey added. "You might as well start making lunch instead. Breakfast is almost over."

Ally ignored us but called us to the table a few minutes later. Our omelets were at our seats, though they didn't quite look how I thought they would. Mine was a runny mess and filled with peppers and onions, both of which I hated. Aubrey's was burnt to a crisp.

"This is disgusting," I muttered, pushing my plate away. "Why would you put peppers in my food? You know I hate them."

Ally threw her spatula in the sink. "Well, make it yourself then, Aiden!"

I threw my arms in the air. "Why would I make it? I didn't even want whatever this is. I wanted cereal."

Aubrey slapped the table. "Shut up, Aiden. She is trying."

"Do you like your omelet, Aubrey?" Ally asked, hopeful.

"Uh, it's kinda burnt, Sis. I don't think I can eat it."

"You guys hate me!" Ally shouted, taking off her apron and throwing it on the ground. "You don't think I can do anything right! I just wanted to do something nice for you."

Aubrey got to her feet, shoving her chair back. "Don't be screaming at me. I was trying to defend you, but I'm not going to anymore if you're going to be a little brat."

Before we knew it, we were all yelling at each other. The argument escalated until Dad entered through the front door, his voice cutting through the chaos like a blade.

"Enough!" he barked. We froze immediately. Dad was usually calm, but when he raised his voice, we listened.

"Where's your mom?" he asked, his tone softer now.

"Still asleep," Aubrey answered.

Dad disappeared into the bedroom while the rest of us found something edible to eat. After we finished eating, we returned to the living room to study a little bit.

Soon after, Dad entered the room, his face pale, his eyes bloodshot, and his hands trembling.

"Dad?" Aubrey asked hesitantly. "You okay?"

He tried to speak, whispering to himself. "I wanted to be here with her. I should have been here." He took a step closer with a long exhale. "We've prepared for this," he whispered, looking up at us. "Mom died in her sleep. I'm so sorry, kids."

"What!?" I yelled, standing to my feet. "No, I saw her last night! She was there when I went to bed. I saw her in the hallway all night. She was fine."

"I'm sorry, buddy," he said, pulling us into an embrace. "I'm sorry this is happening to you kids. It isn't fair."

We ran to check on Mom. Dad tried to stop us, but was only able to contain the girls. I slipped by and sprinted into their bedroom. Mom lay on her bed, oddly peaceful, like she was asleep. I grabbed her arm and begged her to wake up. She had to wake up! But she didn't move. Wet tear stains were on her shirt, but they weren't mine.

Dad rushed in, spinning me to him and clinging to me and my sisters who followed. We sobbed as reality crashed down on us. Mom was gone. The strongest person I knew, the one who always made me believe everything would be okay, was gone.

Later in the day, we held a small memorial for Mom in our home, with just us. With so many deaths happening, funerals weren't possible. We had to say our goodbyes on the same day she passed.

As we shared our memories, I noticed something in Dad's eyes. The light that had always been there was now extinguished. A part of him had died with her. I also noticed how he spoke about her. He loved her desperately. I knew I wanted to love someone as fiercely as my dad loved my mom.

"Dad?" Ally asked after we all shared. "How are we gonna tell Grams and Gramps?"

I almost answered for him, suggesting we simply call them. But then remembered we couldn't.

"I don't know, Sis," My dad said.

I tried to remember the last time we talked to my grandparents. I wish I had said more, asked more questions, and sincerely told them I loved them. If only I had known it was the last time I would be able to talk to them, I would have. I wondered if they were even still alive.

For the past two and a half years, the wall around Vegas hadn't just kept people in or out. It cut us off from everyone beyond it. My grandparents, once a regular part of my life, had become distant memories. At first, we were connected to the outside world during the early quarantine days. Supplies, food, and raw materials were brought in to keep Vegas afloat. Engineers worked tirelessly to optimize the power grid and make everything more efficient. The world hadn't forgotten us. They wanted to ensure we'd survive.

But then, the quarantine failed.

It took months for anyone to realize. The infection spread silently, with no obvious symptoms even months after exposure. By the time the government confirmed it had breached the borders, it was too late. The infection wasn't only Vegas's problem anymore. It was the world's.

Vegas leaders acted quickly. They promised us protection, safety, and, most importantly, a future. "We're safest inside," they told us. "This is the only way to survive."

I couldn't help but wonder if my grandparents were even still out there. Was anyone out there?

That night, my sisters and I gathered in Aubrey's room while workers came to take away our mom. Although we didn't say anything to each other, we knew our petty fighting days were over. Our childish behavior was finished. Soon, we were going to be all each of us had. We embraced in the center of the room, making an unspoken promise. We would be there for each other, no matter what.

14

STRANGE VISITS

"People will expect you to be educated and to have all the answers. You can't just sound intelligent, you must be intelligent." — Tasha Hunt

"**G**ood morning, everyone," Cap said over the usual morning kitchen table chatter. "Listen up. Later today, one of the Senators will come by the station around lunch. It sounds like they are looking for help handling the Children situation. Aiden, weren't you at that event a few months ago when KID and the Children made their threats?"

I nodded, remembering that night all too well. "Yes, sir. It's been almost four months now. Do you know which Senator is coming?"

He examined the slip of paper in his hand. "Says here it's North Towns Senator. Hunt."

"Kim?" I said, surprised. "Cool. She's my neighbor. You guys will like her."

The four months had flown by, though the disturbing memory of KID and his mask felt as if it was yesterday. As I processed the news, two tones blared through the station, followed by the now familiar robotic lady's voice. "Rescue 3, traumatic injury. Repeat, rescue 3, traumatic injury."

During the drive, Ryan read the notes, which seemed oddly vague. He smirked at me. "Might be another crazy one, black cloud."

I hated the nickname, but at this point, I couldn't argue. Fires, odd injuries, challenging rescues—I got them all. Each one was difficult, both physically and mentally, but the experiences were priceless. They'd transformed me from a know-nothing rookie to a somewhat capable firefighter. Ryan's and my friendship grew, but our partnership was even better, working like a well-oiled machine.

We pulled up to a vacant-looking house, its faded paint and broken shutters giving it an eerie feel. After confirming we were at the right place, we knocked on the front door, but no one answered.

A moment later, a boy about our age rounded the corner from the backyard. He had a strange burn-type of scar on his arm between his elbow and bicep. It looked familiar to me, but I couldn't quite place it.

"This way," he said warily.

Ryan and I shared a concerned glance as he walked away before we could respond. We cautiously followed him down the sidewalk to the house next door, where he opened the garage. A girl sat on the concrete floor, her face wincing in pain as she cradled her arm.

Ryan immediately dropped to one knee beside her. "What happened?"

The girl stayed silent, her eyes darting to the boy that led us in. He answered for her, his tone callous and disinterested. "She crashed her bike."

Ryan continued, undeterred. "Okay, did you hurt anything besides your arm?"

"No," the boy answered, crossing his arms.

I got closer and inspected the girl's arm, which was visibly swollen and had a sharp lump pressing at the skin, but not poking through. It was broken.

I cradled her arm for her, holding it in a comfortable position. "Your arm is broken. We will splint it here, get you some pain meds, and get you down to the hospital. Sound good?"

The boy stepped forward, placing his hands on his hips now. "Why would she need to go there?"

I raised my brow before answering, not fully understanding if he was serious. "She broke her arm, man. She needs a doctor."

As Ryan splinted her arm, I began preparing an IV, trying to ignore the hovering boy. Her hand had what looked like old burn marks that were nearly healed. She tried to hide her uninjured hand from me. I'd never had people hide their old injuries before.

"So, what's your name?" I asked, hoping to gain a little trust.

The boy didn't allow an answer. "Just do your job."

"I am doing my job. I need to make sure she is fully alert, and I need her to answer."

She glanced at him as if needing permission before answering in a low voice, "Tawny."

"Nice to meet you, Tawny. I'm Aiden. Do you know what day it is today?"

"Tuesday."

"Great, I know these are silly questions. Who is the President?"

Her voice dropped to a near-growl. "Keres."

Curiosity got the better of me, and I couldn't resist one last question. "What happened to your hand here?"

The boy stepped between us, his posture rigid and hostile. "No more questions. Finish up and leave."

"We can't leave her like this, you see," Ryan explained, his voice remaining calm. "We have to transport her."

The boy's hand dropped to his waistband, his eyes cold. "You're not going to do anything except leave. Now get out, or you'll be in much worse shape than she is."

Though still holding her arm, I planted myself on the balls of my feet, ready to move. His shirt bunched around his waistband, and I knew this was not the time to argue. His intent was clear. Ryan and I silently agreed it was best to back off.

"Please get her to the hospital," I said as we retreated to the door. "She needs help."

He closed the garage behind us, and we returned to the rescue. As we climbed inside, Ryan jotted down the address and informed dispatch the patient had refused.

"What do we do?" I asked. "Should we call Cap? Someone needs to help her."

Ryan shook his head. "I don't think so. These two are hiding something, and I think they are dangerous. I'm pretty sure they are with the Children. That would explain the burns on her hands, you see. She's probably been helping start all the fires we've been running on lately."

Once he said it, I felt stupid because it was so obvious, but I didn't recognize it. Something nagged at me though. I still wanted to get her help. "What if we tell Kaylyn? The President has asked everyone to report Children activity. She's a cop. She would know what to do."

"That's a good idea. I'll call her. Now let's get out of here."

Ryan pulled out his phone and called Kaylyn to relay the details. They'd grown closer over the months, and he'd finally started to relax somewhat around her. He'd been saying he'd ask her out next time he saw her, but he chickened out every time.

Kaylyn, who was on duty, said she'd head over to investigate and would keep us updated. But after she did, she text Ryan to let him know the house was empty when she arrived, and they couldn't find the kids. She also asked if Ryan had any other question to ask her. "Any questions at all." Not needing anything further, he replied "no" and thanked her.

"What do you think she meant by that?" Ryan asked, staring at the text before returning it to his pocket.

"I don't know, man. Probably some weird cop thing."

Back at the station, we told Cap about what had happened. He agreed that we'd done the right thing.

Around noon, Kim arrived, looking official in a fitted blazer and slacks. She shook hands with everyone, giving me a warm hug before positioning herself at the head of the table. "Hi everyone. I'm Kim Hunt, the North Las Vegas Senator."

Reed leaned back, folding his arms with a smirk. "Aren't you a little young to be a Senator? Have you even learned to read yet?"

Cap and Mum glared at Reed, but Kim smiled. "Oh, I read just fine. I can even catch a football. I heard you have a little trouble with that."

The room burst into laughter, Reed included, though he threw a crumpled napkin at me. I'd clearly shared his football ambitions with Kim.

She continued, her tone turning serious. "All right, we are meeting with all the first responders in the Valley to discuss the Children. We are looking for help with combating their growing threats and destruction. As you may remember, a few months ago, their leader, KID, made some serious threats against us and against 'traitors.'"

"What does he mean by 'traitors'?" Mum asked.

"We believe it is people who have defected from the Children." Kim's gaze drifted to Reed. "Reed, defect means to leave or betray."

Reed's face flushed, sinking further into his chair, but he managed a grin.

Kim continued. "We believe a handful are leaving the group, but they soon go missing. We don't know if they have been taken or are in hiding."

I looked over at Ryan, but he shook his head slightly. He wanted to keep his past with the Children to himself still.

Kim then explained the methods they'd used to try to track them. They tracked everyone's debit cards, which was our only form of money since we didn't deal with physical cash, to see if they could find anyone who was being paid on top of their monthly stipend, which everyone got. This proved difficult, since even the known Children somehow got some form of extra payment. She then asked us to keep our eyes and ears open for anything unusual.

Cap nodded. "We'll help however we can, Senator."

"Thank you. Captain, could we speak privately? Aiden, you can join us as well."

Intrigued, I followed Cap and Kim into the Captain's office and closed the door behind us. She took a deep breath before speaking in almost a whisper.

"We've only been telling the captains at each station, but I know Aiden, so I trust you to be here too. You must keep what I'm about to tell you confidential."

Cap and I exchanged uneasy glances, but agreed.

Kim's face tightened as she looked over her shoulder. "We believe KID is a bigger threat than most might think."

Cap's eyes widened. "What do you mean?"

"We think he is planning something big. So big that it could destroy our entire way of living. We just don't know what it is. They're leaning toward arson, which I'm sure you've noticed. That's why we need you guys to be on your toes and keep your eyes sharp. We think they are building up to something bigger. We are keeping our fear quiet because we don't want to cause a panic."

I nodded, though in disbelief that something so evil could be happening. After all the devastation we endured to get to this point, why would someone want to put us through the wringer again? More pressure was on my shoulders now than ever before.

Kim said her goodbyes and left.

I found Ryan sitting on a workout bench in the gym, staring at the wall.

"So..." I began, trying to sound calm. "Do you think this KID guy would try to come after you? Do you want to come stay with me and my sisters?"

He looked up, his face conflicted. "I think I'll be okay. My house has lots of cameras and even a panic room. Besides, I left so long ago, way before they got all crazy, you see. They probably don't even remember me. Thanks, though."

I sat next to him. "Yeah, man, of course. I have to ask you something, though, and I want you to be honest. No more secrets."

With Kim confirming that some of the Children had been going missing, I was more curious than ever to know what Ryan said to the girl we found in the closet months ago.

Ryan knew what I was going to ask. "You want to know what I wrote to the girl who ran off after we pulled her out of the house fire."

I nodded.

Ryan exhaled slowly. "Okay. But you can't tell anyone. This is probably the most important secret I've ever kept, and people's lives depend on it staying that way, you see."

My stomach tightened. I didn't expect the secret to be so intense. "I won't say a word."

"There is someone out there who is helping the ex-Children. They help them get anonymous jobs and places to stay and keep them hidden from KID and the rest of the Children. I'm the only one who knows who this person is. That girl earlier was hiding on her own, but the Children found her. That's why I gave her the note. To get her to someone who can keep her safe."

My brow furrowed. "Who's hiding them? How do you know them?"

Ryan shook his head. "Sorry. That's not for me to tell. It doesn't matter, though, you wouldn't know them. I just wanted you to know what I was doing, you see. Just trying to help these runaways."

My mouth went dry. Someone hiding ex-Children from this maniac was dangerous. And Ryan knew who they were. If KID ever found out, Ryan would be dead. I could be, too. Maybe even my sisters. I thought I wanted to know more, but now I was terrified of what I did know.

What Ryan was doing was admirable, and I looked up to him even more now than I already did. Even still, I had an awful feeling that this KID guy was going to cause us a lot more problems, and soon.

15
HILL'S BIRTHDAY

"Did you know that the easiest way to Dad's heart was through music and his stomach? There was nothing he loved more than music and food—except for us." — Precious Hill

Today was Hill's first anniversary on the job, which also happened to be his actual birthday. Hill downplayed every meal he'd made since I'd been there, even though each was better than our family's best dishes. Today was the first time he said he would be putting in some real effort for our dinner. After all the delicious meals, I couldn't imagine what this special chow would taste like.

We offered to help, but he refused and shooed us out of the kitchen. It was raining hard outside, so we played a little hockey game in the bay, where the engine and rescue were typically parked.

Reed had the idea to do a shootout tournament, since we couldn't play three vs three, like usual. We drew names from a hat to decide who would be matched against whom. I pulled goalie against Reed, but Mum would be shooting with Cap in the net first.

"All right, Fisk," Cap said, tossing the battered hockey stick to Mum. "Let's see what you got."

Mum casually handled the puck between her stick at center court. "I think you already know what I got." She confidently jogged forward, trash-talking the entire way. She faked a shot to the right, then to the left, making him dive out of position. With a quick flick of her wrist, she sent the puck straight into the upper corner of the net, raising her stick in victory.

"I can't be stopped!" Mum boasted, high-fiving everyone as she strutted down the sideline.

"Nice shot, Fisk," Cap said, giving her a high five as well.

Then, it was my turn against Reed. He looked bigger than usual, cracking his knuckles across from me. I gulped, bracing myself as he ran like a freight train, barreling toward me and staring me down the entire time.

I crouched and moved forward a few steps, ready to react to his shot. However, no puck ever came. Instead, he lowered his shoulder and plowed right through me, knocking me back into the net. Somehow, he kept control of the puck and casually pushed it into the net with only one hand on his stick.

"That's one for Reed!" he said, reaching his hand to help me to my feet. "You good brother?"

"Yeah," I chuckled, dusting myself off. "Good shot. I wasn't ready for that."

We cycled through the rounds, taking turns being the goalie and the shooter. Reed and Mum proved unstoppable, but I was starting to get the hang of it. For someone who had never played hockey in the Before, I was picking it up quickly.

When it was my turn for a break, I wandered inside to grab water. As I walked down the hallway, a strange noise came from the kitchen—a rich and soulful melody unfamiliar to the firehouse, but distinctly Hill's voice. I stopped, lingering just out of sight to watch and listen. Hill glided between counters, softly singing as he cooked, his voice passionate and smooth. His eyes glistened, obviously lost in his own perfect world. I had no idea Hill could sing so well; he rivaled any of our professional singers in the After.

I listened briefly before slipping back to the bay, not wanting to disturb him. We played until Hill called "Chow!" around 3pm, much earlier than usual, but we'd skipped lunch for this special meal. We quickly cleaned up, eager to see what he'd prepared.

The moment we stepped into the kitchen, the aroma hit us. A savory blend of roasted potatoes, smoky bacon, and buttery bread. Each of our plates was already prepared and set with a giant porterhouse steak, covered in a sauce so fragrant my mouth watered instantly. Next to the steak were bacon-wrapped green beans, roasted potatoes, and a slice of homemade sourdough toast. Hill stood by his seat, dropping his headphones around his neck, looking surprisingly nervous.

"Hope you guys like it," he muttered, rubbing his arm. "Not sure it turned out as I hoped."

"I doubt that," Mum said, giving him an encouraging smile. "If it tastes anything like it smells, it will be amazing. Thank you!"

I took a bite and any doubts Hill might've given me disappeared. The steak was perfectly tender and juicy, and the sauce was unlike anything I had tasted. Buttery, smokey, and with a slight kick. Each part of the meal was delicious.

We ate in near silence, too focused on the food to speak. By the end, only Reed managed to clear his plate since there was so much. We leaned back in our chairs, groaning in painful satisfaction.

Hill stood up, clearing his throat. "I, uh... I just wanted to thank everyone for all you've done for me and for being such good friends. You made this last year here feel like I was with family."

He paused as his voice cracked, taking a shaky breath. We sat quietly, allowing him to gather his thoughts. He looked up, managing a small smile. "Anyways, thanks. I hope you liked it."

Cap gave him a firm nod. "We are lucky to have you as a member of our crew and as a brother, Hill. And this food was the best I've ever had."

As per usual, three bells rang out, cutting through the sentimental moment.

"Engine 3, Rescue 3, water rescue. Engine 3, Rescue 3, water rescue."

We moaned, trying to find the strength to stand after the feast, and hurried pathetically to the rigs. Though it didn't rain a lot in Las Vegas, when it did, it was frequently a heavy, short downpour. The flood channels quickly became overwhelmed, especially in the springtime, like now.

Cap reminded us to wear shorts and sneakers instead of our turnouts and boots. That gear would weigh us down if we ended up in the water. I threw our swift water equipment on the rig—helmets, life jackets, and rescue throw ropes—and we sped off toward the incident. Reed and Hill followed us in the rescue.

Dispatch stated a boy had been swept away down one of the storm channels. We raced farther east, hoping to get far enough ahead of him and find a spot where we could perform a rescue. Cap coordinated with the other crews over the radio, planning out positions along the route.

We found an adequate place to reach the channel and geared up. Ryan was assigned upstream and had to call out hazards and when he saw the boy. Reed was spaced about 100 feet downstream from him, with a rope bag. Hill and I were spaced out further down the channel. Cap directed from the bank, and Mum got in the rescue, ready to reposition when needed.

"Everyone stay alert and be careful," Cap ordered. "This water is moving fast. Do not fall in!"

The wait felt endless while standing in the pouring rain. I scanned the muddy, fast-moving water, my heart racing as I went through the motions of throwing the rope correctly. Then I noticed something on Hill's neck and tried to get his attention. "Hill! You have your headphones on!"

"What?" he questioned, holding his hand to his ear.

"Your headphones!"

He didn't hear me over the roar of the rapids and the splash of the rain drops, but then a sharp whistle sounded from upstream. Ryan waved his arms, signaling he had spotted the boy.

The kid floated down the channel, his legs out in front, bobbing through the waves. He looked tiny against the powerful current, his face pale and frightened as he fought to stay afloat.

Reed steadied himself as the boy approached, swinging his rope and casting it in a smooth arc—but it landed just out of reach, drifting with the current.

Hill was up now. He squared his stance, took a breath, and threw the rope underhand, straight into the boy's outstretched arms.

Hill gripped the rope, bracing himself, but the force of the pull yanked him forward, and he stumbled on the slick embankment, half-falling into the water. Desperately, he grabbed onto a piece of rebar embedded in the concrete wall with one hand, his knuckles white as he held the rope with the other.

"I got you!" he shouted, his voice strained as he fought to hold on.

The boy clung to the line and acted like a pendulum, slowly drifting to the bank. Hill grunted in pain as Reed and I ran to pull the boy to safety. Once we grabbed him, we carried him up the embankment to the rescue.

The boy was shivering, his skin cold but mostly unharmed. Just some bruises, scrapes, and in the early stages of hypothermia. We wrapped him in blankets and began treating his injuries. Only then did I notice Hill was missing.

"Where is Hill?" I asked, scanning the area outside the rescue.

No one knew, and a flood of dread hit me. I jumped out of the rescue in a panic, racing back to the channel with Cap behind me.

"He was right here, Cap!" I said, peering down the channel.

We stood at the edge, desperately looking downstream. Cap was about to notify the other crews of our missing firefighter when we heard a faint voice, "I'm here."

Hill sat up on the bank, water and mud dripping off his shoes and shorts and severe rope burns across his hands. He looked exhausted.

"Are you okay?" Cap asked, inspecting his hands.

Hill looked down to the ground, appearing strangely sad for someone who made a fantastic rescue. "I'm not hurt," he muttered, though tears welled in his eyes. "It's just... my headphones. They're gone. How could I be so stupid?"

Cap eyed me curiously, unsure how to respond. I shrugged my shoulders. They were old, crappy headphones. Why did he care so much? It would be easy to buy a newer pair.

"Sorry, Hill," Cap said, touching his shoulder. "Let's get you dried up."

After transporting the boy to the hospital, Ryan and I returned to the engine to head back to the station. The rescue arrived shortly after. Hill, with his now-bandaged hands, went straight to his dorm, and Reed joined us in the kitchen.

"Devin seems pretty upset about his headphones," Mum said once Reed sat down.

"Yeah," Reed responded. "Why are they such a big deal, though? They were so old. They look like they are from the Before."

I wondered if they were from the Before. Maybe they were special to him. I contemplated asking him about them but decided against it, thinking he would say something if he really wanted to.

Mum shrugged. "I'm not sure. I wish there was something we could do for him. That was an amazing save he made."

"What if we bought him a new pair?" I suggested. "His were worn out anyway, and we could get him a really nice set if we all chipped in."

"Great idea," Cap said. "Would everyone be willing to put in some money for it?"

Reed rolled his eyes, leaning back. "I don't see why we should buy them. He was the one that left them on."

Cap raised an eyebrow, amused. "Mistakes happen. I'm sure I don't need to remind you of the time you forgot to wear your helmet in a house fire, or the time you left your SCBA mask in the engine, or the time you didn't put the rescue in park, and it rolled away and hit a wall, or the time..."

Reed laughed. "Okay, okay. I get it. I'll pitch in money, but Aiden is going to go pick them out for us, right?"

I nodded. "Yeah, I'll get them, no problem."

"Great, thanks, Aiden," Cap said. "Let us know how much we owe you, and be sure to charge Reed double!"

16

KWIKY KLEAN

"We need to prepare the youth for every career. They'll need doctors and firefighters. Government officials and engineers. Miners and farmers. Store owners and restaurant workers. We should strive to create a society comparable to ours. Maybe it will even be better. We can make it so they won't want for food and water. Money can be an afterthought. We can make them prosperous!" — Mayor Cathleen Goodson

Ryan and I walked together to the parking lot at the end of our shift. We were laughing about something Reed had said earlier when we spotted Kaylyn, arms crossed and toe-tapping beside Ryan's car. She didn't have on her usual approachable smile, either.

"Ryan Mitsuya!" she called out loud enough for him to flinch. "I am sick of waiting for you."

Ryan stopped, looking like a deer in the headlights. "Waiting? For what?"

"I've been dropping hints for months now. Are you really that slow, or are you just that afraid?"

Ryan looked at me, concerned, but I just shrugged.

Kaylyn stomped closer, her arms swinging and her brow ruffled. "Are you going to ask me on a date or not? I keep thinking the next time I see you, you will. But you never do. Don't you like me?"

Ryan's rambling, which he'd mainly overcome around her, returned. "No, I didn't. I mean, yes. Dates are fine. I like them, I mean you. I didn't know if you liked me, you see. I wasn't sure if, I didn't know how, I, uh..."

"Yes or no, Ryan!"

"No, I mean, yes. Yes! Kaylyn, do you want to go out with me?"

She stared, her stern look softening before grinning. "Yes, Ryan. You can take me out tomorrow. And you better plan something nice for us."

She hugged him and then walked to her car, leaving Ryan standing, mouth open in shock.

I stepped in front of his frozen body, waving my hand in his face. "You okay, buddy?"

After a few seconds, he blinked, returning from his daze. "Yes! Yes, yes, yes, I did it. I finally did it!"

He took off sprinting from one end of the lot to the other, pumping his fists in the air. When he came back, panting and sweating, he leaned against his car, looking triumphant.

I patted him on the shoulder, grinning in amusement. "Now the real question is, what are you going to do for the date?"

All the excitement instantly left his face. He faced the car and lightly banged his head against the driver's door. "Oh, no. What am I going to do? I don't know how to plan these things."

"Sorry, man," I said. "I'm no help. I've never been on a date before."

Ryan groaned. "You gotta help me. She is expecting something amazing, you see."

I thought for a moment before coming up with a possible solution. "Come over sometime today, and we can ask Aubrey if she has any ideas? She is pretty creative and likes romantic stuff. I bet she can come up with something."

Relieved, he agreed to come over to the house later that afternoon. When he showed up, Aubrey was in the garage cleaning her car. Ryan pulled up to the house, and I went downstairs to meet him outside, but he went right to Aubrey.

"Hey Aubrey," he said, waving to her. "Aiden said you were a creative genius and were gonna help me out today, you see."

Aubrey stared at him, confused. "I don't see. What am I helping you with?"

"Aiden didn't tell you?"

They both peered at me.

"Why didn't you tell her?" Ryan asked.

I threw my arms up in defense. "She just got home! I haven't had a chance yet. Aubrey, Ryan has a date with Kaylyn tomorrow, and he is freaking out because he doesn't know what to do. We were hoping you could help come up with something."

Aubrey rolled her eyes at us as we tried to look as cute and lovable as possible. "I guess I can. Let's go inside."

She removed her cleaning gloves and led us into the living room, where she sat on the couch with an exasperated look.

"Well," Aubrey began. "First off, you need to clean your car. It's filthy, and if the inside smells anything like you two, you'll need to take care of that, too. As for the date, what do you know about Kaylyn? What does she like?"

Ryan hesitated, thinking hard. "Uh, well, she is a cop, and she is really pretty. Oh, and she is nice!"

Aubrey blinked, dumbfounded. "Uh, huh. Anything else, like hobbies or something?"

Ryan glanced at me as if I should have come up with the answer. I shrugged my shoulders, stumped as he was.

Aubrey stood up with a hopeless gasp. "You guys are impossible."

"No, wait!" Ryan said, lightly grabbing her arm. "What would you want to do for a first date?"

Aubrey rubbed her temples as she sat back down. "It doesn't matter what I want, Ryan. I'm not Kaylyn. You should know what she likes and what she would want to do."

Ryan sat next to her, grabbing her hand and batting his eyes. "Come on, please. Maybe it will help us come up with another idea. You'll be the greatest person ever."

Aubrey contemplated for a moment, looking annoyed, but eventually gave in after letting out a sigh. "Well, if you were taking me on a date, Ryan—I mean, if someone was taking me on a date—I would want it to be thoughtful and creative. Start out by doing something active and a little competitive. Maybe frisbee golf. That way, you can walk and talk together while still playing a game. You can learn a lot about someone by how they win and, more importantly, how they lose."

Ryan and I glanced at each other. We had obviously never thought that much about a date, and she was barely getting started.

Aubrey closed her eyes, seemingly imagining this date she was describing. "Then a picnic. We would each pack our favorite sandwich, snack, and drink for the other person to eat. Finally, I'd want to drive up to one of the hills at the edge of town on a warm, clear night to watch a movie on a projector screen. The winner of frisbee golf gets to choose the movie. Hopefully, the movie would be something funny but romantic. And it would be because if I won frisbee golf, then I would pick the movie I brought, and if he won, he better pick the movie I brought! After the movie, he would drive me home and walk me to my doorstep where we would share a... "

Aubrey shook her head, coming out of her daydream. "Anyway, that's a simple idea I came up with just now. It's not hard. Put a little effort into it, and you'll be fine. I need to get back to cleaning."

She returned to the garage, leaving us feeling more inadequate and ill-prepared than before.

Ryan looked even more lost than before. "That was an intense date. I'm not sure I can pull something like that off."

"I'm sure you could. It did sound fun. We still have to figure out what she likes, though. What do cops like?"

We sat silently for a moment, thinking our hardest. Finally, I came up with an answer so obvious that I couldn't believe I hadn't realized it earlier. "Donuts! Cops love donuts."

Ryan jumped to his feet. "Of course! I can take her out for donuts. She'll love that!"

Now that we had the perfect date idea, we needed to clean Ryan's car. The best place for that was Kwiky Klean, a drive-thru wash with industrial vacuums, ideal for deep cleaning Ryan's car. I agreed to help him, and Ryan drove us to the nearest location.

During the drive, we saw multiple graffiti spots that the Children had tagged, on a couple road signs and even a few buildings. Then we passed a small office building that was burned to the ground. That fire happened while we were off duty, and the building didn't appear to be in use by anyone.

"They are getting bolder," I said.

"Yeah," Ryan answered. "What's the point of burning down vacant buildings, though? Who is that gonna hurt?"

"They are getting better, though, at getting the fires going faster, and burning hotter. Almost like they are practicing for something."

"I'm not sure they're that organized. They were never much for preparing when I was with them, you see. But who knows anymore. This KID guy seems like a full-blown terrorist."

Once we arrived, we drove to the automated window to buy a wash, then pulled into the tracks and let the machinery take over. Something about these washes made me feel like a little kid again. I imagined most had a similar feeling because every time I went with someone, we all had the same look of bewilderment.

Colorful bubbles engulfed the car, and I couldn't help but lean forward in fascination as the soapy aroma filled the car. Ryan had the same expression.

As we moved to the rinse cycle, I glanced out the side and froze. Through the large glass storefront window, there was someone I recognized, but I couldn't believe it. I pressed my head against the glass to get a better look.

"It's her!" I exclaimed, smacking Ryan on the arm several times.

"Who?"

"The Australian girl from the game!"

Ryan raised an eyebrow. "What are you talking about?"

I forgot I hadn't told anyone about her since I was so mad at myself for not getting her name. I hadn't even mentioned anything to my sisters. I had thought about this girl far too much for someone I'd only had one conversation with. At night I would replay our talk in my head, recalling her touch on my hand when I handed her a soda. I had given up hope that I would ever see her again. But there she was.

The car was still on the track, inching forward much too slowly for me. "We gotta get out of the car!"

I frantically searched for a way out, feeling like a leashed dog waiting to chase a squirrel. I needed to get out and couldn't wait any longer. The rinse was done, so I threw open the door, sprinting ahead of the car, only to be hit by the blast of the dryers. The powerful blowers sent me stumbling backward, but I pushed through, heading straight for the entrance of the Kwiky Klean.

Ryan was yelling at me, but nothing could stop me. I made it through the wash and burst through the front doors, drawing some questionable looks from the patrons inside. The girl hadn't noticed me, though.

Attempting to slow myself down, I took a deep breath and walked over to the desk she stood behind. She was just as breathtaking as I remembered.

She wasn't as dressed up as before. She wore a Kwiky Klean t-shirt, a different pair of large dangling earrings, and her hair in a ponytail—which, for some reason, made her look even better to me.

She was writing on a tablet as I stood there staring. With my incredible sleuthing skills, I deduced that she worked here.

Too excited to take a moment to think, I approached the counter without a second thought about what I would say to her. Focused on her work, she didn't notice me, and all that came out of my nervous mouth was the sound of me clearing my throat.

"Welcome to Kwiky Klean. How can I help..." she began, looking up. "Hey! The ginger-ale hero!"

She remembered. That realization alone made me forget to respond.

She eyed me with a smirk, her gaze drifting to my hair. "I like your new style. You really got a 'walked through a tornado' kinda vibe going on."

I checked out my reflection in a nearby window. She was right. My hair had been blown straight up with mud speckles on my face.

"Oh yeah," I said, trying to fix it. "It's pretty windy outside."

She pointed outside to a set of trees in the parking lot, which weren't moving in the slightest. "It doesn't look too windy to me?"

I laughed, searching for an answer. "Well, you know, those crazy gusts of wind come out of nowhere. I guess one of them got me as I walked in."

She smiled and leaned forward on the counter. "Hey, I was kicking myself during the rest of that game because I never asked your name, especially when I saw you on the field helping that player. What you guys did for him was pretty incredible."

"Me too! I've been so mad at myself for not asking for yours."

She leaned back, seemingly waiting for something. "So, go on, tell us."

"Oh yeah, I'm Aiden, Aiden Brann. What's yours?"

"Truly Taylor."

"Truly," I repeated, shaking her hand. "That's a beautiful name."

Before I could say any more, Ryan burst in, looking both annoyed and amused. "Are you crazy, Aiden?! What in the world were you doing, jumping out like that? You could have gotten hurt, or worse, messed up my car!"

"Ryan?" Truly questioned. "You know the ginger-ale hero?"

I was surprised to see that these two seemed to know each other. Ryan had never told me he knew the most beautiful girl in the world, which was strange to me. This was good for me, though, because maybe Ryan could vouch for me.

Ryan looked at me, puzzled. "A ginger hero? You mean Aiden? Wait. Are you the Australian girl, Truly? I didn't know you were Australian."

Truly laughed and shook her head. "Are you serious? You never noticed my accent? Or my parents' accents?"

Ryan shrugged. "I just figured you talked weird. Never thought to ask. How do you know Aiden?"

"I met him for a second at the football game. You guys must work together."

Ryan peered at me, as I stood awkwardly off to the side. "I was at the game. He didn't say anything to me about it. Didn't you see me on the field helping that player?"

Truly blushed. "Uh, no. But to be honest, I wasn't really looking at you."

She glanced at me, then looked back at Ryan.

Ryan began slowly backing away. "Well, I'd better let you two talk. Your ginger hero here almost destroyed my car trying to get to you, you see. Remember, Aiden, you promised to help me clean. I'll see ya later, Truly."

Ryan went back outside, and I nervously tried to fill the silence. "So, how old are you?"

"I'll be 15 next month."

"And you work here?"

Man, my questions are lame! Get it together, Aiden!

"Well, actually, I own all the Kwiky Kleans in town. I just happened to be here getting some inventory and whatnot. Boring stuff."

"Oh, wow, that's cool. I love your car washes." I rubbed the back of my neck, contemplating if I was brave enough to do what I'd been dreaming of since I met her. "Hey, so, I was thinking. I know we kinda just met, but would you maybe want to go out and do something with me tomorrow or sometime, you know, if you want to?"

"Like a date?"

My face flushed. "No, it doesn't have to be a date or anything, I was just thinking..."

Truly smiled, interrupting my nervous stammers. "A date sounds great! Hand us your phone."

I handed it over, and she typed in her number before returning it. "There, now you have my number. Text me when and where tomorrow and I'll be there. Now, you better get back to Ryan and help him out like you promised."

Barely able to contain my astonishment, I simply smiled and walked away without saying anything further. Once around the corner, I investigated my contact list and found Truly Taylor, except she put a heart instead of a 'u' in her name. I jumped up in the air as I exited the building, feeling how I imagined Ryan felt earlier.

"Things go good in there for ya?" Ryan asked, while vacuuming his car.

"Maybe," I said, grinning like an idiot. "How do you know Truly?"

Ryan stopped vacuuming and handed it to me. "Uh, we're just old friends. I knew her parents during the Preparation, you see. Now, why don't you help me like you said you would. This car is a mess."

17

THE MISSION

"If things work like they say they will, you'll still need nonessential jobs. If we get you set up early, you can have a lot of businesses, and then you'll be able to help those having trouble finding their place." — Kolter Taylor

The following morning, I jolted awake as someone shook me hard, and nearly fell out of bed. Blinking through bleary eyes, I found Ryan standing over me, looking disheveled and anxious.

"What are you doing here?" I asked, still groggy. "How did you get in?"

Now that he'd succeeded in waking me, he plopped down on the middle of the floor, covering his face with his hands. "I can't do it, Aiden. I couldn't sleep all night. I'm freaking out, you see. You gotta help me."

"Ryan, I already helped you come up with the date idea. What else am I supposed to do?"

"I don't know!" he groaned, still hiding behind his hands. "I think if you were just, like, there... I'd feel better."

"I can't," I said, shaking my head. "That would be weird. Plus, I have my own date with Truly, remember? How can you be so stressed about this but so chill on our crazy medical calls?"

He sighed, looking completely defeated. "It's different, and I can't do this. I'm gonna call Kaylyn and tell her I'm sick or something."

"I wouldn't lie to a cop. She could arrest you if she found out."

He glared at me, sitting up straighter. "I'm being serious, Aiden. What should I do?"

I swung my legs off the side of the bed, realizing he wouldn't be convinced to do this alone. After a moment, I devised a plan to allow me to be close enough to help him if needed while still enjoying my date with Truly. I explained it to Ryan, and he brightened, finally calming down. He went home to prepare.

Later that afternoon, I arrived at Kwiky Klean to pick up Truly. She'd told me earlier she'd be working until our date. When I parked, I spotted her through the window, looking effortlessly beautiful in a black shirt and jeans, her hair down and slightly curly, wearing yet another pair of unique earrings.

I took a deep breath, trying to keep my heart from racing, and cranked up the A/C to try and help with my nervously sweating palms. But before I could calm myself, she noticed me and waved. There was no delaying anymore, so I climbed out of the car and walked to the entrance.

I met her at the front door and handed her a single rose. She accepted it with a smile, held it up to her nose, and took a whiff. She examined it, puzzled. "Is this... plastic?"

"Yeah! Well, it's wrapped in plastic," I said proudly. "I made it myself. It's chocolate! I never understood giving flowers. They look nice for a day or two, and then they die. I think chocolate is way better."

She laughed, unwrapping it and handing one of the two pieces of chocolate inside to me. "That's the greatest thing I have ever heard."

I popped the piece in my mouth, and she did the same.

"So, what are we doing tonight?" she asked, sucking on the chocolate.

"We will be going on the most daring undercover mission imaginable. Top secret. In fact, I might get in a lot of trouble for telling you that much, let alone bringing you along."

"Oh, cheeky. Will it be dangerous?"

I leaned in, pretending to listen for eavesdroppers. "Oh, yes! Very dangerous. Have you ever seen Mission Impossible?"

"No."

"Good," I said, putting my hand on her shoulder. "Because that movie would give you hope that this mission is possible. This mission is beyond impossible. It's improbable!"

She burst out laughing, shaking her head. "I think improbable means there is a better chance of success than impossible, Aiden."

I blushed, realizing she was right. "Oh... uh yeah. Well, either way. It's going to be hard, so we are going to need a disguise. And we are going to need to take your car. Mine has been compromised. To the thrift store!"

She laughed as we climbed into her car. At the thrift store, we picked out the most outlandish outfits we could find. Clothes, scarves, hats, anything and everything was fair game, and we modeled and gave fashion critiques for each one. They were getting more and more ridiculous and hilarious as we went. Somehow, no matter how wild the outfit, Truly still looked amazing. The same could not be said for me. We laughed so much that my face hurt, which hadn't happened to me in a long time.

Trying on clothes was an oddly surreal experience. I felt as if I was living out one of the cheesy movies my mom used to always watch.

After a while, we settled on outfits for each other. Truly dressed all in black, complete with a scarf and beanie. She already had a black shirt and looked like a super spy with a purple wig. To top it off, she found a pair of pineapple sunglasses that she had to have, since it was her favorite fruit from the Before.

For me, she picked out mismatched camouflage, an orange hunting cap, and giant white-framed glasses. We purchased our things and left the store for part two of the covert mission.

"Now that no one can recognize us," she said, inspecting our handiwork. "Where to?"

"That's classified."

She dangled her keys just out of my reach. "Well, I'm the one driving. How are we going to get there if you don't tell me?"

I held out my hand, looking as serious as I could. "You have two options. You can drive with your eyes closed while I give directions. I don't recommend that one. Or you'll just have to let me take the wheel."

She peered at me, looking skeptical. "I don't know... Are you a good driver?"

"Come on, I drive ambulances around the city all day. I think I can handle it."

"Fine, but if you crash my car, you're dead."

She reluctantly handed me the keys, and I stood at the driver's door and rushed in a quick joke before entering. "And I've only wrecked the ambulance twice!"

"You cheeky bugger!"

I started the car and told her to close her eyes. She protested at first, but I told her I was keeping the classified location from her for her own safety. She finally agreed, covering her eyes with a dramatic sigh. I turned on the radio, singing along to the music as we drove.

When we arrived at our destination, I guided her to a nearby bench. "Okay, you can open your eyes now."

She uncovered her eyes and looked around, confused. "Why are we sitting across from a donut shop?"

"You'll see."

She scanned the area, looking for clues. "So... what exactly are we waiting for?"

"Shhh! Patience, Agent Taylor. Patience."

She squinted at me, and a few minutes later, she gasped and pointed. "Wait. Isn't that Ry..."

I covered her mouth quickly. "Shhh."

I kept my hand there while we watched Kaylyn and Ryan enter the donut shop. Once they did, she licked my palm, and I quickly pulled away and wiped it off on her shoulder. "Ewww."

Her eyes glistened with amusement. "That was Ryan, right? Are we here for him?"

"Yes," I whispered. "He is our mission. We are here to spy on his date and make sure things go well. If it starts to take a turn for the worse, we will have to run interference."

She grinned, clearly intrigued. "Interference? How are we going to do that?"

"I have no idea," I said, with a slow smile. "But those are my orders."

From our hiding spot, we watched Ryan and Kaylyn looking over the menu. We couldn't see what they were saying, so Truly decided to fill in their conversation.

Putting on a playful and heavy American accent, she said, "So, your idea of a romance is donuts?"

I tried to imitate Ryan's voice, replying, "Nothing says love like a maple donut, you see."

We went back and forth like this, inventing ridiculous lines for them and trying not to laugh too loudly. It was strange to think that just a few days ago, Kim was warning me about an impending threat from KID. At this mo-ment, however, nothing felt threatening. A day of joy was much needed for me. I just hoped my black cloud wasn't following me today.

By the time Ryan and Kaylyn finished, we were nearly in tears from laughter. Ryan seemed to be doing a decent enough job on his date. We couldn't tell what they were saying, but we saw Kaylyn laugh multiple times. Hopeful-ly, she wasn't laughing at him.

As they walked out of the shop, they looked in our direction. We panicked and threw ourselves over the back of the bench and onto the ground on the other side. I fell first and onto my back, and Truly landed on top of me with her face close to mine.

We giggled for a moment and tried to remain quiet. Our laughter faded as our eyes locked, staring intimately for several seconds. I got nervous and cleared my throat, glancing back under the bench. They were crossing the street and coming right for us.

"We gotta run!" I said.

I helped her to her feet, and we sprinted down the side-walk. Truly held her wig atop her head so it wouldn't fly off and we ducked into a nearby alley.

"I assumed Ryan knew we were spying," Truly said, trying to catch her breath.

"He does. Kaylyn doesn't, though. I told him we would stay hidden and wouldn't get caught."

We snuck back to Truly's car just in time for Ryan and Kaylyn to enter theirs and drive off. Truly was driving again, and we followed behind Ryan and Kaylyn since I didn't know where they were going next. We continued following them until we arrived at a mini-golf course.

"Okay," I began in my most serious voice. "This will be the most difficult part. Not only do we have to infiltrate this secure facility, but we also have to navigate the interior, undetected by the person of interest. Are you ready for this?"

"Oh, I'm ready."

We crept to the front entrance, playfully conspicuous, crouching and spinning as we approached the front counter.

The worker, tall and lanky and looking older than he probably was, watched us suspiciously. "Ummm, can I help you?"

I looked over each shoulder, whispering and lowering my sunglasses. "Yeah. We are going to need two mini-golf games, STAT."

"I'll need the purple ball," Truly added. "And he'll take the orange."

I slowly slid my debit card across the table. Then, with my eyes peeled, I looked him dead in the eyes, attempting to look intimidating. "No one needs to know about this. Understand?"

"Or else we will be back for you, Bradley!" Truly said, reading his name tag.

The worker stared blankly, returning my card to me. "Uh, okay. Do you want a receipt?"

Truly slapped the countertop, startling both me and the worker. "No paper trails!"

Outside, we trailed a few holes behind Ryan and Kaylyn, creating more dialog as we went. We kept the secret agent gag alive, taking our shots while rolling, crawling, and diving behind bushes to avoid detection. I couldn't think of the last time I had this much fun in the After. A part of me kept waiting for it to all fall apart or for another Children attack, but none came.

Things seemed to be going well for Ryan and Kaylyn. However, if I was being honest, we were having so much fun playing our own game that we stopped paying much attention to them. I wondered if Ryan had gained the ability to talk to her properly. Either way, there was no possibility they were having a better time than Truly and me. My stomach was beginning to cramp from all the laughter.

When we finally looked up from our antics, we saw Ryan and Kaylyn standing at the end of the final hole, arms crossed, looking directly at us.

"Why have you been spying on us all day?" Kaylyn asked, raising an eyebrow.

I glanced at Ryan, who was wide-eyed and shaking his head slightly, signaling to stay quiet.

I tried to look innocent, but our outfits weren't helping. "Spying? Us?"

Kaylyn rolled her eyes. "Oh, please. I saw you guys at the donut place. You sat outside watching us the whole time. Then you walked in here behind us and ridiculously rolled around trying to hide from us." She looked at Ryan accusatorily. "How would they know where we were going?"

"I didn't tell them we were going to golf."

That was actually the truth. He only told me about the donut shop. I simply had to follow them to the next locations. I had no idea they were going to play mini-golf.

"Sorry, Kaylyn," I said. "I just wanted to see how the date was going for you guys. I thought it would be fun to spy on you. I'm sorry if I ruined it for you."

Kaylyn began laughing, and the rest of us nervously chuckled along.

"Oh, you didn't ruin it," Kaylyn said. "We spent most of the time making fun of your ridiculous outfits and how you thought you were so sneaky. Did you really think we never saw you?"

I shrugged. "Uh, I mean, kinda, yeah."

She laughed again and turned her attention to Truly. "I'm Kaylyn, by the way. Since these boys have no manners, I'll introduce myself."

"I'm Truly. Sorry we had to meet this way. I don't usually spend my time stalking people. I'm a tad more boring than that. Maybe next time we can give a double date a go, unless donuts for your first date were a deal breaker."

Kaylyn tossed her arms in the air. "Thank you! What in the world was he thinking? Did he really think that because I'm a cop, I love donuts?"

Truly rolled her eyes. "Boys don't understand much, unfortunately."

Kaylyn stepped closer, laughing with Truly. "Do you have an accent? Where is it from?"

"Australia."

Kaylyn stared at her momentarily before responding. "Australia? Interesting. Well, I like the idea of doing a double date. We should totally do that soon. But today, I can't wait to see what else Ryan has planned for us," she said sarcastically. "Nice to meet you. You guys don't need to follow us anymore."

Kaylyn and Truly exchanged numbers before she and Ryan left for their car together, leaving Truly and me alone on the putting green.

"So, I guess the donut idea we had wasn't a good one?" I asked.

Truly gave me a playful shove. "Don't tell me you helped him come up with that?"

I gave a sheepish smile and a shrug. She linked her arm to mine and turned toward the exit. "You guys are adorable, but that was a terrible idea."

We returned to her car and didn't say much during the drive back to her work. I felt like I had just had the best night of my life, but I got self-conscious after hearing the donut idea was terrible.

When we arrived back at her work, she parked, and we both got out. Truly walked over to me and wrapped me in a hug, surprising me.

"That was the best first date I could have ever asked for, Aiden," she said softly.

I barely believed I heard her correctly. "Really?"

She removed her wig and sunglasses, revealing those gorgeous green eyes. "Absolutely! That was the most creative thing anyone has ever done for me. I can't wait to see what you do for our next date!"

I blinked. "Next date?"

She pulled me back just enough to kiss me on the cheek. I stood there dumbfounded, holding my hand to my cheek. "Cheeky," I said, regretting the cheesy joke almost immediately.

"Ha! I see what you did there," she said, giving me a playful shove. "Let me know when you want to go out again, okay?"

She returned to her car and drove off while I sat back in mine. I remained there momentarily, replaying everything in my head, then let out a triumphant yell as I punched the air. When I eventually made it home, still buzzing with excitement, I walked in and found Aubrey and Ally waiting on the couch.

Aubrey stood up, marching over to me. "Where have you been?"

"We have been worried about you," Ally added. "You didn't tell us you would be gone today and haven't been answering your phone. With all this KID stuff going on, we were freaking out."

"Oh, sorry. I had it on silent," I mumbled, trying to hide my grin.

Aubrey narrowed her eyes and moved even closer. "What are you smiling for? Were you out with a girl?" Her eyes widened as she covered her mouth with both hands. "Oh my gosh, you were! You were out with a girl!"

Ally sprang to her feet. "What!? A girl! Why didn't you tell us?"

I lightly pushed through them, trying to play it cool, and walked through the living room. "Because you guys would act all crazy like you are now."

"Oh no, you don't," Aubrey said, grabbing me by the arm. "You're going to sit down and tell us everything, buddy, and I mean everything."

"Fine," I said, immediately jumping onto the couch.

I didn't need much convincing. I was more than happy to recount my story. I walked them through the date step by step until the kiss. That was just for me.

18
New Headphones

"I use my headphones when I need to block out the bad out there. They help me get lost in my own little world, surrounding me with only the things I love. They can do the same for you." — Precious Hill

The morning sun was warm against my face as I practically skipped through the parking lot to work, feeling like I was floating. I couldn't remember the last time I felt this good or happy. Life in the After didn't feel so heavy today, not with my date with Truly still fresh in my mind.

When I got inside, Cap and Mum were already planning the day in the captain's office. I knocked lightly on the door frame, holding up a package.

"Here are the headphones for Hill, Cap," I said. "My sisters made me wrap it for some reason, but I'm not very good, so... this is the best I could do."

The wrapping paper was wrinkled, one corner oddly bulging, and quite possibly more tape than decorative paper held it all together. Mum stifled a laugh as Cap took the package with a raised eyebrow.

"This is perfect, Aiden," he said, smirking. "It's the thought that counts. Thank you for picking these up. Make sure you let us know how much we owe you."

Mum inspected me curiously. "You're looking chipper today. Good couple of days off?"

"Yup!" I replied, unable to hide my grin.

Before she could press for details, I slipped away to the bay to start my morning checkout. Ryan arrived a few minutes later, wearing the same goofy grin as me.

"All right, let's hear it," I said as we sat in the engine, pretending to go over the inventory.

He smiled. "Kaylyn wants to go out again. Can you believe it? Somehow, I didn't blow it!"

"That's awesome," I said. "I was glad the girls seemed to hit it off. It will be fun to do a double date sometime."

We began sharing more details about each of our dates, but the moment was interrupted when Reed poked his head into the engine.

"What are you guys doing? Still checking out the rig?"

"Uh, yeah," Ryan responded. "Just doing a quick inventory."

"Inventory? It's not truck day."

Ryan hesitated, so I chimed in. "Yeah... well, you know C shift, never restocking stuff."

Reed snorted. "Whatever, I don't care. Have you guys seen Devin yet?"

"No," I replied. "Why? Hill's not here yet?"

"Reed hasn't seen him, and he's usually here by now. Maybe he slept in by accident. I'll try calling him."

Reed walked off and dialed his phone. Ryan and I exchanged uneasy glances, but I shook it off and finished restocking supplies.

Muster began as usual, with Cap outlining the day's plan. But partway through, he looked up, his brow furrowing.

"Where's Hill?" he asked.

"I don't know, Cap," Reed said, holding up his phone. "I've tried calling him a few times, but he isn't answering."

Cap's expression shifted, concern flickering in his eyes. He glanced over to Mum, who had the same look.

"All right," Cap said. "Engine mount up. We're going to Hill's house to check on him. Reed, stay here in case he shows up while we're gone."

Ryan and I followed Cap and Mum to the engine. I whispered to Ryan, asking him what was happening, but he didn't know. Mum carried the headphones we got for him and placed them inside, next to the driver's seat.

The drive was unusually quiet, Cap's voice breaking the silence only to inform dispatch we were out of service. Aubrey's voice acknowledged Cap over the radio, and a moment later, my phone buzzed with a text.

My chest tightened as we pulled up to Hill's house. It was a sleek, modern home with white walls and black trim, but the curtains were drawn tight, blocking out the outside world.

Cap and Mum shared a cryptic look before they stepped out.

"You two stay here," Cap ordered.

I turned to Ryan as they walked toward the front door. "What is going on? Why does he want us to stay here?"

"I have no idea."

We watched as they knocked on the door and rang the doorbell, but no one answered. Cap jiggled the handle, but it was locked. They disappeared around the side of the house, leaving us alone with our growing unease.

"I don't feel good, Ryan," I admitted. "My stomach feels sick."

Suddenly, the front door flung open, and Mum stumbled out, her hands covering her face. She paced on the patio, her shoulders trembling as if she were about to collapse. Cap appeared moments later, grabbing her and pulling her into a hug. They slowly sank to their knees, Cap's arms still wrapped around her as she cried.

"What is going on?" I asked, my voice cracking.

Ryan didn't answer. We remained frozen in our seats, confused and helpless, as Cap eventually left Mum crying on the ground and walked toward the engine. He climbed in the front seat, his face pale, and stared blankly straight ahead.

"Cap?" Ryan asked.

Cap's voice was barely audible. "Devin is dead. I'm sorry, boys."

The words hit like an axe to the chest. Ryan flung the door open, sprinting toward the house, but Mum caught him, pulling him into her all-encompassing hug as he struggled to free himself.

"Let me in!" Ryan screamed, his voice breaking. "Let me through! I can help him. Let me help him!"

"No, Ryan," Mum whispered in a shaky plea. "Please stop, please. You can't help him."

I remained in the cab, my mind spinning. This didn't make any sense. Hill was fine last shift. He just saved someone's life. We had headphones to gift him. How could he be gone?

"Captain Jefferson, what do we do, sir?" I asked.

"I don't know, Brann. I don't know."

Cap gathered everyone back into the engine before stepping out and calling our Chief. The inside of the cab was disturbingly silent, except for the occasional sniffles. Mum held the wrapped headphones we bought for Hill in her lap. None of us said a word, even when Cap returned.

A few minutes later, our Chief and police officers arrived at the house. Cap spoke with them before returning the engine.

"Fisk, take us back to the station, please," Cap said. "Chief is sending the rest of us home and will have another crew come replace us."

No one answered or questioned the order given. We began the long, quiet, and confusing drive back. Once we arrived at the station, the weight in the air was palpable. We all entered the captain's office except for Cap, who went to break the news to Reed.

Reed sat at the kitchen table. After a minute, his voice erupted, his screams echoing through the station. "This is on you, brother! How could you let this happen? You're in charge of us. You're supposed to lead us."

More slamming sounds came as we ran toward the noises. Reed smacked the table, throwing the contents on top before punching a hole in the wall.

Reed continued yelling at Cap, "You're supposed to protect us! You're supposed to keep us safe! That's your only job! This is your fault. Why didn't you do your job?"

"Marion Reed!" Mum barked, stepping between them. "That's enough!" Her petite frame was a wall, unyielding.

Reed glared at her, tears streaming down his face. Then, he suddenly flipped the table and stormed out, tires screeching as he drove off.

Cap didn't move. His eyes were vacant, the light from them gone. I recognized that look. It was the same emptiness I saw in my dad's eyes after Mom died. We waited for him to say something, but nothing came.

Mum broke the silence, still fighting her tears. "Okay, everyone. We are all going to follow our orders and go home. If you need anything or want to talk, call me or Captain Jefferson. Understand?"

We nodded our heads, staring at the floor.

"Good. Go home and get some rest. Cap will reach out with more details later. Right, Cap?" Cap didn't answer. "Right, Captain Jefferson?"

Mum looked at him sternly, knowing we needed his leadership now more than ever, but obviously trying to control her emotions as well.

"Yes," Cap answered. "I'll let you know what happens next. Go home."

Ryan and I walked out of the station solemnly, not even bothering to remove our gear from the engine. We didn't say anything to each other as we got into our separate cars. What was there to say?

The drive home was surreal. I turned my music off, which I never did. It didn't feel right listening to anything upbeat or joyful. I drove home with only my jumbled thoughts bouncing around. They were so many and scattered that I couldn't focus on one single thought. My mind was a mess, but it felt empty as time seemed to stand still.

My route took me past the flood channel where Hill saved the boy and lost his headphones. The water had dried up, and the channel was clear. For some unknown reason, even to me, I pulled over and walked to the same place where the rescue happened. I scanned the area looking for Hill's headphones, even though I knew I wouldn't find them.

Maybe if I found them, I could wake up from this nightmare, and the last hour would never have happened. After about thirty minutes, I gave up, though I still didn't fully accept Hill was gone.

When I got home, I hoped Ally would be in a massage so I wouldn't have to explain why I was back already. I snuck in quietly, but she was pacing in the living room with scrubs on and her massage oil holster on her hip, seemingly waiting for me.

She looked at me in a way only my mom ever had—with care, love, and concern, like she could see inside me and feel my pain. She had never looked so much like Mom than in that moment.

"I'm giving you a massage, Aiden," Ally demanded. "Go get on my table."

"Ally, please don't start this again. I'm not in the mood."

Not only did she look like my mom, but she sounded like her now, too. "I'm giving you a massage! Now go lay on my table."

"I'm serious, Ally. Stop it."

Tears welled in my eyes as I tried to walk by her, but she held her arm out and stopped me. I attempted to go around the other side, but she wrapped me up this time and hugged me. I tried to wiggle free, but she squeezed tighter.

"Please, Aiden. Let me do this for you."

"Ugh! Fine! Then, when I hate it, will you leave me alone?"

"Yes, now go get on the table. The table warmer is already on and ready for you."

How could the table be already warmed up for me? How did she know I was coming home? I entered the massage room, and Ally closed the door behind me and told me to lie face-down under the sheets.

I looked suspiciously at the table and sheets. "I don't have to get naked, do I? Because if I do, I'm out."

"Nope. I put a pair of your shorts on the chair for you. Just put those on and take your shirt off. Don't be weird about it, and it won't be weird."

She definitely knew I was coming, but how? I begrudgingly put on my shorts and took off my shirt. I laid face down on the warm table and covered myself with the sheets. Despite my initial reluctance, I found myself beginning to relax, sinking into the warmth of the table.

"Okay, you ready?" she asked from the closed door.

"Yeah, let's get this over with."

Ally entered and turned on relaxing music. Whatever relaxation I felt vanished the second she touched my back, and I immediately tensed.

"I can't believe you are actually letting me massage you, gross!" Ally said.

"That's it!" I said, pushing myself slightly off the table before she shoved me back down.

"No, no, I'm sorry," Ally begged. "I'm just trying to lighten the mood. I'm sorry, I won't say anything else."

I laid my head back down on the headrest. Ally's hands began working out knots I hadn't realized were there. If I'm being honest with myself, it started to feel wonderful after the initial shock. She continued massaging, only speaking to remind me to relax throughout.

"Why did you say you already had the table warm for me?" I asked. "And how did you know to put my shorts in here? Did you know I was coming home?"

"Aubrey called me before you got home and said something bad happened at work today. She wouldn't tell me what, but she said you were on your way home. It sounded serious, so I canceled my appointments for the day. Do you want to tell me what happened?"

I contemplated my answer for a moment. "I don't think I'm supposed to talk about the bad things I see at work."

Ally's hands stopped moving. "Who told you that?"

"Um, well, no one, I guess. I just figured we see bad things, things most people shouldn't have to, so I didn't think I should tell anyone. Dad never really told us about everything he saw. He only talked about the fires and funny calls."

Ally began working again. "Well, that's just not true, Aiden. Dad talked about his calls all the time."

I lifted my head a bit. "What? He never told me any of those stories. Even during the Preparation, he only said I would see hard things like he did, but he didn't specifically say what."

"He didn't tell me those stories either."

"Well, then, what are you talking about? How do you know he talked about it?"

"He didn't tell any of us kids. We were too young to hear that kind of stuff. He talked to Mom about it all the time, though."

"How do you know that?"

She told me that during many of Mom's massages, she would sit outside the door and listen in. She would listen to Mom's clients talk about their problems, fears, and worries. She said sometimes Mom would offer support, but most of the time, she only listened. Even Dad talked about the things he saw and was struggling with.

"I wanted to be like her so bad," Ally said. "I think she helped so many people just by offering an ear, especially Dad. I wanted to help people the way she did."

I was shocked. "Dad struggled with things?"

"Of course, Aiden. He wasn't a robot. He just learned how to deal with it. So, if you want, I can listen for you, like Mom listened for Dad."

"That's okay," I answered, trying to remain tough. "I'm good."

"That's fine. I'm here if you change your mind."

I wanted to be strong, though deep down, I wanted someone to know what I had seen. She continued the massage as I remained determined to be a locked vault. That determination, however, didn't last long.

Without warning, the dam broke, and I spilled everything that happened to me since I started the job. Going unconscious my first day; Jenny and the fiery car crash; telling Chris his sister died; how the Children were making me nervous for our future; all my doubts and insecurities. Finally, I told her about today with Hill. I told her I didn't understand why he was gone and if I was somehow to blame. I even rhetorically asked her what we should do with the headphones we bought for him.

I was sobbing uncontrollably into the headrest and struggled to form complete sentences. Ally simply listened and handed me a tissue. She didn't try to fix me or offer empty reassurances. She only listened, like Mom used to do for Dad.

To my surprise, the hour was already over. "That's it?" I asked.

"Yup, that's it. Since you're my brother, the first one is free."

I felt lighter, like I'd shed hundreds of pounds I didn't know I was carrying. Kim was right. The massage was both physically and emotionally therapeutic.

"Thanks for making me get a massage, you jerk," I said, my voice hoarse. "Do you think I could book another one for next week?"

"Of course you can. But don't expect another freebie. You're gonna have to pay like everyone else."

19
LAST HONORS

"Unfortunately, you won't be able to do funerals for us. There won't be time for everyone to have one, so you'll have to do something with your siblings at the house." — Ashton Brann

The day I dreaded had arrived. Hill's funeral wasn't just another event. It was my first ever funeral, and it was a real confrontation with loss and a reminder of the people we couldn't save. Even the ones closest to us.

To make matters worse, cell phone service had gone down that morning, which had never happened in the After. No calls, no texts, nothing but silence. I wanted to think that the world paused to acknowledge Hill's absence, but I had an eerie feeling that it was something else.

Surprisingly, few people were accustomed to funerals. Since the adults all died in such large numbers and in a short period, the typical service was eliminated. There was no way to accommodate every person. Instead, everyone was taken to cremation centers after they died. Since millions were dying, we weren't even able to keep the ashes.

Some had small gatherings of close family members in their homes instead of funerals, sharing a few memories and a meal. My dad's was regretfully less than that. He survived longer than most, so we kids had to handle arranging for his body to be cremated ourselves. No neighbors or families were available to help us anymore. By then, the cremation center was run by kids.

After dropping off my dad, we didn't have a meal or share memories like we did for Mom. I have always regretted that, but we were in shock, trying to wrap our heads around the fact that we were alone. My dad deserved more than we gave him.

Today, however, we would hold a typical funeral for Devin Hill, like they did in the Before. Truly insisted on coming. When I told her about it, she didn't hesitate. She said she wanted to support me, even if it meant meeting my sisters under the strangest circumstances. I was grateful she would be there, even though I couldn't imagine a less ideal way for an introduction.

I stared at my Class-A uniform hanging in the closet, hoping that if I waited long enough, the day might magically undo itself. But time pressed forward, dragging me along with it. My class-A was a crisp, formal black suit with silver bands on the sleeves. A shiny badge hung over my heart. It was only my second time wearing it, the first being my swearing-in ceremony, which felt like a lifetime ago.

The uniform was uncomfortable, and the hat was stiff and awkward on my head. I wanted to call Ryan to make sure everything looked right, but the phones were down, so I had to figure it out on my own.

"Ready?" Ally asked, poking her head into my room. Her voice was softer than usual, sounding like Mom.

"Yeah," I muttered, adjusting my tie. "Let's go."

The funeral home was simple but beautifully adorned. Engine 3 was parked out front, standing guard. Truly stood by the entrance, talking with Kaylyn and Ryan, who nodded at me as I approached.

"Hey," she said, pulling me into a quick hug. Her warmth grounded me for a moment.

Behind me, Aubrey and Ally lingered, clearly curious but polite enough to hold back their questions, for now at least.

"Truly, these are my sisters," I gestured to them. "Aubrey and Ally, this is Truly."

"Nice to meet you," Ally said with a guarded but polite smile. Aubrey just nodded, shaking her hand, clearly appraising her.

The room was maybe half-full, primarily of firefighters in their class-As. Our crew sat in the second row, with Truly and my sisters behind us. Cap and Reed sat on opposite ends, the space between them a chasm of unspoken tension. Mum greeted us with hugs, while Cap and Reed acknowledged us with a silent nod.

Before the ceremony began, we sat reverently. This still didn't feel real to me, and I didn't fully understand why he was gone. I wondered if I should have known something I didn't. Should I have helped in some sort of way? I even pondered if I was somehow to blame.

The ceremony began as the honor guard entered, their uniforms immaculate, movements precise. They carried the Las Vegas flag gracefully, which bore a silhouette of the Strip with the sun rising in the background, signifying a new dawn. A female member sang the Vegas anthem, her voice steady and clear, though it trembled on the higher notes.

As the anthem played, I scanned the room. My gaze landed on a girl in the front row, who looked strikingly like Hill. She stared at the ground, her eyes puffy and red, her exhaustion apparent. It had to be his sister. I couldn't imagine how difficult these last few days must have been for her.

After the anthem, speakers took turns at the podium, recounting Hill's love for music, his talent in the kitchen, and his quiet but infectious humor. I listened, but their words blurred together, and my mind drifted to memories of my first experience with loss I'd had in the Before.

I remembered Michelangelo, our black family cat with an orange stripe across his eyes, who had been around even before I was born. He took an immediate liking to me as an infant and quickly became my constant companion, watching me like a furry guardian. We became inseparable, and he would even wait for me by the window when I went to school. One night, after a birthday party for Aubrey, Michelangelo didn't come home. I searched the house, then the yard, panic rising each minute.

My mom graciously accompanied me down the street as we searched for him. We slowly approached a black lump in the middle of the asphalt. He'd been hit by a car and was already dead.

We walked him back as I tried to stifle my tears. Mom laid me into bed and asked how I was doing. Trying to be a big boy, I told her I was okay, though the tears streaming down my face told otherwise. I'd never thought about what she would say next until now. She tucked me in, kissed me on the head, and told me, "It's okay to not be okay." I didn't understand these words until now, sitting in a room filled with people struggling to be okay.

To my surprise, no one approached the podium when the floor was opened for other speakers to say something. The long silence stretched, heavy and oppressive. My mom's words pulsed louder in my mind until they pushed me, almost involuntarily, to my feet.

I walked to the podium, my hands trembling. As I looked out over the crowd, my eyes stopped on Hill's sister, who still stared at the ground in front of her.

"I just wanted to say something on my mind as I was thinking about Devin," I began, my voice unsteady. "I don't know why Devin left us. I don't know what he was going through on and off the job. We can never really know what is going on in someone's life. I'm not sure if there's anything me or any of us could have done to help him."

Hill's sister's gaze moved from the ground and locked onto me, her eyes glistening with unshed tears.

"What I do know is that every single person here needs to know that it's okay to not be okay. It's okay to need to talk to someone and tell them you're struggling. It's okay to not feel strong. It's okay to be sad. It's okay to be hurt. We are all in this life together and need to support each other in good times and bad."

I paused, my words hanging in the air. All eyes were fixed on me. I gripped the edge of the podium, my voice breaking. "It's okay to not be okay... and I'm not okay."

I stepped down quickly, avoiding everyone's eye contact as I returned to my seat. Truly leaned forward, gently pulling my head close to her, her voice low and teasing. "I thought our first date was unique, but somehow, you managed to outdo yourself."

A tearful laugh escaped me, and I gave her a grateful look. I liked this girl. I really, really liked this girl.

Reed stood next, his broad shoulders tense as he approached the podium. His voice was gruff but firm.

"Devin was no quitter," he said. "Anyone who thinks differently doesn't know him. They don't know that he just saved a kid in the strongest way imaginable. He never let go, not slipping, even once. It was the strongest and bravest thing Reed had ever seen. Devin was strong, stronger than me even. He was my brother and... I'm not okay."

Reed returned to his seat, sniffling. I was surprised he'd repeated the phrase I'd used. Next, Cap stood up to speak.

He surveyed the room with the same empty look in his eyes I'd noticed back at the station.

"Devin was a great firefighter and a great friend," Cap began. "I should have done more for him. As his captain, I feel like I failed him."

He paused, staring down at the podium, fighting back his emotions. He remained in that position for nearly a minute until he finally spoke softly into the microphone.

"I'm not okay."

He hurried back to his seat, only glancing at me momentarily, before returning his attention to the floor. Mum and Ryan spoke as well, along with many other people—some firefighters and some I didn't know. Everyone shared a memory of bravery, strength, or humor about Hill, with stories from the Before and the After. No matter what they said, they all finished by saying, "I'm not okay."

The service ended, and we moved to the gravesite. I instinctively checked my phone. I was surprised to see it still had no service. Strange. At the gravesite, I examined his tombstone. The words *Protective Brother, Fearless Hero'* were written on the face of the stone, along with an etched picture of the headphones he always wore. Those headphones must have meant more to him than any of us realized, though I still didn't understand why.

One of the honor guard members started the graveside service by performing Amazing Grace on the bagpipes, the mournful notes cutting through the dry air. I was amazed we had a member who knew how to play. The instrument seemed challenging to handle, but he played it flawlessly.

Two members then took the flag from his casket and delicately folded it into a tight triangle. One then walked reverently to Hill's sister and knelt on one knee before her, presenting her with the flag, which she clutched tightly to her chest, her silent tears mirroring my own.

Watching this moment unfold put me over the edge, and tears streaked down my face. Hill was really gone.

Our crew lined the closed casket to say our final good-byes. Mum, who held the still-wrapped headphones we bought to replace the ones he lost, gently placed the package on top so he could be buried with his unopened gift.

As we walked away together, his sister stopped us. "Can I ask what you put on his casket?"

"We bought him a new pair of headphones since he lost his during the water rescue," Mum said. "He seemed upset about it and we thought it would help."

Hill's sister began to weep, wrapping her arms around Mum. "Those headphones were the last gift he ever got from our mother. They were probably the most important thing in his life. I think when he lost them, it broke him. I tried to talk to him, but I couldn't get through. He was just so devastated and felt like he lost the last piece of our mother. I never thought he would..."

She paused without finishing the sentence.

"Anyway," she continued. "I wanted you all to know that you were good friends. Devin talked about all of you all the time. He loved going to work and considered you his brothers and sisters. He loved each of you!"

I touched the wristband my dad gave me before he died, looping my fingers in it and inspecting it, thinking about how important it was to me. I now understood what Hill's headphones meant to him. Everything.

20
IV's in the Before

"That's it, buddy," my dad whispered, with his head next to mine. "Now push the needle in a tiny more and advance the catheter."

I nodded, my hand shaking slightly. I'd done many IVs on my dad over that last year. This time he was making me practice on a smaller vein on the back of his forearm. The angle was difficult, but I forced myself to breath like Dad taught me—slow and calm, like I knew what I was doing.

I used my index finger and slid the plastic catheter further into the vein, and removed the needle, holding pressure above the puncture site so he wouldn't bleed before I could connect a lock.

"Push harder, Aiden," Dad commanded as some blood trickled out and onto the floor.

"I'm trying, Dad."

I quickly connected the lock and taped it down, looking up at my dad for his approval. He gave it to me with a smile and a smack on the arm.

"Nice work, buddy. I think you're ready for the final level."

"Where else am I supposed to poke you?" I asked as I grabbed a bandage to begin removing the IV I'd just placed.

He grinned, though the smile didn't reach his eyes. I hadn't seen his real smile—the one where light practically beamed from his eyes—since we lost Mom a month ago. I didn't have the heart to ask him if we weren't enough for him. That would be selfish. He had lost the love of his life and on top of that, he knew he would be following her any day now.

I knew my time with Dad was limited and wanted to enjoy every moment with him, even through my exhaustion. I had barely been able to sleep most nights, wondering if each night would be his last. I even checked on him periodically throughout the night, as if that would somehow stop his death from coming.

"You're going to be practicing your IVs on Ally from now on," he said, rising to his feet.

"What!?" Ally gasped.

I didn't realize she had been listening to us. She was sitting in the opposite room, supposedly doing her homework for the Preparation. She walked over to us hesitantly, covering her arms.

"I don't want to get poked with a needle, Daddy."

"I know, Sis," he replied, wrapping her in his arms. "But you remember what I said about you guys all helping each other. Aiden needs your help now. He shouldn't be practicing IVs on adults anymore. He should be practicing on kids like you, because that's who he is going to be doing them on once he is working."

Tears began forming in my little sister's eyes. Aubrey entered from the kitchen, with an apple in her hand.

"Aiden is gonna stab Ally?" she asked, taking a bite. "I gotta see this."

Aubrey's tone soon changed when she noticed Ally turning pale, with pure fear in her eyes.

"It's gonna be fine, Ally. Aiden is really good. He can do it on me instead."

"No," Dad said firmly. "Thanks, Aubrey, but Ally needs to be the one to do it. Aiden, get your stuff set up while I go talk with Ally for a bit."

I nodded as they left the room. Aubrey sat next to me, continuing to eat her apple.

"Why does it have to be Ally?" she asked.

"I don't know. Maybe he just wants me to practice on someone smaller than me."

I finished setting up as Aubrey continued eating. Minutes passed. Aubrey and I began talking about our day. She told me about the calls she had taken in the dispatch center today and if she thought she was ready. I told her how much I hated working at the chicken farm, and showed her the scratches I had gotten that day.

Since I was going into one of the few professions for which the adults believed you needed to be a certain age, due to physical ability and seeing traumatic events, I had to do another job in the meantime. Working with the chickens, gathering eggs and feeding them, was a convenient job for me. I was able to work early in the mornings, which gave me time to study and prepare to be a firefighter in the afternoon.

Unfortunately for me, I had only been doing this job for a few weeks, and I still had three years until I turned 14 and could be a firefighter—even though some of the firefighters working now were still under 14. But there was no way around that; they had to take the oldest kids they had for the time being. I, however, would have to wait. It was going to be a long three years, but I knew it would be worth it.

Dad and Ally finally returned. Ally wiped her nose, trying to hold back her tears.

"I'm ready," she said.

I had her sit down next to me on the chair.

"This is gonna be a little tight," I said as I wrapped the rubber tourniquet around her arm.

She winced, tugging her arm away from me slightly, before allowing me to tie it off around her bicep. I took my gloved hand and began softly tapping around her arm, looking for a suitable vein. She had a decent one in her forearm, and that's the one I chose.

I took out an alcohol prep pad and wiped my chosen site. Ally began whimpering. I slowly unpackaged the needle and uncapped it, examining it closely. Ally's whimpers grew louder as she reached for my dad. He remained out of reach, watching me.

"Okay, Ally," I said. "Little poke."

"No!" she screamed, pulling her arm away. "I don't want to do it."

She looked to Dad, begging him silently to call off the assignment, but he remained silent.

"Ally," I said, reassuring her. "If you just hold still, it will be over fast. It only hurts a little."

She cautiously returned her arm to me, allowing me to hold it on my lap. Again, I held the needle up and slowly moved it closer to her arm.

"I can't!" she screamed, pulling away yet again.

"Dad!" I protested. "Tell her to stop moving." He shook his head. "Well, what am I supposed to do? I can't make her sit still."

"Can't you?" he finally said.

I glanced back at Ally, tears freely flowing down her face now, before I looked back at Dad, who nodded, approving of what I was thinking.

I got to my feet, recapping the needle and placing it next to the chair. Ally wrapped her arms around her knees, begging me to leave her alone. Aubrey did the same on the couch, shifting her attention between Ally and my dad.

"Sorry, Ally," I said as I grabbed her by the arm and pried it away from her knees. She screamed and squirmed, attempting to free herself, but even with only a six-teen-month difference, her nine-year-old frame was much smaller than mine. I wrestled her to the ground, laying her flat on her back and sitting on top of her.

Now pinned, I once again grabbed the needle, trying my best to keep her from moving, but she continually swatted at me with her free hand.

"Dad, hold her other arm," I demanded.

"I can't," he answered, his voice cracking. "I'm not gonna be here to help you when things get hard. Sometimes your patients will fight you and you are just going to have to figure it out."

Attempt after attempt, I tried to bring the needle closer to her vein, but each time she moved just enough to keep me from poking her. Her cries softened but remained desperate.

Aubrey's eyes welled as she grasped a pillow in a tight squeeze. Again, I looked to my dad, who once again nodded. But this time, it seemed different, like he was trying to tell me something. I looked to my crying sister below me, then back to Dad. An idea popped into my mind that must have shown on my face, because my dad mouthed the word, "Yes."

I got off Ally, releasing her arm from my grip, and helped her back into the chair. Her chest hitched, as if there wasn't enough air in the room. Tears fell to the ground, forming a puddle.

"I'm sorry, Aiden," she said into her hands. "I'm too scared."

"That's okay, Sis," I said, placing my hand on her knee. "I'm scared too."

"You are?"

"Yup. So why don't we talk about something different for a little bit? Have you decided what job you want to have yet? You can be a therapist, a nurse, or a manager kinda person, right? That's what your testing showed?"

She nodded. "But I don't know if I want to do those things."

"Do you have something you do want to do, then?"

She looked around at the rest of the family before her eyes fell onto a picture of Mom on the mantel. "I want to do what Mom did. I want to do massage."

I glanced at Dad, who had his arms crossed with one hand over his mouth. His eyes were beginning to water.

"Do you think you should be doing something that you didn't test into? You could probably help a lot of people being a nurse."

"I think I will help a lot of people. Just like Mom."

I nodded slowly, though I didn't quite get it. Sure, Mom's massages felt nice, but that didn't seem quite as helpful as stitching up wounds or pulling someone from a fire. But, if it made Ally brave, I wasn't gonna argue.

"I bet Mom would be super proud of you for wanting to help people like she did. She was always willing to help people, huh?"

Ally looked at her arm, then looked me in the eyes. "She would want me to help you, Aiden."

She extended her arm to me, placing it back on my lap.

"Just close your eyes," I said. "And think of Mom. You'll barely feel it and I promise I'll be fast."

She did as I said and closed her eyes. Aubrey ran over and grabbed Ally's free hand. Dad didn't stop her. I quickly inserted the needle, Ally barely flinched when I did. Then I set the lock and taped it.

"All done," I said. "You did it!"

Dad stepped in, wrapping Ally up into his arms. "Great job, Sis. I'm so proud of you for being so brave and willing to help your brother. And I think you're right. You doing massage will help so many people."

Releasing Ally, he motioned me over and grabbed me by the shoulders. "You rocked that, Aiden!" he said, giving me a fist bump. "This is what you were meant to do. This is who you are meant to be."

I accepted the compliment but was slightly confused. Starting IVs was such a small part of being a firefighter. And it wasn't even the exciting part.

He then gathered all of us kids and knelt in front of us. "You all have made me and Mom so proud. Each one of you has a special light that you are going to shine on this world of yours, and I will be watching over each of you with sunglasses on."

And for the first time since Mom died, Dad truly smiled.

21
FEAR AND TENSION

"You'll have to learn to like Rusty sooner or later, Marion. I know he isn't your father, but he's a part of our lives now. Why don't you try and give him a chance?" — Tiffany Reed

Returning to the station felt like stepping into a shadow. Hill's absence lingered in the air like a thick fog. The kitchen, usually lively with teasing and banter, was quiet. Even the clang of dishes and closing cabinets seemed muted.

But work-life marched on, and emergencies were still called in. We couldn't be short-staffed, so whether we were ready or not, Hill's position had to be filled. It felt cruel and unfair, like they were trying to erase Hill—though deep down, I knew we needed the six-man crew.

They'd sent a new rookie to Station 2 and reassigned one of their members to us—Adrian De La Cruz, or "De La," as most called him. I worried how the crew, still raw with grief, would treat him. It wasn't his fault he'd been sent here, but I hoped he would understand the delicate situation he was walking into.

Before muster, I found De La near the lockers and introduced myself. He stood about my height, with short, neatly trimmed dark hair and an easy smile that seemed at odds with the somber mood around the station. The smell of cologne wafted from him, sharp and overpowering. I tried not to react as I extended my hand.

"Aiden Brann," I said, managing a small smile. "Welcome to Station 3."

"De La. Thanks, I've always wanted to get down here where all the action is."

During muster, Cap welcomed De La and asked him to introduce himself. He stood confidently, his voice laced with optimism.

"I've been at Station 2 for the last six months," he began. "I live in Henderson with my older brother, who manages a grocery store and will bore you to death within a few minutes of talking to him, so I'm always happy to come to work and run some crazy calls."

His humor landed with most of the crew, though the smiles were subdued. Reed, however, remained stone-faced, his arms crossed as he stared at nothing in particular.

When De La finished, Reed unexpectedly stood up, causing the room to tense.

"I wanted to apologize," Reed said, his voice genuine. "The way I acted... the way I treated Cap was wrong. I was sad and angry and took it out on you, my brothers and sisters. Cap, nothing I said about you was true. You are a great Captain, and Devin was lucky to have you. We all are. Reed is sorry, and I hope you can forgive me."

Cap bowed his head, fighting his emotions. A long but not uncomfortable silence filled the room.

Mum was the first to respond with her delicate voice.

"Thank you, Reed. This has been hard for everyone, and we are in this together."

Reed nodded, his expression grateful. "Thanks, Mum. I was wondering, Cap... Could we hang Devin's helmet above the door out in the bay? That way, we can start and end the shift seeing it and remembering him."

"I think that's a great idea," Cap said.

Reed carried Hill's helmet to the bay, the rest of us following. He climbed a ladder, carefully and reverently hanging it above the door. When he stepped down, he touched the helmet, and one by one, we followed suit, each of us placing a hand on it, and taking a moment to reflect.

And just the way every good moment was ruined at the fire station, the sound of tones broke the solemn silence.

"Engine 3, building fire, engine 3, building fire."

Mum sped through the streets, barking at every car in her way as always. Normally, Cap would have read us the notes and prepared us for what might be coming. But today, he sat silently, staring out the windshield. Ryan had to prompt him for instructions, and even then, his response was hesitant, his usual confidence replaced by uncertainty.

When we arrived at the incident, a red car parked in front sped off. Probably some bystanders wanting to watch the fire. The medium-sized house had flames licking out the Delta-side window. For now, the fire seemed to be contained in one room. Ryan and I pulled the hose while Mum grabbed some tools, but Cap lingered in the engine longer than normal. When he finally emerged, he was untangling his radio from his seatbelt. When he got free, his initial radio report was uncharacteristically garbled and confusing.

"We're defensive," Cap announced.

"Did he say defensive?" Ryan asked, looking at me. "That can't be right."

"I'm sure he meant offensive," I said, shrugging.

I scanned the house, attempting to find something dangerous that maybe I hadn't noticed, but I didn't see anything unusual. The small amount of water we applied through the window quickly knocked down most of the flames, but we would need to get inside to fully extinguish it. We moved the nozzle to the front door, preparing to enter. But as we tried to open it, Cap grabbed us, pulling us back.

"I said defensive!" he yelled. "Stay outside!"

"Cap," I responded, "the fire is mostly out."

Before he could respond, a girl frantically ran up to us, screaming about her dog trapped in the house. She begged us to save him, tears streaming down her face.

"Let's go in, Cap!" Ryan pleaded.

But Cap was immovable. "We're defensive. Now pull back!"

Ryan hesitated, glancing between Cap and the house. I knew we could probably save the dog, and for a second, I wanted to go in despite Cap. However, I knew better than to disobey an order.

Then, without a word, Ryan connected his regulator and disappeared into the smoke. Cap shouted after him, but he didn't stop. I stood frozen, torn between following my friend and obeying my Captain.

"Cap," I said, forcing calm into my voice, "we need to back him up. He doesn't have a hose."

Cap stared into the house, his eyes empty like they were after Reed yelled at him. He'd previously led us into far more dangerous situations, but now he looked paralyzed. Finally, he closed his eyes, taking a deep, shaky breath.

"Okay," he said. "Go. I'll be right behind you."

I connected my regulator and stepped inside, dragging the hose alone with all my might. Before I made it too far, Ryan emerged from the smoke, a limp dog in his arms. Relief flooded through me as we hurried back outside.

Ryan carried the dog, who wasn't breathing, to the front of the lawn and laid him down. Another engine arrived, and Cap assigned them to take over fire attack while we cared for the dog. Mum brought us the pet oxygen mask and O2 tank from the engine. The girl knelt beside us, sobbing as we worked to revive her dog. Minutes felt like hours, but eventually, its chest rose and fell, and its tail twitched.

"Bob!" the girl cried, cradling the dog. "Thank you, thank you, thank you!"

Ryan and I backed away a little, admiring our work and exchanging a small, weary smile. I noticed the red car was back, watching us fight this fire just down the street.

Cap stood nearby, his gaze distant and empty. I approached him cautiously.

"Hey, Cap," I said. "I'm gonna grab a water from the cooler. Would you like one?"

He didn't respond, so I touched his shoulder lightly. He flinched, then looked at me as if waking from a dream.

"What?" he asked.

"Do you want a water?" I repeated.

"Oh, uh, sure, thanks."

I grabbed some waters from the cooler and passed them out. The girl still sat on the lawn, holding her dog, so we gave her space. We stood nearby, drinking water and watching the girl get her faced licked off by her dog.

The red car began creeping forward. I assumed they were leaving, since most of the action was over. Suddenly, they slammed on the gas, speeding into the scene, and screeched to a halt. Two masked figures jumped out, grabbing the girl and dragging her, kicking and screaming, toward the vehicle.

Without time to think, I sprinted toward them, slowed down by my turnouts, shouting for them to stop. Bob the dog also attempted to chase them, letting out pathetic barks, but was far too weak. I grabbed one masked person from behind, but the other shoved me hard, sending me sprawling. They threw her into the car and sped off. I ran after it, grabbing the door handle, but I couldn't keep up. I slid along the car for a moment, but my grip slipped. I hit the pavement with a thud, skidding to a stop, and the car disappeared.

Ryan helped me to my feet, his face in shock. "Aiden, are you okay?"

My whole body trembled as I attempted to process what happened. I scanned the area, looking for anything fast enough to chase them in. "We gotta go after her!"

Cap called in the incident to dispatch, but his voice was panicked. I paced frantically, desperate to do anything, but knowing there was nothing to be done.

"What do we do? We need to do something," I demanded.

"They are gone," Mum reasoned. "We would never catch them in the engine. The cops are on their way."

We returned to the lawn where Bob lay whimpering.

"Why would someone take her like that?" I asked.

"She is probably a 'traitor,'" Ryan said. "Those were Children, and they must have found her. I bet they started her house fire."

"I described the car and girl to dispatch," Cap said. "The police are looking for her right now."

"What do we do with the dog?" I asked.

Mum kneeled next to him, patting him. "We can have animal control come get him."

"Can I take him home?" I asked. "Maybe the police will find her, and I can return him then."

"I don't see anything wrong with that," Mum said. "Cap, is that all right?"

Cap nodded. "Have one of your sisters come pick him up at the station."

Feeling helpless and in disbelief, we didn't know what to do besides begin to clean up. While doing so, I pulled Mum aside to speak in private.

"I think something is up with Cap," I said. "He wasn't acting right. I'm worried about him."

Mum sighed. "Yeah, he doesn't seem to be himself, does he? When we get back, I'll talk to him."

While driving back to the station, Cap stared blankly out the window for a while before breaking the silence.

"Brann and Mitsuya," he said sternly. "I appreciate you trying to help that girl from being taken, but we need to talk about what happened during the fire. I'm the Captain, and I make the strategic decisions. That was the last time you will disobey an order. I'm in charge. If I say we are defensive, we are defensive."

"But, Cap!" Ryan protested. "That should have been an offensive fire. Only one room was involved, and we had a dog inside..."

"I'm the Captain!" he interrupted, voice cracking. "Not you, not Brann, not Fisk. I am! It's my job to make the decisions. It's my job to keep everyone safe. It's my job to protect you!" He paused, his voice lowering. "It's my job to keep you alive. Mine, and only mine."

No one responded. We understood now. He wasn't just mourning Hill. He was drowning in guilt and terrified to lose anyone else.

When we returned, Cap informed us he had tweaked his back and would be going home for the rest of the day. We knew better. He wasn't injured, at least not physically. He called the engine out of service, and we would have to wait for another captain to come in from home.

Before he left, Mum pulled him aside near the turnout lockers. Whatever she said to him was quiet but firm, her hand resting on his arm in a gesture of support.

I waited for him in the parking lot and quickly called Ally to ask if she would pick up Bob, the dog, and squeeze Cap in for a massage later. She said she could come to get the dog right away, and would also be able to massage Cap later this afternoon.

As Cap approached his car, walking stiffly, I called out. "Hey, Cap. Can I talk to you for a sec?"

He stopped, his expression weary. "What's up, Brann?"

"I know your back is bothering you, and I thought maybe I could help. My sister Ally is a massage therapist. I've already booked an appointment for you today at 2:00. It's on me, so all you have to do is show up. I'll text you the address."

He frowned. "You didn't have to do that."

"I know," I said, stepping closer. "You've done so much for me, though, and I wanted to try and repay you. You deserve it. Please. I promise she is great and can help you... I mean, help your back feel better."

"I'm really okay, Brann. I don't need anything."

I wasn't about to let another crew member battle their demons alone. I couldn't allow that twice in one lifetime. "It's okay to not be okay, Cap."

For a moment, I thought he might argue. Instead, he nodded, his shoulders slumping. "All right. Thanks, Brann."

As he drove off, I felt a slight sense of relief. It wasn't much, but maybe the massage would help.

I headed to my dorm to grab a change of clothes and shower, only to stop short at the door. Something was missing, and by something, I meant everything. My bed, desk, lamp, all of it was gone. My room was completely empty.

"What the...?" I muttered, stepping inside and spinning in place. I double-checked the door, wondering if I had somehow wandered into the wrong room. No, this was definitely mine.

Confused, I walked toward the kitchen, and that's when I saw it. My entire room, bed, desk, lamp, and even my duffle bag were set up neatly in the kitchen, perfectly replicating my dorm room.

Ryan, Mum, and De La sat around the table, struggling to keep straight faces. De La, in particular, looked as if his face might explode if he held in his laughter any longer. He was the obvious culprit.

"Well," I said, strolling over and plopping onto the bed. "This is as good a place as any for a nap."

I pulled the blanket over me, flipped the nearby light switch, and laid my head on the pillow. The room erupted into laughter, De La's the loudest among them.

"Shhh," I said, "I'm trying to sleep."

Before I could milk the joke any further, the lights snapped back on, and Reed walked in, his face fuming red.

"What's going on in here?" he demanded, glaring at all of us. "Why is your bed in the kitchen, Brann?"

"It's just a little prank," De La said, still grinning.

"No one was talking to you!" Reed snapped. His gaze swept the room, his voice rising. "This is how we're acting now? Like everything is fine. Hill is gone. We barely put him in the ground. Cap went home. And you're all screwing around like nothing happened. De La, we don't need you in here acting like a freaking child. You're all pathetic."

The room went silent. De La's grin faded, and I sat up, shame prickling at my skin. Reed stormed out without waiting for a response. Even Mum, who could usually calm any situation, remained quiet.

Maybe this time, Reed was right.

22

KIM AND THE PRESIDENT

"Leadership isn't about knowing all the answers. It's about finding them with the people who trust you and you trust."
— Ryder Hunt

It was rare for my sisters and me to have dinner together. What once was a daily occurrence was now a special event. The aroma of lasagna wafted through the air as Ally hummed in the kitchen, her apron dyed with sauce. It smelled so much like Mom's cooking that it almost felt like she was there with us.

All day, I felt stuck in a funk. I didn't feel like going out, but staying inside felt just as miserable. Reed's words from the other day, calling us pathetic, clung to me like tar. This dinner was a welcome distraction.

We sat at the table, eating in a comfortable rhythm. After a few bites, we complimented Ally on her meal. She had a way of perfectly replicating Mom's old recipes every time. As the conversation moved from mundane topics to the usual sibling teasing, I casually reminded my sisters that Truly, Ryan, and Kaylyn would be stopping by later.

"And please, I'm begging you," I said, gesturing dramatically, "don't embarrass me."

Aubrey's eyes gleamed with mischief. "Us? Embarrass you?" she asked with a grin that could only be described as sinister. "We would never do such a thing."

"Yeah," Ally chimed in, holding back a laugh. "We've never done anything embarrassing in our entire lives. We definitely wouldn't start today."

I rolled my eyes, knowing full well they would be finding new and creative ways to mortify me.

They were in the middle of teasing me when the doorbell echoed through the house. My heart jumped. "Is Truly here already?" I asked, my voice laced with panic. "Quick, do I have any pasta on my face?"

My sisters burst out laughing, ignoring my sincere concern. They eagerly ran to answer the door.

But instead of Truly, it was Kim, standing there with a solemn expression, and a relaxed Blazie cradled in her arms.

I sprang to my feet, snatching Blazie from her and scratching the cat's ears. She purred in delight, but Kim's face remained serious, and the mood shifted instantly.

"What's wrong, Kim?" Ally asked, grabbing her by the arm and gently leading her inside.

Kim sank onto the couch, covering her face with her hands.

"I don't know if I can do this anymore," she said, her voice muffled. "It's all too much, too fast, and everything seems to be going wrong."

Aubrey knelt by her side. "What's going wrong?"

Kim shook her head. "Everything! This KID guy, the Children, and now... now..."

"Now what?" I asked, my curiosity clawing at me.

Kim dropped her hands, revealing teary eyes. "Now the President is missing!"

Ally gasped, sitting beside her. "What do you mean, missing?"

Kim's voice broke as she continued. "We don't know what to do. Everyone's looking to me for answers, but I don't even know where our President is. How am I supposed to lead people? I just barely turned 10. How am I supposed to do this?"

Ally took Kim's hand, looking her dead in the eyes. "Kim, you are one of this city's smartest, most prepared, and awesome people. If anyone can do this, it's you."

Kim shook her head, but Ally's encouragement seemed to steady her. I knew what she was feeling. With Hill, Reeds' comments, and the kidnapped girl I couldn't save, I was wondering if I was cut out for this.

"But what happened to the President?" I asked.

Kim sniffled, wiping her face. "Well, KID's threats have been getting worse and worse. You know he's been starting all these fires, but we think that's just the start. Almost like he's... preparing for something."

"Preparing for what?" I pressed.

"I don't know," she admitted. "Remember the phone outage the other day? We think that might have been him. We aren't sure why, though, but whatever his plan is, we think it involves the President. We told her she should lay low, but she refused and said she'd be fine, and she'd take care of it."

Aubrey finished her thought. "And now she is missing?"

"Yeah," Kim said. "What's weird, though, is all the Senators got a text from her. 'Don't give up, keep everything running, and keep the peace.' That was three days ago, and we haven't heard from her since."

"That's strange," Ally said. "It almost sounds like she knew something was gonna happen."

Kim nodded. "We thought the same thing. But how could she know she'd disappear? The Senators are meeting up again tomorrow to try and figure out what we are going to do. The only thing we know for sure, is we need to keep her disappearance quiet. If people found out, there could be panic."

The doorbell rang again, startling us. My eyes widened.

"She's here," I whispered.

"Who's here?" Kim questioned, quickly straightening herself and wiping away the remaining tears.

"His girlfriend," my sisters said in unison, their voices dripping with mockery.

I glared at them, blushing furiously. "Shut up."

When I opened the door, Truly's smiling face greeted me, and Ryan and Kaylyn stood behind her. Somehow, the sight of her made all the fear, sadness, and doubt from the current moment wash away. She gave me a quick hug before stepping inside.

"Everyone," I said, gesturing toward the living room. "You've already met Aubrey and Ally, but this is our neighbor, Kim Hunt."

"Hunt?" Truly asked, shaking her hand. "Are you Senator Hunt?"

Kim nodded, a shy smile tugging at her lips.

Truly's eyebrows shot up. "I didn't know you were so..."

"Beautiful?" Kim interrupted, grinning.

Truly smiled back. "Well, yeah, but I was gonna say young."

Kim shrugged, looking away. "Yeah, I know I'm too young to be a Senator."

Truly quickly stepped forward, grabbing Kim's hand. "Oh no, I didn't mean it like that. I mean, yeah, you're young, but I think that's amazing. I've heard you're doing a cracker job. Who cares how old you are as long as we got the right person in that position? I'm glad I got to meet you."

Kim blushed, looking genuinely touched. "Thank you. You have no idea how much I needed to hear that." She grabbed Blazie and turned toward the door. "Well, I better go. Thanks for letting me vent. It was nice to meet you guys. And Ally. This is why I can't miss my massages, like I have been. Everything falls apart!"

At least Kim was still able to find some humor during this awful time. After Kim left, I braced myself for the onslaught of humiliation from my sisters.

Aubrey wasted no time. "So, Truly, did Aiden ever tell you he used to love dressing up in our clothes? Modeled them on a pretend runway for us and everything."

"No, I didn't!" I protested, but my sisters were already laughing. "You guys made me do that. I hated it."

"Oh, Aiden," Ally teased. "Like we could make you do anything. We are just two weak little girls."

Truly raised an eyebrow, a mischievous smile spreading across her face. "I bet he looks gorgeous in a dress and heels."

"I bet Ryan would look better," Kaylyn added.

The girls debated for a bit on who would look best, and their stories of my childhood humiliation continued, each one worse than the last. I might have been more annoyed if not for the occasional smirk or wink Truly sent my way.

It felt strange laughing and joking when such wild news about the President was just dropped on our front doorstep. But we were a family of first responders. If we shut down and ignored life around us every time something bad happened, we would always be powered down.

Eventually, the teasing subsided, and we moved to the kitchen to bake cookies. My sisters never seemed to get the hint that I wanted them to leave, and instead "helped" us with the baking. The process was as chaotic as ever. Flour ended up everywhere, but mostly on me. Aubrey somehow managed to get dough stuck on the ceiling.

Once the cookies were in the oven, I had to change my shirt before settling into the living room to watch a movie, thankfully a decent one from the Before.

Truly leaned forward during the opening scenes. "So, have you guys known Senator Hunt for long?"

"Since she was born," Aubrey said. "Her parents even let me hold her the day they brought her home from the hospital."

"She must be brilliant to already be a Senator," Truly said.

"I don't know," Ryan said sarcastically. "She might be one of those crazy cat ladies. Can she really be trusted?"

"She's the smartest person I know," Ally said. "Most kids her age needed help when the adults were gone. Or they had to go live at the Hotel. Kim didn't need anyone. She probably helped us out more than we helped her."

"She doing okay with all this Children stuff?" Truly asked.

"Actually," Ally said, leaning closer. "She was just telling us..."

Aubrey discreetly kicked her leg.

Ally paused, rubbing her leg. "Uh... telling us that they are doing okay."

The oven timer chimed, and I got up to pull the cookies out. When I returned with a plate and glasses of milk for everyone, they were still conversing about the Children.

Aubrey shared some calls she'd taken about them and how dangerous she thought they were. Ally talked about how worried she was for everyone.

Truly surprised us by sharing her insights. "I've met some of them," she said thoughtfully, brushing a stray hair behind her ear. "Not all of them are bad, you know. Some are just... stuck. Maybe misunderstood."

"Really?" Kaylyn asked. "I've never heard anyone defend them before. Why do you think they are misunderstood?"

Ryan and I shared a glance but let the girls keep talking.

Truly hesitated for a moment before speaking. "I've run into some of them before and had conversations with them. They're not all like KID."

"Do you think KID is misunderstood, too?" Kaylyn asked.

Truly thought for a moment. "He seems like he has a lot of unresolved issues. A lot of rage. I just don't believe they are all like that. Some are for sure, but not all."

"Sounds risky," Ally said. "Talking to them, I mean. You never know what they might do."

Truly shrugged. "Exactly. You never know what they're capable of. Could be something great. They might just need the chance to show us."

A silence settled over the room as we pondered her perspective. I watched Truly as she stared at her hands, clearly thinking hard about what she'd just said. Her optimism was strangely difficult to hear but refreshing at the same time.

As the movie continued, we sat quietly, enjoying our time and eating cookies. I was next to Truly and had difficulty focusing on the plot because my attention was on her hand and mine. My mind raced back and forth as I contemplated holding hers, which sat invitingly on her thigh. Ryan was holding Kaylyn's hand, so maybe I should follow their lead.

Just as I thought I might have found the courage to go for it, Truly's phone buzzed. She glanced at the screen, and her expression shifted immediately. For a moment, she looked like she might say something, her eyes darting toward me. But instead, she stood abruptly.

"I'm sorry," she said, forcing a smile that didn't quite reach her eyes. "Something's come up at work. I have to go."

"Is everything okay?" I asked, standing as she grabbed her jacket.

"Yeah, it's fine. Just... a work emergency."

Kaylyn stood as well. "We carpooled, remember? You need me to get you home?"

"Oh, I forgot," Truly sighed. "Would you be able to? I'm sorry to cut this date short."

Ryan offered to go with them, but Kaylyn refused, saying she would like some girl time with Truly. I told them I would get Ryan home.

Truly went to the door, her fingers lingering on the doorknob as she glanced at Ryan and then stared back at me. She almost seemed to want to say something important, but changed her mind. "I'll call you later, okay? Thanks for the cookies. They were delicious."

Before I could press her further, she was gone, leaving me staring at the closed door, a sinking feeling settling in my chest. My sisters exchanged a look but said nothing, returning their attention to the movie. Ryan grabbed more cookies, and I sat back down, trying to shake the unease that lingered long after she left.

If she was hiding something, I wasn't sure I wanted to know what.

23

COWARDS AND HEROES

"I hope you keep that smile, Adrian. The way you can find the good and fun in anything is spectacular. Please don't ever lose that." — Rosa De La Cruz

Captain Jefferson's absence began causing tension among us crew members at Station 3. We hoped he'd return each shift, but each shift was a letdown. Cap was taking more time to "recover" than we anticipated. His back wasn't the problem—we all knew that. Grief had a way of twisting even the strongest into unrecognizable versions of themselves.

Mum checked in on him when she could, and Ally told me he'd been booking more massages with her. But he hadn't set foot in the station since he left, and seemed to be avoiding us. The hole he left seemed impossible to fill.

In his place was a revolving door of fill-in captains. Some were decent, some not so much. Today, we got Captain Carmichael, a notorious micromanager from station 5, B shift, the slowest in the department.

"Why isn't the TV working?" Reed grumbled, stabbing the remote like it owed him money. The screen only displayed the dreaded black-and-white static.

"Mine was out at home too," Mum said, leaning against the counter with her coffee. "Must be out everywhere."

De La, still new to the crew but ever the optimist, grinned from his seat at the kitchen table. "Don't worry, Reed. I'm here. Wanna hear a joke?"

Reed shot him a glare, then tossed the remote across the table. "No."

Before De La could reply, Captain Carmichael's voice boomed as he strutted in from around the corner, startling us. "I called muster five minutes ago! Why are you not in the office?"

We exchanged weary glances as Mum explained. "Sorry, sir. We usually meet in the kitchen."

Carmichael rolled his eyes and walked toward the captain's office. We groaned and followed. Carmichael waited in Cap's seat, his expression a mixture of impatience and superiority.

"First of all," he barked. "As long as I am here, muster will be in its proper location in the captain's office, and you will come when it is called."

"Sorry," Mum said. "Our crew always meets in the..."

"Second," he said, raising his hand. "Don't interrupt me while I'm speaking. I would say you all know what unit you are on today, but since no one came to talk to me this morning to see what they were riding, I can't possibly understand how you would know."

"They are following their normal rotation, sir," Mum said. "It's Mi's and Brann's rescue shift, and Reed and De La are on the engine."

Carmichael stood up from his chair and held the empty seat out to her. "I didn't know you were the captain here. Why don't you make the roster then? Why don't you come sit in my chair while you're at it?"

"I didn't mean..." Mum said before stopping herself and remaining quiet.

"Well, since you don't want it," he said, sitting back down, "I guess I'll remain in charge. I'll allow you to stay where you all are today, but next time, you need to check in with me, and I will assign you. Also, no more nicknames. Call everyone by their full last name. No more of this, De La and Mi garbage. They are De La Cruz and Mee...zoo...yeh. Any questions?"

We kept our mouths shut, not daring to correct his horrible pronunciation of Ryan's last name. Mum's jaw tightened, her hand gripping her mug so hard I thought it might break. Reed crossed his arms, glaring at the empty table in front of him. Even De La, usually unfazed, seemed deflated.

Carmichael then began "teaching" us every step we should take in every scenario imaginable. This went on for a long time. Too long. But, to my delight, Ryan and I caught a call—escaping, for the moment, this ridiculously drawn-out muster.

We sped off down the street for a reported traumatic injury.

"What's with Captain Carmichael?" I asked Ryan.

"That guy is the biggest micromanager we got. Funny thing is, when things get serious, the guy disappears. He talks a big game but is a coward."

"That's strange," I answered before changing the subject. "Speaking of serious, have you heard anything about the girl that got taken?"

Ryan shook his head. "No. I asked Kaylyn, and they said they hadn't found her either, you see. Pretty scary. How's her dog, Bob, doing? He must have been hiding during the movie at your house."

"He is fine," I shrugged. "He's no Blazie, but he's nice to have around and is a good dog."

During the drive, dispatch notified us that a lot of screaming was occurring on the other side of the phone, and they heard someone yelling about a sword. Ryan asked for Engine 3 to be added to the call for assistance.

As we approached, Ryan looked over at me. "Be ready. Calls with all that screaming are either really bad... or nothing. Hopefully, it's the second."

Two kids were in the front yard, waving their arms hysterically. One boy shouted repeatedly, "It was an accident! I didn't mean to!"

The girl with him paced the driveway, frantically pointing to the backyard. We hurried to the back and froze as we turned the corner. A boy sat slumped in a lawn chair, his face white as a ghost. Blood poured from his arm, which dangled grotesquely by a portion of muscle and skin. The bone had been cut clean through. Another boy pressed a towel to the wound, his hands trembling, looking pale himself.

Ryan moved first, applying a tourniquet to the boy's arm. "What happened?"

The boy who was holding the towel backed away slowly. "We were just playing around and trying some tricks, but he missed!"

"Missed what?" I asked.

He pointed to the grass where a blood-streaked samurai sword lay. "It was an accident, I swear."

While Ryan finished tightening the tourniquet, I began working on an IV, talking to the fading boy. "Hey, stay awake," I said, squeezing his shoulder and standing in a pool of blood. "What's your name?"

"Ty...ler," he said faintly.

The engine arrived as soon as I finished establishing the IV.

"What do you guys need?" Reed asked.

"Get the gurney over here so we can load him up," I said. "De La, come hold his arm in place so it's not flopping around. Mum, will you..."

Before I could finish, De La, who'd just grabbed the dangling arm, turned his head and vomited spectacularly, projecting chunks of undigested cereal and white milk across the stone patio. He continued vomiting, all while somehow maintaining the arm in a stable position.

Reed groaned in frustration. "Are you kidding me?"

"Sorry," De La responded, throwing up one last time.

"Okay, Mum, why don't you hold it," I said. "De La, you can drive us to the hospital."

De La gave a thumbs up and stumbled away, gagging as he went.

We needed to load Tyler onto the gurney; he was fading by the minute. De La could not help, so I looked around for more hands.

"Where is Captain Carmichael?" I asked.

Mum rolled her eyes in disgust. "Sitting in the engine."

We loaded Tyler onto the gurney and rushed him to the rescue. Inside, we worked fervently, attempting to replenish his lost fluids and establish more IV access points. Reed complained loudly about De La's driving, though I didn't notice anything particularly wrong with it.

"You need to warn us when you are going to hit a bump," Reed demanded.

"He's doing fine," Ryan said. "Why are you being so hard on him?"

"Because he is being worthless!"

At the hospital, the reality of the After hit hard. The young doctor admitted she didn't know how to save Tyler's arm. It was too advanced a procedure. I'd never thought about these limitations until now, but they were painfully obvious once she said it. Adults worked for eight or more years to learn how to perform surgeries. We kids weren't even close to that.

Instead, they finished the amputation and closed the wound, following an instructional video from the Preparation archives. Many occupations had similar videos to assist with progression and problem-solving for things we kids weren't quite ready for. The doctor's hands trembled, sweat beading on her forehead, but she managed to close the wound. It was both awe-inspiring and heartbreaking to witness.

They gave him some medication through the IV to ensure he remained unconscious but still breathing. The doctor used a scalpel to cut the remaining skin, removing the arm entirely from his body.

I finally noticed my blood-stained gloves and carefully removed them, tossing them into a nearby biohazard bin. My gurney was even more soaked than my gloves, so I would need to hose it off in a decontamination area.

After doing so, I found De La in the back of the rescue, cleaning.

I leaned against the opened door. "So, uh, what happened back there?"

De La grinned sheepishly. "Yeah, I don't do well with gross stuff like that. I don't know why, but it makes me so nauseous. That's probably the third time I've thrown up on a call. I can't be perfect at everything, you know."

I laughed. "Well, I was impressed with how you kept hold of his arm while puking. That's some serious talent."

"I still got a job to do, right?"

"Yeah," I said, shifting tones. "Hey, I'm sorry Reed has been a little hard on you. Hill being gone has been hard on all of us, but especially him."

De La shrugged. "It's fine. I understand. I'll win him over eventually."

On our way back to the station, Ryan and I caught another call. The notes were vague and only stated someone needed our help.

When we arrived in the neighborhood, Ryan recognized something. "Hey, Cap lives around here, a few streets down."

"Oh really?" I answered. "Maybe we can stop by when we are done."

The house we found seemed a little odd. There were no cars in the driveway, the windows were all covered, and it didn't look like it had been lived in for years. We confirmed the address, cautiously walked to the front door, and knocked. No answer.

After no response, we heard faint cries for help coming from a nearby house. Ryan and I glanced at each other, confirming we both heard the strange sound. We heard it again and began running toward it. Finally, a third yell confirmed which house it was—and this one didn't look vacant like the other.

Once we opened the door, we heard another plea.

"Help!" I need help!" a voice from upstairs called.

"Are you okay?" Ryan yelled up.

"I'm just stuck," the person said. "Please help me."

After climbing the stairs, we saw a light on at the end of the hall. When we entered the room, we found no one. My stomach felt sick as I noticed the barred windows. When we turned around to leave, there stood a masked figure with a symbol we knew all too well. The Children.

"Ryan Mitsuya," the masked stranger said. "I've been hunting for you for a long time now. Do you know how hard it is to corner you into a room like this?"

"How do you know my name?" Ryan asked. "And why are you looking for me?"

The masked stranger took a small step forward and spoke with a menacing tone. "Oh, I've known you for a long time. You could even say we were friends once. Until you became the first traitor of our little group. The first to leave. The first to abandon their friends. The first to break an unbreakable oath!"

"Kaleb?"

He removed his mask, revealing a boy maybe two years older than me. He had black, slicked-back hair and was taller than both of us. A prominent scar crossed his upper lip, one that indicated he'd been born with a cleft lip. What stood out the most, however, was that despite his sinister smile, he had a deep, dark hatred in his eyes.

Kaleb ran his hand through his hair. "I'm surprised you remember your old friend. I would have thought you forgot all about me when you left me to work for the enemy."

"I left to help people," Ryan said. "I wanted you to come with me. Are you the one hunting and taking innocent kids from their homes?"

Kaleb snapped. "They are not innocent. And neither are you. They are weak, they are liars, they are traitors. I know you've been helping them. Hiding them from me."

"You don't know what you're talking about. Now let us go!"

Kaleb shook his head. "I do know. And I know you are not doing it alone. You've had some help."

The static from my radio went off, and dispatch called for us. "Rescue 3 from dispatch. What's your status?"

"Don't answer that!" Kaleb yelled.

I held up my radio. "If I don't answer, they will send someone here looking for us."

Kaleb pulled out a gun from his waistband and pointed it at me. "Well, then tell them you are fine. Or else you won't have a chance to say anything else."

My heart dropped as I stared down the barrel. I had never been threatened in such a drastic way before. I cleared my throat and tried my best to sound calm. "Dispatch from rescue 3, we are code 444."

"What's that?" Kaleb yelled, taking a step closer to me.

"Copy," dispatch replied.

"It means we are available," I said. "We talk using numbered codes."

I lied, however. Although we use codes occasionally to talk, this code meant we were in trouble and needed help immediately.

"Kaleb," Ryan pleaded. "Why are you doing this?"

"You'll find out soon enough. Now, the real reason I brought you here is I need your help."

Ryan scoffed. "I'm not helping you with anything."

"Oh, I think you will. I know you are hiding President Keres, and I need to know where she is. She is the last piece to my plan and has magically disappeared. I'm thinking that you may have something to do with it. You and that stupid Australian girl!"

I glanced at Ryan, puzzled. Was he talking about Truly? Ryan also looked surprised that Kaleb knew his secret.

Kaleb smiled at me, noticing my confusion. "Surprised I know so much, Ryan? I see and hear everything. And it looks like your friend here isn't helping you hide them, which means he is no good to me."

He pointed the gun back at me, straightening his arm, ready to fire.

Ryan stepped between us, putting his hand up. "No! Stop! He has nothing to do with this. Just let him go! You can keep me."

"Oh, I won't be letting anyone go," Kaleb said, lowering the gun. "Maybe you can save him for now if you tell me what I need to know."

"I don't know where the President is," Ryan said.

"How could you not know? You and that dumb girl have been hiding all the traitors from me. I know you hid the President, too!"

He raised the gun back at me, though Ryan still stood between us. "Tell me where she is! Or I'll kill your friend right here."

"I swear I don't know," Ryan pleaded. "Yes, we have been hiding the Children, but I don't always know where, and I don't know where the President is."

"Well, then tell me where the Australian girl is."

"I don't know that either. We only talk by text. I don't know where to find her."

Kaleb directed the gun at Ryan now. "That's not what I heard. Stop lying to me!"

I stepped forward beside Ryan. Kaleb stared back intently with hate-filled eyes. To my shock, I noticed something in the hallway behind him. Another figure was creeping closer. The mysterious person approached and lunged forward at Kaleb, knocking him to the ground.

"Run boys!" Captain Jefferson yelled.

With too much adrenaline, I had no time to stop and wonder how Cap was here. We sprinted toward the door past the startled Kaleb. Running for my life downstairs was more difficult than I imagined as I tried not to lose my footing. Ryan led the way, followed by Captain Jefferson and me.

The front door was open, and I saw freedom in the daylight. Just as we were about to pass through the door, Kaleb jumped from the second-story overlook to the floor below, landed on his feet with an impressive thud, and blocked our path.

He shook his finger and held up his gun. "No, no, no. I'm not done with you yet. Who's your new friend here?"

"Let these boys go!" Cap demanded, pushing us behind him.

"Oh, you must be the captain," Kaleb said, looking him up and down. "You definitely look the part."

"I said, let them go!" Cap said again. "Or else."

Kaleb admired his gun. "I don't think you are in any position to be making threats. Now, why don't we sit down and have a little chat."

Suddenly, Reed bolted across the lawn like a blitzing linebacker hidden from Kaleb's view.

"Why don't we not!" Reed yelled as he tackled him to the ground.

Mum and De La followed, waving for us to run outside. Ryan ran, and I almost did as well before I looked back at Reed. He wrestled with Kaleb, trying to pry the gun away from him. Reed was larger, but Kaleb was athletic and quick. I reached to help Reed, but Kaleb pulled free as I did, rolling to his feet.

"Where are all you people coming from?" Kaleb questioned, frustrated. "I guess it's time for me to go. You'll be seeing me soon enough… except for you."

He pointed the gun at Reed and pulled the trigger.

Bang!

Reed crashed hard to the side as De La shoved him out of the way and collapsed to the ground next to him. Kaleb fled through the back door and out of sight as the rest of us surrounded De La, who lay face down, motionless.

Kaylyn also entered in uniform with a gun drawn, and we directed her out the back door to pursue Kaleb.

Reed rose to his feet and saw De La's body lying below him, wide-eyed and in shock. I rolled De La to his back. His eyes were closed, and he didn't appear to be breathing. I lowered my ear close to his mouth to listen for a breath and watch for his chest rising.

"I told you I would win him over," De La whispered.

"De La!" I exclaimed. "Are you hit?"

Somehow, De La still managed a smile. "He just nicked me," he said, lifting the sleeve of his shirt to show a superficial graze wound below his left shoulder. "I'm fine."

I helped him to his feet, and Reed stepped closer, bringing himself face to face with De La.

"Thank you, brother," he said, wrapping him in a bear hug. "Reed thought you died."

De La winced. "Ow, ow, ow."

Reed released him, sobbing and begging for forgiveness from De La for how he had been treating him. "Let me get you bandaged up," Reed said, leading De La out of the house.

Another officer arrived, responding to my initial distress call, and Kaylyn returned, stating he got away. Kaylyn was panting, her brow furrowed, and inspected Ryan to make sure he wasn't hurt. Ryan assured her he was okay, and she and the other officer left to continue the hunt for Kaleb.

We stood as a crew on the front porch.

"Cap," I said. "How did you find us? How did you even know we needed help?"

"I was listening to the radio from home and heard your distress call. I live a few streets over and knew I could get to you faster than anyone. I saw your rescue on the street and saw this house had an open door."

"Well, you saved our skin, Cap," I said, then turned to Mum. "Where is Captain Carmichael?"

She rolled her eyes. "We heard your 444, but he said we had to wait for the police to clear the scene before we could come to help you. Claimed it wasn't our job. So, we left without him."

Ryan placed his hand on Cap's shoulder. "Cap, we need you to come back. We need a good captain with us. That coward Carmichael is no good for us. We need a hero like you leading us. We are safest with you. Please. We miss you."

Tears welled in his eyes. "I'm not sure you are safest with me. I already let Hill down. I don't want to let you down too."

Mum grabbed him by his shirt before embracing him, as did the rest of us. "You've never let us down," Mum said. "And you didn't let Hill down either. We need you."

Cap nodded, wrapping his arms around each of us. I was happy to be getting our captain back. But in the back of my mind, I knew KID had escaped, and he would be coming for all of us now.

24
TRULY'S SECRET

"We must ensure no one enters or leaves the borders we created. If these kids are to have any chance, they must remain isolated from the potential dangers outside the wall. We'll need to set up cameras and monitors to alert the kids' leaders of any movement near the wall." — Mayor Cathleen Goodson

De La's injury, though minor, earned us an early release from duty so we could be with him at the hospital. While he assured us it was "just a flesh wound," the hospital insisted on thoroughly evaluating him. The staff bandaged the wound, and De La remained his cheerful self, smiling through it all as if gunshot wounds were just another part of the job.

"You see what happens when you leave us for too long," Mum teased Cap, standing near De La's hospital bed.

Cap chuckled softly, but his face grew serious. "I'm sorry, guys," he said, shifting uneasily. "I guess I should tell you what's been going on with me."

We exchanged uncertain glances, sensing something significant was coming. Cap looked at each of us, drawing a deep breath.

"I'm sure you noticed I wasn't quite myself after Hill," he began. "It hit me hard. Harder than I ever expected. I blamed myself. I let someone I was responsible for get hurt. I kept thinking if I had done something different, maybe he'd still be here."

He paused, his voice faltering for a moment before he continued. "I couldn't stand the thought of seeing anyone else get hurt. I started doubting everything. My leadership, my judgment, even whether I belonged here. As the captain, I felt there was no place for weakness, never letting anyone see you struggle. Eventually, I realized I couldn't handle it alone."

Cap's gaze softened. "I got in touch with someone who has been helping me work through it all. I wasn't sure I was ready to come back yet, but then I heard your 444 on the radio. When I knew you needed help, all my doubts disappeared. There was no time to second-guess. I just... acted. I knew it was what I needed to do."

Mum stepped forward, hugging him in her all-encompassing way. "None of us think you're weak, Cap. You're the best leader we could ask for. We're lucky to have you."

"Thanks, Fisk," Cap said, his voice thick with emotion. "And thank you, Brann, for sending me to your sister."

"Of course," I said. "I'm glad you liked her massages."

"Well, about that..." Cap scratched the back of his neck. "I didn't really like the massage. Not that Ally isn't great at it. I just can't stand the feeling of the oil on me. But I kept coming back because she was a great listener. Talking to her helped me deal with things I didn't even know were weighing me down."

"She is pretty cool," I admitted. "Most of the time."

Cap chuckled. "Seriously, though, I think all of you should find someone to talk to. Even if you think you don't need it, you'd be surprised how much it helps."

We lingered at the hospital for a while, joking and catching up, but eventually, we went our separate ways, though Ryan and I met back up immediately after getting back to our cars.

"So, how do you know this KID guy?" I asked.

"Kaleb Ian Drexler," Ryan answered, a shadow passing over his face. "I can't believe I didn't see it earlier. K. I. D. It's the same guy we confronted at the store awhile back. I don't think I wanted to believe it was him. He's changed so much, you see.

"So, you knew him before?" I asked.

He nodded, his expression heavy. "We were best friends growing up, practically brothers. We lived in the same foster house for years. It wasn't a good place, but we looked out for each other. Took care of each other."

"So, what happened?" I pressed.

Ryan hesitated, his voice dropping. "This sucks to say, but you have to see it from my point of view." He paused again. "The adults dying was, unfortunately, the best thing that ever happened to me. To me and Kaleb. No more foster homes, no more rules and terrible living. We were finally free. At first, it was exciting. We thought we could do whatever we wanted, but after a while, I realized I wanted more. I wanted to help people, to make it so no one had to suffer like me. Kaleb... didn't. He didn't understand why I wanted to leave that life. Felt like I betrayed him."

"And now he wants to kill you?" I asked.

Ryan sighed. "I never thought he would get so extreme. I mean, he was even willing to kill Reed. But I don't think he is just after me. He wants the President for some reason."

"So, what do we do?" I asked. "He is probably going to come after you, right? Do you want to come stay with us?"

"Yeah, he might," Ryan admitted. "I'll be okay, though. I don't want to show him I'm scared and I don't want to put you or your sisters in any more danger than I already have. Besides, I think he wants the President more. He must have some plan that involves her."

"So, about that. I know you knew Truly, but are you working with her to hide the Children that have left KID?"

Ryan shook his head. "I should let her talk to you about that. Aren't you going out with her tomorrow? You should ask her then."

The following morning, I found Aubrey and Ally waiting for me downstairs. A lamp was aimed dramatically at a kitchen chair, next to which our new dog Bob was curled up.

"Have a seat," Aubrey commanded, gesturing to the lighted seat.

"Uh, what's going on?" I asked warily, approaching the chair.

"She said sit!" Ally barked, failing to suppress a grin.

I sat cautiously, scanning the room for clues about their latest scheme. They studied me with exaggerated seriousness as though I were under interrogation.

"We need to talk about your relationship with this Truly girl," Aubrey said.

"What? Why? What's wrong with Truly?" I asked, genuinely confused.

"That's adorable," Ally interjected. "He thinks we are worried about Truly." She turned to Aubrey, shaking her head. "He's so clueless."

"Wrong!" Aubrey announced dramatically.

I sank further into my chair, unsure whether to laugh or defend myself.

"We are worried you are going to screw it up somehow," Aubrey continued. "You'll get cocky, stop trying, and then BAM! She'll dump you for someone taller, funnier, and better looking."

"Better looking than me? Come on."

They both groaned, exchanging looks of mock despair. Since Hill's funeral, Truly and I had hung out a couple of times, and each time has been as fun as the first. My sisters had taken a liking to her.

"We're gonna lose Truly," Aubrey declared.

"Yup," Ally agreed. "Just a matter of time. I hope you'll let her stay friends with us after she dumps you. Oh! Maybe she can move in with us, and we can kick Aiden out!"

"Now there's an idea," Aubrey said. "She would be a huge upgrade from him."

Their banter continued as if I wasn't there until I finally interrupted. "You two are hilarious, but I've got stuff to do. Besides, I know I'm not getting dumped, so you can keep dreaming."

I grabbed breakfast and went about my day, holding back a smile as I thought about their little performance. Beneath the jokes, I knew it meant they liked Truly. And that mattered more to me than I would like to admit.

Since Truly was choosing what we did that evening, she came to pick me up. I went downstairs to meet her, but my sisters stood in front of the door again to evaluate me, inspecting me up and down with disapproving eyes.

"Ugh, just look at him, Ally," Aubrey said.

"Yup," she answered. "He is never going to be able to keep Truly around looking like that."

I checked myself in the nearby mirror. "What's wrong with how I look?"

The doorbell rang, and I eyed the door, then turned to my sisters, concerned.

"Well, it's too late now," Aubrey said.

"Maybe we should say our goodbyes to her," Ally added.

"You guys are the worst!" I said as I answered the door.

Truly looked amazing, as she always did, and her outfit was similar to mine. I wore shorts and a dark blue T-shirt, while she wore a burnt orange top and jeans.

Truly stepped inside. "Hey Aubrey, hey Ally."

They sauntered to her, taking turns embracing her and dramatically saying their goodbyes. I ushered Truly out with a confused look on her face.

"What was that about?" she asked.

"Nothing, they're just weird. So what are we doing today?"

"You'll see."

She drove me toward the northern outskirts of town, far beyond most residential communities. The street grew quieter, the buildings fewer and farther between, until the city's lights faded in the distance. Finally, she pulled off the road and drove along the 30-to-40-foot-tall wall surrounding the city.

We drove for only a few minutes until she stopped, put the car in park, and shut it off. Then, she grabbed a backpack from the trunk.

I got out also and looked around in every direction. "So, what are we doing here? Are we allowed to be here?"

During the Preparation and even now, in the After, it was ingrained in us how important it was to remain within the walls. We were never to leave, for our safety and everyone else's. To me, it made sense to stay inside. My family was here. There was nothing out there for us anymore. I've never considered going near the wall, let alone over it.

Rumor had it that the wall was monitored, and if you tried to leave, you would be stopped.

"I want to show you something," Truly said.

We walked a little further through the dirt and the weeds, until we came to a spot with multiple pegs sticking out of the wall, forming a ladder to the top.

She placed her hands on the pegs and began to ascend. "Follow me."

I hesitated momentarily, curiously inspecting the area and pegs. Then I watched her climb to the top.

"You coming?" she asked.

I yelled up. "Are we allowed to do this? We aren't going to get in trouble, are we?"

"Just get up here, ya big baby!"

I stepped forward, placing my hands on the first peg. I wasn't nervous to make the climb, but getting in trouble was another story. Though I wasn't sure who I would be in trouble with, or what the punishment would be, I was still hesitant.

I examined the area around me one last time, took a breath, and began to follow her up. The rough rungs provided a textured grip, so they weren't slippery. After a few steps, I glanced back up, and Truly was now sitting at the top with her legs dangling over the edge.

"Today, Aiden!" she yelled, laughing. "I don't want you to miss it."

I finished the ascent and sat next to her, catching my breath.

She patted me on the back. "Glad you made it."

"Me too. What do you have to show me?"

She smiled. "We still have a little time."

She unpacked her backpack, which contained sandwiches, fruit containers, and a couple of sodas. We started eating and talking as we sat on the wall overlooking Las Vegas. I had not seen this view of the city since the Quarantine. My family would occasionally hike some outer mountains to get a similar view.

From way out here, the city appeared to be the same. The buildings were the same, the size was the same, and even the streetlights were the same. Besides the lights on the strip—which we only turned on for special occasions—the lack of noise, and the clean, crisp air, you would never know Vegas was drastically different.

"So, I thought these walls were monitored so we don't climb them," I said.

"Oh, they are," she replied.

"What? Then why are we here? Is someone going to come for us?"

"Don't be such a squib."

Thrown off by her unusual insult, I forgot about my fear of getting in trouble.

"What the heck is a squib?"

"Well, you are right now," she laughed. "Now quiet. It's time for me to show you why we came here."

She turned me to the west, and we sat beside each other with our feet on the wall now.

She pointed to the horizon. "Look over there. You will see the most beautiful thing ever in just a few minutes."

I glanced at Truly, thinking I was already looking at the most beautiful thing, but I knew that was way too cheesy to be said out loud. I smiled and focused my gaze back on the mountains without responding.

"Wow, Aiden," she said, playfully shoving me. "You were supposed to say I was the most beautiful thing. I set you up perfectly."

"Ugh! I knew it. I was totally going to, but I thought you would think it was dumb or something."

"Uh-huh, sure you were."

We turned back to the mountains and waited. Soon, the sky's colors changed. Oranges, reds, and purples filled the backdrop behind the mountains, lighting up the few clouds, turning them into giant puffs of cotton candy. I had seen these sunsets before at home, but Truly was right. From here, they were more impressive. However, I didn't know if the company or the different views made it so.

"Isn't it beautiful?" she asked.

"You're beautiful," I responded.

"Oh no! It's too late for that. You had your chance, and you messed it up."

She laughed and put her hand down by her side next to mine. Our pinkies touched, sending my heart racing. Did she want me to hold her hand? Should I try to? What if she didn't want me to, and I got rejected? She wasn't moving away, so she had to be okay with it, right?

My mind frantically played out good and bad scenarios. I couldn't focus on the sunset any longer as the stress continued to build. Finally, I went for it, speaking simultaneously as I grabbed her hand, trying to create some sort of distraction or cover-up.

"How did you find this place?" I asked, placing my hand over hers. "And how do you know the walls are monitored?"

To my surprise, she didn't pull away, and instead intertwined her fingers with mine. The stress subsided, which was good because I wanted to pay attention to her answer.

"I've been caught out by the walls before," she said. "Some security people will come if you trigger a sensor. They don't really do anything, though, besides make sure you go back into town and tell you not to come near the wall again. I spent a lot of time searching and found this blind spot. No one will be coming for us here."

"Do you come here a lot?"

"Kind of. I come out here if I'm having a bad day or something. I love the view. This place helps me feel like I can get away from it all. Helps me not feel so trapped. Sometimes, I just sit here and dream about leaving."

I sat up straighter and looked at her, involuntarily letting go of her hand. "Leaving? Why would you want to leave? What's out there?"

"I don't know. My family maybe, my friends, anything."

I looked at her, speaking sympathetically. "They're gone, Truly. Everything that happened here happened out there. Who knows how those kids are handling it? They could be running wild, they could be killers, they could all be dead. We are safe here. Life is good here. I'm here."

She grabbed my hand again and turned back toward the sunset.

"Yes, you are," she said with a smile. "And I'm glad you are."

We sat longer, enjoying the view and each other's company. The sun dropped below the mountains, and the colors faded. I never wanted this moment to end.

She soon tensed and her tone hushed a bit as she looked me in the eyes. "I wanted to talk to you about something."

"What is it?"

She grabbed my hand with both hands now. "Ryan told me what happened to you guys yesterday. That must have been scary."

"Yeah, kinda. You know Ryan better than I thought you did. Why would you keep that a secret?"

"Well, Ryan and I met during the Preparation. My parents were involved in helping orphans get set up for the Preparation. Without my parents, they would have probably been forgotten about." She paused, holding back tears. "My dad and Ryan got super close. Ryan looked up to my dad a lot. Since I was around them quite a bit, I became friends with Ryan and many of the others."

She continued explaining that many of the Children went to her when they got tired of doing nothing, much like Ryan did. With her multiple businesses, she got them jobs and made sure they got set up.

Recently, though, KID declared himself the Children's leader and decided he wanted to tear down our way of living. Some of the Children were willing to follow him, but a lot were not. They wanted to leave, but he wouldn't let them. Since she helped them get jobs, some started coming to her to be hidden.

"Over time," she continued, "I became the person they ran to, to disappear. That's where I had to go the night we made cookies with your sisters. Ryan left the Children long before it was a big deal to leave, so no one was after him right after he left. But I asked him to help me, and he has been. I think you can understand why we don't tell people what we are doing. I wanted to tell you earlier, but I'm telling you now because I trust you, and Ryan trusts you."

"Wow, that's crazy. And yeah, you can trust me."

"Thanks," she continued. "I also have another favor I want to ask. I'm getting a little overwhelmed with keeping these kids hidden. More and more keep coming, looking for help. On top of that, KID found Ryan, so he might be close to finding me, too. Ryan told you we have been hiding the President, right?"

I nodded. "Yeah, he said he didn't know where she was though."

"That's true, he doesn't. But I have a terrible feeling that KID is close to finding me. Like I'm not the best option to keep the President safe anymore. I can't send her to Ryan either. You're the only other person I really trust. I was hoping you could help."

My initial gut reaction was to help. I wanted to be that person. But then doubts began flooding my insecure mind. Was she only being friendly to me so I would help her? Why would I want to get involved with KID when I knew how dangerous he was? What if he came after my sisters?

I didn't answer for a long time, though Truly watched me, desperate for an answer.

"Aiden?" she questioned, squeezing my hand tighter. "I don't have anyone else to turn to. We have to keep the President safe until we can figure out how to stop KID."

I let go of her hand. "I want to help you, I really do. I think what you're doing is amazing, but I don't know if I can be a part of it. I promised my parents I would always protect my sisters. I don't want to put them in danger."

"But everyone will be in danger unless we stop KID," she contested.

"I'm keeping people safe by being a firefighter. That's what my dad did, and that's what I'm going to do. Be a firefighter."

The disappointment in Truly's eyes pierced me. "That's a pretty narrow-minded way of thinking, Aiden. I thought you were more than just your job title." She looked toward the mountains, which had completely hidden the sun now. "It's getting dark," she said. "Maybe we should go."

The ride back to my house was silent. Truly kept her eyes on the road, her usual warmth replaced by a chilly distance. I wanted to say something, to explain myself better, but the words wouldn't come. When we pulled into my driveway, the air between us felt impenetrable.

As I stepped out of the car, she called after me. "Goodnight, Aiden. Call me when you figure out who you really are."

Her words lingered long after she drove away, cutting deeper than I expected. I stood in the driveway, staring after her car until the taillights disappeared around the corner. My stomach churned as I imagined what would happen if KID found her, but I couldn't put my sisters in danger. And I knew who I was. Didn't I?

I entered my home to find Aubrey and Ally eagerly waiting, along with Bob, who ran to greet me. I lightly pushed him aside.

"Well?" Aubrey began. "Has Truly finally wised up and realized she could do better?"

She spit the words out too fast before really looking at me.

"Oh no!" Ally said, jumping off the couch. "What happened?"

I shrugged, avoiding eye contact with them. "I don't know. Truly wants something different than what I am, I guess."

"Aiden," Aubrey said softly. "I'm sorry, I didn't mean to..."

"I know you didn't," I answered. "I don't want to talk about it right now. I'm gonna go to bed. Sorry."

I crawled into bed but couldn't sleep. My thoughts haunted me. Did I make the right decision?

25

SCAVENGER HUNT

"We should make a new game or something. Trapped in here, watching TV is boring. Oh, I know! What about a scavenger hunt?" — Ashlynn Brann

The next shift at work started with a call that matched my mood. Sluggish and out of sync. Ryan and I were dispatched to a boy who was reported unconscious. As we rode silently in the rescue, Ryan eyed me from the passenger's seat, noting that something was off.

"You okay, Aiden?" he asked.

"I'm fine," I lied, staring out the windshield.

"You don't look fine," he pressed. "Things not go good with Truly?"

I opened my mouth to respond but realized we arrived at the house. "We can talk later," I muttered, grateful for the excuse to drop the subject.

At the door, we were greeted by a teenage girl who seemed far too calm for someone who'd called 911.

"My stupid brother is in his room," she said flatly, turning on her heel. "Follow me."

We followed her to a bedroom, where a boy lay sprawled on the bed, snoring loudly.

"Did you really call us here because your brother's asleep?" I asked, more sharply than I intended.

"He's not sleeping!" she snapped. "I'm not an idiot. He's a diabetic and must have taken too much of his insulin without eating again. Usually, we catch it in time and feed him, but I can't wake him up this time."

Ryan stepped between us, sensing I wasn't in the right mindset.

"Okay, let's see what we can do," he said, kneeling beside the boy and pinching his trap muscle to check for a response. Nothing.

Ryan grabbed the glucometer and tested the boy's blood sugar while I pulled out supplies for an IV. The glucometer beeped, and Ryan read it. "Yup. His sugar's low, you see. 21. We'll fix him up."

"I'll start the line," I said, pulling out a blue tourniquet. But as I wrapped it around the boy's arm, my hands fumbled. The knot slipped, and the rubber snapped loose. I tried again, but it popped off once more. My gloved palms were filling with sweat, and frustration built in my chest.

"Come on," I muttered, finally managing to tie it, though it looked sloppy.

I located a vein and prepped the site with an alcohol pad, but when I inserted the needle, there was no flash. No blood. I adjusted slightly, then again, trying to find the vein, but each movement felt clumsy and off-target. I let out a groan.

"Here, let me try," Ryan said, taking over without judgment. Within seconds, he had the IV secured. He connected the line, spiked a bag of D10, and began the medicine infusion.

The boy stirred as the sugar solution worked its way through his system. Slowly, his eyes fluttered open, and confusion turned to embarrassment as he realized what had happened.

"I'm sorry," he mumbled.

"You're okay now," Ryan reassured him, finishing his vitals and assessment. "Make sure you eat something once we leave."

As Ryan filled out the report, I stood off to the side, gripping the medical bag and staring at the floor. It was the first IV I'd missed, and it didn't just feel like a mistake. It felt like a personal failure.

Once Ryan finished, we left their home, carrying our bags. I shuffled in front of him down the sidewalk.

"You look like a mindless bag dragger," Ryan said teasingly.

"What's that?" I asked, managing a weak smile.

"It's exactly what it sounds like, you see. Seriously though, what's going on?"

I sighed, getting in the rescue and putting the rig into drive. Then, slowly, I began to tell him everything. The night with Truly, her request to hide the President, and my hesitation to get involved.

"So, you don't think she is worth helping?" Ryan asked.

"I didn't say that," I said quickly. "I just don't think I can handle all that extra stuff and this job. And I want to keep my sisters safe, too."

Ryan shook his head. "You can do both. I do. You remember that night I took off right after the movies?"

I nodded.

"Well, it was Truly who text me. She needed help with one of the Children. We have been doing this alone for a while now because we never knew who to trust with the secret. I trust you, and she does too, which is no little thing, you see."

"I can be trusted," I said, defending myself. "But I'm still trying to figure out how to be a good firefighter. You're already great at it. I need to focus on that."

Ryan nodded thoughtfully. "I get it, Aiden. You may not think this is your battle, but it probably is going to become yours whether you get involved or not. And let me tell you something. Truly is a special person that deserves someone equally as special, you see. You gotta decide if that can be you or not. You got some decisions to make, but either way, I got your back."

His words lingered with me as we returned to the station.

As soon as we walked into the kitchen, Ryan clapped his hands loudly. "Well, it's over!" he announced to the crew.

They gasped dramatically, except for De La and me, who exchanged confused looks.

"No!" Mum groaned. "When did it happen?"

"Just barely," Ryan answered.

"Well, who is the winner then?" Cap questioned.

"Winner?" I asked. "Winner of what?"

Ryan grabbed a notebook, flipping through the pages. "Let's see... ah, here it is. Cap guessed 8 months. Reed, you said, and I quote, 'the very next call he runs,' so you definitely lost. I guessed, 1 year, 2 months, and 6 days. Hill, the optimist, said it would never happen. And finally, the winner of the 'How long will Aiden have on the job until he misses an IV' bet is... drum roll... Mum! With a guess of 6 months. Congratulations!"

"You guys bet on when I would miss an IV?" I asked, though no one responded.

Mum stood up and pretended to accept an imaginary trophy which Ryan handed to her. "Thank you, thank you. I'd like to thank all of you for making such terrible guesses and Aiden for finally missing an IV on this beautiful day. I'm thankful you'll all be paying for my chow next month!"

The crew burst into laughter and applause as Mum bowed dramatically.

Still somewhat confused, Ryan explained that after about two months of me being on the job, they noticed I hadn't missed an IV. So, they decided to make a bet on when I would miss my first one.

"You guys are insane," I said, shaking my head. "Sorry I ended my streak and let you down. Not you, Reed. I'm glad you were way off."

After lunch, I headed to the gym, determined to refocus. But my mind wandered as I half-heartedly lifted weights. Truly's words bounced around in my head: *Call me when you figure out who you are.* It didn't make sense. I knew who I was. I was a firefighter.

Still unable to concentrate, I gave up lifting and lay back on the bench, staring at the ceiling. I didn't move for several minutes, thinking about my dad and how he was probably the best firefighter ever. He probably never even missed a single IV.

While thinking about my dad, I saw something strange: a faint marking in the corner of the room on one of the ceiling tiles. My heart skipped a beat when I got closer. Was that what I thought it was?

I rushed to grab a ladder to inspect it better. It was! Our family scavenger hunt logo. The @ with the connected letter b. I pushed the tile up and reached around blindly, feeling each side eagerly until my fingers brushed against something. I pulled out a folded, triangular piece of paper with my name on it, written in my dad's handwriting.

"Hey buddy," the note said, as I read aloud through teary eyes. "I thought you might like one more scavenger hunt. Happy hunting, and good luck!"

This couldn't be real. I stared at the note, waiting to wake up from this dream. I carefully examined it, front and back. It sure felt real, and the note wasn't disappearing from my hand. This couldn't be some sick prank, could it? Nobody knew about our hunts though. This had to be from my dad, so I opened it.

Excitement bubbled up inside me. I hadn't done a scavenger hunt since he died. Did he really leave a special gift from the past, just for me? I read the first clue, my heart beating out of my chest. My dad's hunts were always my favorite.

Clue #1. When your clothes get dirty and smell, you don't have to walk a well. Check behind me to find where I dwell.

I smiled, answering the riddle, "The washing machine!"

I pulled the washing machine away from the wall, searching frantically until I saw it. Our symbol written on the corner of an outlet cover. After unscrewing the cover, I found the next clue.

Okay, that was an easy one! But don't get too confident. This next one will be a little trickier. You hope this cold box won't lose its power. Otherwise, things could become real sour.

I thought momentarily, springing to my feet once I figured it out. "Ha! That wasn't hard. The fridge."

I sprinted to the kitchen, smiling at Ryan when I passed him in the hall. Under a broken tile behind the fridge, I found the next clue.

Nicely done! She let down her hair from way up high, though this one is used when these must dry.

This clue made me think of Truly and her beautiful hair. I wished I could call her and tell her what I was doing. I thought about at least texting her, but decided against it. She didn't want to talk to me.

This clue was a little tricky, and I had to sit and think about it for a few minutes. The first person I thought who would let their hair down was Rapunzel. But we didn't have a tower at the station, so it couldn't be that, right?

"Wait," I said aloud. "Yes, we do! The hose tower."

I carried the ladder into the hose tower, which used to dry hoses but was no longer utilized due to modern hoses. I climbed high into the tower, looking for anything out of place or our family symbol. I found the clue inside a cinder block with a broken hole in it.

The hunt continued throughout most of the day. With each clue, memories surfaced: Dad's voice, his laugh, the way he'd always make the clues just hard enough to make you think, but not impossible. This was easily the longest hunt I had ever been on, and it went well into the night. I only stopped for dinner and running calls, though I didn't tell anyone what I was doing.

Eventually, I found what was most likely the last clue.

You're about done. All that's left is one. Go to my desk to see what you have won. Underneath, you'll find, unless you're blind, a tiny compartment where I stashed the last piece of parchment.

This was the easiest one yet. In the Before, I visited my dad at the station all the time and knew exactly which desk used to be his. I ran into the captain's office and crawled under it, searching methodically for the note. But it was nowhere to be found.

Did I remember wrong? I checked the neighboring desk and then every other desk in the station. Still nothing. Desperate, I inspected each recliner in the TV room. Then under every table and desk in our dorms. But still nothing. I had to be right with my first guess.

Long after everyone went to bed, I tore that desk apart, losing hope with each passing minute. Hours passed, and the weight of everything came crashing down on me all at once. Truly, my missed IV, the job, KID, the memory of my dad. It all felt so overwhelming. Paralyzed, I remained under the desk, hugging my knees, until the sun peered through the blinds.

Cap walked in, noticing my curious position. He knelt on one knee in front of me. "Aiden? Are you okay?"

"I can't find it, Cap. I can't find the note." Tears gushed down my face as I struggled to speak. "My dad... left me a note... it has to be in this desk... but I can't find it... I need to find it!"

Cap placed his hand on my shoulder, a sympathetic look in his eyes. "Aiden, I had those desks replaced last year. There was a roof leak that ruined them. They had to be torn out."

My head dropped as I let out an uncontrolled sob. The last letter my dad ever wrote to me was gone. Cap softly patted my shoulder and walked away, leaving me sobbing on the floor.

The devastation sunk in, quickly turning from sadness to anger. How could my dad have done something so irresponsible? He should have known that any of those clues could have been lost at any time. Why would he give me hope just to have it ripped away? If he wanted me to read something special, he should have just handed it to me before he died.

I felt a tap on my shoulder, startling me, followed by Cap's voice. "Here, Aiden."

I looked up through watery eyes, and Cap held out his hand, grasping a triangular folded piece of paper.

My eyes widened as I wiped away my tears and stood to my feet. "What? How?"

He smiled faintly. "The worker who tore out the desks found this with your name on it. They gave it to me, and I held onto it, thinking I would give it to you at a special moment in your career or something. Seems like you need it now, though."

I snatched Cap up in a hug. "Thank you, Cap!"

I left for my dorm to read my letter in privacy. My hands trembled as I carefully unfolded it, and my dad's familiar writing brought a lump to my throat as I tried to catch my breath.

Hey buddy, looks like you finished the scavenger hunt! I hope I didn't make it too hard for you or too long! I wanted the last hunt I made to be the best one you ever did. I put the first note in the weight room because that's where I would go when I was having a rough day. I would lay on the bench and stare at the ceiling. I wanted you to find this when you were in a time of need and I had to hope that you somehow did the same as me. So, hopefully, you found this note when you needed it most.

I smiled, wondering how it was possible that my dad and I were so alike and how he seemed to know me so well, even after years without him. I eagerly kept reading.

I wanted to let you know how proud I am of you. I hope I said it enough when I was around, but I have always been proud of you. The fact that you became a firefighter is great. But I want you to know that even if you didn't, I would still be just as proud. I wanted to leave you this letter to hopefully teach you one last lesson. A lesson that took me much too long to learn myself.

Ryan popped his head in. "Hey, man. Your relief is here."

I nodded and told him I'd be right there, trying to hide my expression. Once he walked out, I continued.

You are more than just a firefighter. You are Aiden Brann. Aiden is a brother, a son, a friend, a firefighter, a caregiver, a competitor, and a protector. Aiden is someone who helps those in need, who stands up for what's right, who never gives up, and who is passionate and caring. Even though being a firefighter is a tremendous calling, that is not all you are. You are so much more. It took me years to figure this out on my own. To figure out that I was a husband first and a father first. A neighbor first and a friend first. Once I learned that, my life was so much better. Your mom and I loved each other more. I was a better father, a better brother, a better neighbor, and a better friend. I was more willing to help others, and not just because it was my job. Aiden, I need you to know this! YOU... ARE... MORE... I'm sorry I can't be there to see the man you have become. But I truly know that you have become someone better than I could have ever imagined. I love you so much, buddy! Love, Dad.

I pressed the note to my chest, tears streaming freely. His words felt like a lifeline, pulling me out of the cavern of fear I was trapped in. For the first time in a long time, I was certain about what I needed to do. I would be more.

26
MISSING

"I know you have been dealt a bad hand in life, Ryan, but you have the chance to make something of yourself, you see. To help others never have to experience what you have. To create a new society that is peaceful and fair. To make this world a better place." — Kolter Taylor

By the time I finished reading my dad's letter, my relief arrived at the station. I hadn't slept the entire night, but something inside me was more awake than before. My dad's scavenger hunt had reminded me of who I was and what I stood for. And there was someone I needed to see.

But first, I needed to talk to Ryan. I waited for him in the parking lot, pacing back and forth, eager to leave. When he finally approached, I could tell he knew something was on my mind.

"Hey," Ryan said, his brow furrowed. "I didn't hear you go into your dorm last night. Everything okay?"

"Yeah," I replied. "Better than okay. I need to ask you a question, though."

"Shoot."

"Do you regret getting involved in hiding the runaway Children? If you had to do it all over again, would you?"

Ryan didn't hesitate. "Leaving the Children was the second-best decision I ever made. The first was helping others who wanted out. People can change, Aiden, but they need a chance to. Why shouldn't we help them? The more people are willing to do their part, the better off we'll all be. I'd do it all again in a heartbeat."

His words hit exactly where I needed them to. I nodded. "Thanks, Ryan, that's what I hoped you'd say. I'll call you later."

Despite my exhaustion, I drove straight to Truly's house. On the way, I rehearsed what I wanted to say to her. How I would apologize, explain my hesitation, and ask for her forgiveness. I was nervous, but couldn't let things end the way they had.

When I knocked on her door, there was no answer. I rang the doorbell and waited, but still nothing. Her car was parked in the garage, so she had to be home. Or so I thought. Maybe she was ignoring me because she was still upset.

"Truly?" I called, knocking again. Nothing but silence.

A voice behind me startled me as I stood there, contemplating what to do.

"Hello, can I help you?"

I turned to see a girl with short, curly hair standing on the sidewalk, her head tilted judgingly.

"I'm looking for Truly," I said. "Do you know her?"

"Yeah, I do," she replied. "And who are you?"

"I'm her friend, Aiden."

Recognition lit up her face. "Oh, you're Aiden? She talks about you all the time. I'm Cairn. Her neighbor."

I couldn't stop the blush that crept up my neck, nor the slight grin that tugged at my lips.

"Do you know where she is?" I asked.

Cairn's expression shifted to something more serious.

"Truly got arrested last night," she said. "She came home late, which isn't unusual for her. But as soon as she parked in her garage, a cop pulled up behind her. Next thing I knew, she was in handcuffs and being put into the back of the car."

"What?" I asked, my stomach dropping. "What did she get arrested for?"

"I was hoping you'd know," she said, narrowing her eyes. "You two weren't doing something illegal, were you?"

"No," I said quickly. "Nothing like that."

"Well, I caught the whole thing on my security cameras," she said, pulling out her phone. "Can't be too safe, even in this neighborhood. Look at that house down the street. They are always playing loud music at night. And that house over there, they..."

"I'm sorry," I interrupted. "But can I see that video?"

She handed me her phone and I watched as the footage played. Truly parked her car in the garage, got out, and waved casually at the officer who pulled up behind her. Moments later, she was turned around, cuffed, and led to the patrol car. The officer even took the time to close the garage door before returning to their vehicle.

My chest tightened as the officer's face came into view.

"Can you drop me this video?" I asked urgently.

"Sure," she said, tapping her phone to mine.

Once the video was on my phone, I sprinted toward my car, nearly bumping into Cairn.

"Sorry! I gotta go!" I yelled.

"Nice meeting you!" she called after me. "Follow the speed limit!"

I called Ryan as I sped toward his house, ignoring the speed limit.

"Ryan, I'm coming over. I'll explain when I get there."

He accepted my strange request without hesitation. When I arrived, I burst into the living room, pacing back and forth, unable to sit still. Ryan watched me with growing concern.

"What's going on?" he asked.

"Look at this and tell me I'm hallucinating," I said, handing him my phone.

He sat on the couch and hit play. "Is this Truly's house?"

"Just keep watching," I said.

His eyes widened as the footage continued. "Wait... is she getting arrested? What did she do?"

"Keep watching."

Ryan leaned in, squinting at the screen. When the officer's face came into focus, he froze.

"Is that... Kaylyn?"

I nodded, my stomach twisting again. "I didn't want to believe it."

"She wouldn't do this," Ryan said, jumping to his feet and shaking his head. "There has to be an explanation. Truly hasn't done anything illegal, right?"

"I don't think so," I said. "Unless you count going up on the wall."

Ryan rubbed his temples, his mind racing as he took over the nervous pacing. "If that's it, why didn't they arrest you, too? Something has to be up. Maybe that isn't Kaylyn. Maybe she just looks like her."

"Maybe they didn't know I was there. Or maybe... this isn't about the wall at all."

We decided the only way to get answers was to try and find Truly at the jail. As we drove downtown, desperate for answers, we attempted to call Kaylyn but got no response. Truly's phone went straight to voicemail.

We walked into the front office of the jail, and a chill hit my spine. I'd never been to one before. The boy at the check-in desk looked surprised to see us, his feet propped on the counter as he played on his phone.

"We're here to see an inmate," I said.

He raised an eyebrow. "There's only one inmate here right now, and he's getting released in less than an hour."

"What about Truly Taylor?" I asked. "She would've been brought in recently."

He shook his head and leaned back into his chair. "Nope. Not possible. No one's been brought in for over a week."

"Are you sure?" Ryan asked.

"Of course I'm sure," the boy said. "It's my job to know who comes in and out of here, and there is no Truly Taylor."

My heart sank. If she wasn't here, where was she?

As if to make things worse, the boy groaned and tossed his phone aside. "Cell service is out again."

Ryan and I checked our phones. No signal. The boy turned on the TV as we stood back, discussing our options, but the TV screen just cycled through flashing red, green, and yellow colors.

Ryan continued flinging ideas, but I stared at the TV, mesmerized at the flashing colors. There was something oddly familiar about it. Then, it clicked.

"Ryan!" I said, pulling him outside. "I've seen those color patterns before."

"On the TV?" he asked. "Doesn't that mean it's just broken?"

"I don't think so. I think someone is doing it, and I think I know who it is. We need to get to the Hotel."

We drove to the Hotel as I reminded Ryan about Chris Goodson, the computer wizard whose sister died in the fiery car crash months ago. He had messed with the jumbotron at the football game and made the screen do precisely what the TVs were doing now. I didn't see the correlation to our dilemma with Truly, but I couldn't shake the feeling that this needed further investigation.

Inside the Hotel, the old casino floor had been cleared out of slot machines, and transformed into an open recreational area. Kids played catch in one corner while others lounged in another.

At the reception desk, a redheaded boy greeted us.

"Hello, I'm Tobias. How may I assist you?"

"We are looking for Chris Goodson," I said. "Can you tell us where he is?"

Tobias frowned. "Goodson? No, we don't have a Goodson here. Are you sure you have the right name?"

"Yes, his name is Chris," I insisted. "His sister, Jennifer Goodson, died in a car crash a while back, and he was brought here."

The boy shook his head. "I remember that car crash. She was a Senator. Just terrible. But I'm certain we didn't have her brother check in. We don't get many checking in anymore. Most everyone here has been here for a bit."

Confusion and frustration churned inside me.

"What is happening?" I muttered to Ryan as we walked away. "I've talked to Chris since he's been here. He even told me about the Hotel."

Ryan sighed heavily. "I don't know. But you're right. Something weird is going on. I mean, Kaylyn brought him here. How could they not know him?"

Suddenly, the pieces fell into place.

"It's Kaylyn," I said.

"What?" Ryan asked, startled. "What about Kaylyn?"

"She is working for the Children!" I said. "Think about it. She's been at almost every attack. The movie theater, the banquet, and she was first at the warehouse fire with the threatening message. She took Truly home the other day and knows where she lives. Now she's taken her."

"No way. Why would she be going out with me?" Ryan asked. "If she figured out who Truly was, she had to have known who I was, right?"

"Maybe, maybe not. I don't know. But if they found Truly, they probably have the President too."

"What do we do?" Ryan asked. "If they have the President, things could get real bad."

I clenched my fists, determination replacing fear. "Whatever they are planning, it's gonna be big, and we need to stop them. Whatever it takes."

27

THE FOSTER HOME

"I can't believe how good you are with computers, Chris, especially since me and your mom know nothing about them. You will do some really cool things with these someday."
— Christian Goodson

R yan and I returned to my house to try to form a plan with my sisters and Kim. As I suspected, no one's cell phones or TVs were working, nor were our debit cards or the internet. After a long time contemplating how to find Truly and the President, we dozed off on the couch, with the TV still flashing its patterns of colors.

The TV turned to static, giving off a low hum. We were startled awake by the sudden sound of a voice in the living room with us. KID! His masked face was stark white against the dark background in the center of the TV screen.

"Good morning, Las Vegas," KID began. "I couldn't think of a more perfect day to speak with all of you. The day we celebrate our independence. July 4th!"

Today was the 4th, and we celebrated it as we did in the Before. However, our definition of independence was slightly different now.

"You may be wondering why I am addressing you," KID continued. "You may be wondering why your cell phones, internet, TVs, and debit cards have not worked for the last day. Let me assure you. This is how it is going to stay! I have no demands. I have no ransom. There is nothing you have that I want. Everything I want is right here."

KID stepped to the side to reveal President Keres tied to a chair behind him in the center of a room. She squirmed, attempting to say something, but the ropes around her wrists and ankles and the gag in her mouth kept her bound and helpless.

He went on to explain how there was nothing we could do to stop him and to enjoy our last day in our supposed utopia. The video ended with him stating he would address us again later today to commence the festivities. The video then started over and played on a loop.

No matter which channel we changed to, he was there, somehow becoming more sinister with each channel change. We put it on mute and allowed it to play in the background.

"Kim, do you have any ideas?" I asked.

Kim shook her head. "I don't know. We need to find out where he is and what he plans to do."

"How do we do that?" Ally asked. "We have no idea where to even start."

The hopelessness in her voice mirrored the knots in my stomach. I stared at the floor, guilt gnawing at me. If I'd supported Truly when she asked for help, maybe we wouldn't be in this mess. It was my fault the President had been taken.

Ryan clapped his hands suddenly. "Well, I need something to eat," he said. "Can't think on an empty stomach, you see."

"I do see," Aubrey said, standing up with a smile. "I'll help you. The rest of you want something?"

The rest of us stayed in the living room, the muted broadcast looping endlessly in the background. My thoughts spiraled, each one darker than the last. What if we were too late? What if I never saw Truly again?

When Aubrey and Ryan returned with plates of pancakes, the smell of food did little to break my despair. Each person filled their plate while I remained motionless, staring blankly into the void.

"You too, Aiden," Aubrey said, nudging me with a plate.

I took it reluctantly, forcing myself to eat. I barely tasted the food. My mind was still filled with the worst possible scenarios.

Ryan was halfway through his plate when he froze, his fork in his mouth. He stood slowly, pushing his plate to the side and walking toward the TV, wide-eyed.

"I know where they are!" he shouted, facing us.

"What?" I asked, startled. "How?"

He turned back to the screen. "That room! The wallpaper, the carpet, the chair. I've been there before. That's my old foster house!"

The urgency in Ryan's voice lit a fire under all of us.

"We have to go now," I said, already walking toward the door.

"Shouldn't we call the police?" Ally asked.

"No," Ryan said firmly. "We don't know who we can trust anymore. What if someone tips Kaleb off?"

Aubrey nodded. "He's right. It's too risky."

"But we'll need backup," Kim said. "We can't go in there alone."

Ryan's face brightened. "What about the crew? I know where they all live. We can go pick them up."

With no other options, we split up and drove to gather everyone. None of our crew hesitated to join us. They'd seen firsthand what KID and the Children were capable of, and getting them on board didn't take much convincing.

With a full caravan, we headed to Ryan's foster house, parking a few blocks away. The area was run down, and few people, if any, lived in it. Ryan and I volunteered to scope out the house and report back.

The house was a pale, battered green, the kind of place that seemed forgotten by time. The roof had missing shingles, and the windows were cracked, some lined with aluminum foil and cardboard.

Ryan stared at it for a long moment, his jaw tight. "It doesn't look much different than when I lived here," he whispered.

Ryan and I crept closer, using the abandoned houses as cover as we inched forward, our breaths shallow and quiet.

We reached some bushes near the front of the house and peered into the window. The dim light inside revealed a grimy living room, but no sign of anyone existed.

As we debated our next move, the front door creaked open. We ducked lower, holding our breath as KID stepped out, flanked by two of his henchmen.

They escorted a blindfolded girl to a car parked on the street. My heart raced when I realized it was President Keres. She struggled against their grip, but they shoved her into the back seat.

"In the next few hours," KID said, speaking to someone standing in the doorway, "everything is going to change. They are all going to know first-hand what we went through. Make sure you keep our prisoners locked up. And if that Australian girl keeps running her mouth, shut her up. Once this is over, we won't need any of them anymore."

He slammed the car door, got in, and drove off with his goons. I clenched my fists, rage boiling inside my chest. Truly was still inside, and KID was threatening her. We rushed back to the crew, relaying what we'd seen.

"Truly's in there," I said, my voice trembling. "We have to get her out now. They could kill her any second."

"We need a plan," Cap said. "If we just rush in without thinking, we'll get ourselves and her killed."

Reed pounded his fists together. "Just let Reed in. I'll take 'em all out!"

"Here's how we'll do it," Cap said, ignoring Reed's bravado. "Ally and Kim, you'll stay outside as lookouts. If anyone shows up, alert us. Reed, De La, and I will handle any guards we find. Aiden, Ryan, and Aubrey, you come in after us and search for the prisoners. Got it?"

We each gave a determined nod, ready to put everything on the line.

We snuck to the front door, and Ryan constantly needed to hold me back as we did. The door was locked, as expected.

Adult firefighters like my dad kicked doors in all the time. We did not use that practice. We were simply too little. Even Reed didn't kick down doors, so we weren't sure how to gain access without our forcible entry tools.

"Maybe we can use the windows," Cap suggested. "But we won't be able to get in fast."

The crew whispered ideas back and forth, none of which were ideal. I couldn't take it anymore. I needed to get inside.

"Move," I said, pushing the crew out of the way of the door.

Before anyone could stop me, I raised my foot and kicked the door with all my strength. Fueled by the pure need to save Truly, the kick was powerful enough to splinter the frame, and the door flew open.

"Let's go!" I shouted, charging inside.

Cap shot me a glance that could only be described as pride, as he and Reed barreled past me. The first guard, a teenager with a baseball bat, stood in our way. Reed charged him like a linebacker chasing down a quarterback. His massive arms wrapped around the boy, ignoring the boy's weak attempt at a bat swing, and he lifted him off his feet before slamming him hard into the ground.

Another Children member ran up from the basement, wielding a machete. He swung at De La, who dodged it gracefully while Cap grabbed the boy from behind. Together, they disarmed him and pinned him face down.

"Go find Truly," Cap yelled. "We've got this."

Ryan, Aubrey, and I raced downstairs into the dimly lit basement. A narrow hallway stretched before us, lined with doors on either side. I opened the first door and found two terrified girls huddled in the corner. One I recognized as the owner of Bob the dog, who was kidnapped in front of me.

"I'll stay with them," Aubrey said. "Check the rest of the rooms."

The next two rooms were empty. My heart beat faster as I opened each one until I opened the last door on the right, and my heart stopped.

"I told you. I'm not telling you where anyone is," Truly yelled. "But you can give it a go!"

"Truly?" I called, my eyes in disbelief.

She spun around, her eyes wide with shock and immediately filling with tears.

"Aiden?"

I ran to her, pulling her into my arms. "I'm so sorry," I whispered. "I should have been there, helping you. Can you forgive me? I'm here now!"

Though I asked for forgiveness, I didn't feel like I deserved it.

She pulled back just enough to smile at me. "I'm just glad you're here now."

Before I could say more, Ryan called from across the hall. "Aiden, you need to see this."

We followed him into another room filled with computers and monitors. In the center, chained to a chair, was Chris.

"They tricked me," he said, tears streaming down his face. "I didn't mean for any of this to happen."

"What did you do?" I asked as I began to free him. "Why aren't you at the Hotel?"

"I never went to the Hotel. Kaylyn took me to the Children's hideout. She told me she thought what I could do with computers was cool. They were so nice to me, let me practice all kinds of hacking stuff, and brought me everything I needed to try harder and harder hacks. I thought they were my friends."

Released from the chains, he stood up, and covered his face with his hands.

"They had me start practicing shutting down things. Cell phones, TVs, everything. They always had me turn it back on, so I didn't think it was doing any harm. I tried to leave once I found out what they were planning, but they tied me up and threatened to kill me if I didn't do what they said. I'm sorry, Aiden."

I placed my hands on both his shoulders. "It's not your fault, Chris. Do you know what they are planning next? Do you know where they are taking the President?"

"I don't know where they're taking her, but I do know what they're planning, and it will be apocalyptic for us."

"Are you able to turn everything back on?"

He nodded.

"Okay," I said. "Do it, and let's get out of here."

28

KID

"Before we are... gone. There is something I need to tell you. When I was younger, I got pregnant, but I wasn't ready for a kid yet. I was alone and tried to raise him, but I couldn't do it. So, I took him to a fire station and dropped him off. I only left a note with his name. Kaleb... What I'm trying to tell you, Kaylyn, is that you have a brother somewhere out there. Maybe you can find him." — Kristie Keller

W e left the foster house with Truly, Chris, and the other girls. The reunion between the girl we'd saved from the fire and her dog, Bob, was the one bright spot in a bleak situation. She clung to him like he was her family, tears of joy streaming down her face. At that moment, it reminded me why we were doing this. Why we needed to fight.

After sending the two girls somewhere safe, we gathered around the kitchen table at my house. Chris detailed KID's plan.

"He's going to burn down every major production facility in the city," Chris explained, desperation in his voice. "Anything we need to survive. The warehouses, factories, food processing plants, farm equipment, everything."

"If he does that," Kim said, "we won't be able to recover. We wouldn't know how to rebuild those."

"And President Keres?" Ryan asked. "Why does he need her for that?"

Chris swallowed hard. "He's going to make her the symbol of our collapse. He plans on... having her go down with the first building. He wanted to broadcast it, but he won't be able to do that without me. I doubt that will stop him though."

Cap leaned back, contemplating the news. "He is going to have a tough time burning those buildings down. They have amazing sprinkler protection."

Chris shook his head. "He knows that. He's planned for it. I heard him say he had something called a Knock key. Gets him into all the buildings. Says he knows how to shut the sprinklers off."

Cap's face darkened. "A Knox key?"

Chris nodded. "Yeah, that's it."

The room fell silent. The scale of KID's plan was staggering. If he did have a Knox key, he could easily get into any commercial building and could shut down the sprinklers. We would have a hard time controlling the fires in such giant buildings with so much material inside.

Fortunately, Chris restored the city's communication system, and we could make phone calls again. Cap wasted no time calling the Chief and briefing him on the situation.

"We need every single engine and truck available," Cap said firmly. "Send them to the production district and cover as many buildings as possible."

The Chief didn't argue, and within minutes, crews were mobilizing. There were so many potential sites, however, that we knew we couldn't possibly cover them all.

"Do you know what building he would go to, Chris?" I asked, hopeful.

Chris lowered his head. "No. He never said which one he would start with. If we had his phone number, I bet I could track it. It's pretty simple since all our comms, internet, radios, and pretty much everything else is on a closed grid now. Not like the Before."

That was something I was not aware of, and I wasn't sure if I fully understood it, but it didn't matter right now.

"I have Kaylyn's number," Ryan said. "Do you think she would be with him?"

"It's worth a shot," Mum answered.

With no time to waste, Chris got to work. Meanwhile, our crew raced across town to retrieve our gear and a reserve engine.

As we drove toward the warehouses, Cap spoke up, his voice strong but laced with emotion.

"No matter what happens, I want you all to know how proud I am of all of you. You're the best crew I could ask for, and it's been an honor to be your captain. I know Hill is going to be watching out for us." He paused, then slammed his fist on the dash. "Now, let's go stop this guy!"

We cheered in agreement, ready to take on the world next to our brothers and sisters.

"Captain Jefferson," Chris said over the radio. "I've got a location. The corner of Ann and Sloan. That's where you'll find Kaylyn."

Mum pushed the engine as fast as it could go, weaving through the quiet streets. For once, she didn't scream at traffic, her focus unshakable.

While looking out the window, my mind began to wander, and thoughts of inadequacy flooded my brain. This seemed much too important for someone as ordinary as me. Was I up to the task? I still had so much to learn. This would be a lot for even an experienced firefighter, maybe even for my dad. I clasped my wristband, thinking of my dad and what he would do. A wave of understanding rushed over me and a voice of reason sounded in my head, in my dad's voice.

I didn't need to be someone special. I just needed to be me.

Ryan tapped me on the knee, noticing my new resolve.

"We got this, Aiden. We just have to stick together."

I nodded, determined, as we took our last turn, arriving at the street Chris sent us to. We located a colossal warehouse and drove around it, looking for an opening. This was one of the storage buildings stocked full of various items that had been stored during the Preparation.

That's when we found, to our horror, a loading dock roll-up door open, with thick smoke billowing out the top of it.

"All right, guys," Cap said. "This is it, so listen up. Mitsuya, Brann, Reed. I need two 2 ½'s inside that building. Mum. Hydrant's right behind us. De La, you get to the fire control room and get those sprinklers back on. Without them, we got no chance. Everyone, move fast and stay safe!"

Ryan and I worked together to pull a line, and Cap helped Reed grab his. These lines were much bigger than the ones we typically used and were difficult for us small kids to control because they put out so much water, causing a lot of pressure at the nozzle. It usually took three or even four of us working together to handle one of these hose lines.

The door to the warehouse was massive, and inside was an ominous void of darkness and smoke. The smoke hung high toward the ceiling, leaving a layer of clear air below. If the President was in here, she could still be alive.

After we masked up, I noticed Cap frozen, his eyes fixed on the darkness inside. He held the same empty look he had at our last fire. I knew if we were to succeed, we needed everyone, especially Cap.

I placed my hand on his shoulder. He blinked, coming out of the daze, and locked eyes with me. I nodded, telling him we trusted him. Light returned to his eyes, and he looked back inside, now focused and ready.

"All right, boys!" Cap said, his voice commanding. "Let's go!"

We dragged the dry hoses inside with great effort for a few hundred feet, until we approached the roaring fire. Towering shelves stacked high created a spectacular inferno, lighting the entire room orange. Smoke was banking down farther to the floor. We had little time remaining.

"You guys go to the left," Cap commanded. "Reed and I will handle the right."

Cap keyed up his radio. "Fisk, send the water!"

After a few seconds, our hose lines pressurized, turning hard as a rock and significantly increasing their weight.

I aimed the hose, and Ryan stood behind, bracing me as the pressurized stream shot out, pushing us backward until we regained our footing. The heavy stream slammed into the flames. The intense heat radiated through our gear, but we held our ground, gripping the hose with all our strength.

Though we sprayed copious amounts of water, the fire was already so large that it provided little effect and seemed to be growing faster than we could extinguish it. The flames pushed forward, creeping closer and closer, the heat becoming nearly unbearable.

"De La!" Cap shouted into his radio. "We need those sprinklers now!"

"Almost there!" De La replied.

A minute later, water cascaded from above like rain from heaven, pouring onto us and the flames, slowing its progression. Working in tandem, we began making a difference, pushing forward now with confidence. The black smoke turned to grey, cooling our environment.

Then I heard it. A voice cutting through the chaos. "Help! Somebody, help me!"

"Did you hear that?" I yelled to Ryan.

Ryan looked toward the direction of the voice. "Yeah. Someone's in here!"

We motioned to Cap and he left Reed with his hose line and ran to grab ours. "You two go!" he said. "Reed and I will handle the fire."

There was no time to admire their strength in spraying these lines alone, though Reed used sheer brawn, and Cap used his brain and hooked the handle of the hose onto a bolted down desk to relieve the brunt of the weight.

Ryan and I took off sprinting toward the sound, weaving through the maze of unburned shelves. The voice grew louder, desperate. "Please! Anybody!"

We turned a corner and found President Keres tied to a chair, her face streaked with soot.

"We've got you," Ryan said, working to untie her.

"I'm so happy to see you guys!" she exclaimed. "That psycho KID just left. He might still be close."

With the air clear, we removed our masks, helped her to her feet, and guided her back through the warehouse. The sprinklers rained down on us, turning the floor into a shallow lake.

We nearly returned to where we had left Cap and Reed, when two figures stepped into our path.

KID and Kaylyn.

"You guys can't seem to stay out of my way!" KID snarled, his eyes burning with hatred. "Ryan, you abandoned me years ago and now refuse to leave me alone."

"Kaleb," Ryan said. "Why are you doing this? These buildings are how we survive! If you destroy them, we lose everything. You lose everything, too, you see. All of us will be left with nothing."

KID grinned from the corner of his mouth. "You've always been slow, Ryan. That's exactly what I want. It's what you should want too!"

Ryan and I glanced at each other, confused. Who could possibly want this?

KID stepped closer. "When we had no parents, we were forced to suffer. No one cared about us. No one loved us. Now, no one has parents, and they get to live even better than before? No! It's not right! They deserve to suffer like we suffered! They should know what it's like to be hungry, to sleep in the heat, to feel alone!"

Ryan stepped forward, water dripping off his head. "None of us have to be alone anymore, Kaleb. We can all get through this together."

"No!" KID screamed, desperation and heat seething in his voice. "It's not fair! But I'm going to change that. You think because you shut off my broadcast, you stopped me? Streaming the burning of this building and the President was just for entertainment. It doesn't really matter. And once I give the signal to the Children, your precious firework celebration will be drowned out by your future going up in flames. Then everyone will have to live like we did. Fighting for survival."

"We won't let that happen!" I yelled, stepping next to Ryan. "You aren't getting out of here!"

"Kaylyn," Ryan pleaded, his voice growing softer. "Why are you doing this? Why are you helping him? This isn't you."

She shook her head. "I didn't want you to get involved, Ryan."

"This can't be what you want. You're a police officer. You're supposed to help people."

Kaylyn looked away. "That doesn't matter anymore. It doesn't matter what I want."

"It doesn't matter?" Ryan questioned. "Do we not matter? Do I not matter?"

Kaylyn hesitated, avoiding eye contact with Ryan now. "I didn't know who you were when I first met you," she said. "I really did like you."

"You don't have to follow him, you see!" Ryan pleaded. "Just leave with me now. We can fix this."

She looked back up, tears visible in her eyes, even through the downpour of water. "I can't leave him, Ryan. He's my brother. He's family... I'm supposed to help my family."

KID pushed her back behind him with one arm. "That's enough of that. We have a mission to accomplish, and you two are standing in my way."

He pulled out a handgun and aimed it at Ryan and me. We froze. Kaylyn looked at KID and then back at us, panicked.

"You two need to go," KID said. "I'm sick of you getting in my way. Goodbye, Ryan."

"Kaleb, stop!" Kaylyn cried, stepping between us. "You said you wouldn't hurt them. Let's just leave. Please."

"Get out of my way, Kaylyn!" KID shouted.

She stood her ground. "Please listen to me. I'm your sister. I've done everything you've asked. And now I'm asking you not to hurt them."

Kaleb hesitated, slightly lowering his gun for a moment. Then rage rushed back into his eyes. "You think just because we were born by the same woman, that makes you my sister? The same woman who didn't love me enough to keep me, but had no problem keeping her precious little girl?" Kaleb's voice began to break. "The same woman who abandoned me at a fire station and never looked for me again, even when I rotted in a foster home?"

"I didn't know, Kaleb," Kaylyn said. "I would have found you earlier if I knew you were out there suffering."

"You're not my sister!" he shouted. "You're just some delusional girl who is trying to make herself feel better by helping me. I'm not stupid. But you've served your purpose, and now you're just a problem! But I can fix that."

Bang!

The gunshot echoed through the warehouse. The world around us, even the raining water, seemed to pause as Kaylyn crumpled to the ground.

"Kaylyn!" Ryan screamed, dropping to her side. The pooling water changed to red as he cradled her head.

KID stared blankly at what he'd done, lowering his gun for a moment. It was obvious, despite all his threats, he'd never taken a life before.

"This is all your fault!" KID said to Ryan, with the same darkness in his eyes, as well as tears. "You should have never left! You promised you would never leave me!"

Ryan slowly looked up, fire in his eyes. He charged at Kaleb, screaming as he did. Kaleb raised his gun, but never fired, and was tackled hard to the ground. I followed suit, pouncing on him as Ryan threw wild punches.

Kaleb was quick and strong. He hit Ryan with the butt of the gun, knocking him off. I got in a few good swings, but took an elbow to the gut, causing me to lose my breath. Kaleb bounced back to his feet.

"You should have never left, Ryan!" he said in desperation. "You promised!"

"I'm sorry, Kaleb," Ryan said. "I should have brought you with me. But you've gone too far now. I don't know you anymore!"

KID raised his gun, pointing it directly at Ryan. "Since that's how you feel. Goodbye, Ryan."

I ran to Ryan, praying I wouldn't have to see my best friend die right in front of me. But I was too far away; I would never make it in time.

As KID pulled the trigger, the sound of powerful, rushing water filled the warehouse—then a strong blast of water slammed into KID, knocking the gun from his hand

and sending him crashing violently into the wall. Cap stood at the nozzle, blasting him with gallons of water as Reed sprinted after him and pinned him to the ground, locking him into a painful-looking hold. Once Reed had someone locked up, there was no escaping.

"It's not fair!" KID pleaded. "It's not fair. Why did I have to suffer? Now they'll never understand. They'll never understand what we went through."

With KID subdued, Ryan raced back to Kaylyn, placing his hand gently on her face. "Kaylyn. Come on, wake up Kaylyn. I got you."

The bullet wound in her chest bled profusely. I placed my hands on top of the puncture, trying to stop the bleeding—though deep down, I knew that it was in vain.

With barely enough strength to lift her head, Kaylyn looked sorrowfully into Ryan's eyes. "I'm sorry, Ryan. I wanted to help... my brother. I felt so bad when I found out about him... I felt... like I owed him. I just wanted to be... a good sister. I'm sorry I hurt you. Please... forgive me. I really did like you."

Ryan wept, pulling her closer. "Don't worry about that, Kaylyn. We are going to get you some help. You're going to be fine. We're going to be fine."

Kaylyn managed a smile. "Go easy on... the Children. They're just... scared kids." She coughed, blood pooling in her mouth now. "Ryan, I... I..."

Kaylyn's head fell back. Her body limp as she released one last breath.

"No!" Ryan cried, desperately wrapping her in his arms. "No, Kaylyn, please come back. Don't go. Aiden, help me! Please."

It was no use. I stood back helplessly and watched my devastated friend beg and plead as sprinklers continued to rain upon us, the red-tinted water spreading around us.

Ryan looked at me, broken. "I should have known she was in trouble. I should have saved her. This is my fault. I couldn't save either of them."

29

EPILOGUE

That same night—the night we were supposed to celebrate our day of independence—the mood back at home with Ryan and Truly was solemn and grim. Though Aubrey and Ally were relieved we were okay and told us we saved the city, it didn't feel like we won.

Ryan stood with red eyes. "I think I just want to be alone tonight."

Though we protested and asked him to stay, he insisted and left. As we sat silently on the couch, a text came through to all our phones, asking us to tune in to a statement from President Keres. We turned on the TV to see the President standing in front of a podium, looking worn down and wearing a backward hat.

"Fellow citizens of Las Vegas," she began. "I am pleased to report that KID is in custody and is no longer a threat to our beautiful valley. Though he held me captive, I was saved by a small crew of heroic firefighters. Captain Roger Jefferson, Wendy Fisk, Marion Reed, Adrian De La Cruz,

Ryan Mitsuya, and Aiden Brann courageously put their lives in danger to save me and the rest of us from certain destruction. I will be forever grateful for them."

My sisters looked at me like proud moms. I did my best to avoid eye contact with them and continued watching the address. It was hard to feel heroic when we'd lost Kaylyn.

"This day is not without loss, however. Officer Kaylyn Keller died today, putting her life on the line to save her friends. A truly selfless sacrifice that should never be forgotten. Due to these traumatic events," she continued, "you may feel the need to cancel our Independence Day festivities. But we have more reason to celebrate now than ever. Go out! Enjoy yourselves. Spend time with your family and friends and appreciate what we all have here. Our independence remains intact! Happy 4th of July and remember, this valley is our home. Together we live. Together we thrive!"

The threat of KID and the Children was over. No other fires were started. KID, now in custody, never gave the signal.

Too exhausted and heartbroken to enjoy the festivities, Truly and I decided to sit atop the roof to watch the fireworks coming from the strip. As the show lit up the sky, Truly leaned her head on my shoulder, her hand in mine. For the first time in a long time, the world felt peaceful.

Over the next few days, with the help of Chris and other Children who had defected, those behind the attacks were located and placed in prison, along with KID.

Most of the Children only remained incarcerated for a few weeks. After serving some time, they were released on the condition they would find jobs, become functioning members of society, and be placed on probation. Kaylyn was right; they'd been scared to cross KID and felt they had no choice but to follow his orders.

As for KID, he would remain imprisoned indefinitely. Whether he was remorseful or not, we may never know. KID hadn't spoken a word since his capture. I personally believed the realization that he'd killed his only sister rocked him to his core. But since he committed the first and only murder in the After and attempted to destroy the city, he was someone we would not have to worry about for a long time. Life in the After was wonderful again, especially since Truly was a part of mine now.

A few weeks after all the chaotic events, Truly convinced me to take her back to the wall. We sat in the same spot as the sun dipped behind the mountains, painting the sky in fiery hues. Silently, we watched, holding each other and soaking in the moment.

"I never properly thanked you for saving me," she said. "Your parents would be proud of the person you have become."

I shook my head, still disappointed in myself. "I should have never let you get taken in the first place."

She turned, locking eyes with me. "Just promise to never let me go again."

Before I could respond, she leaned closer, stopping a few inches from my lips. I became lost in her emerald eyes, my heart racing. She wanted me to kiss her, right?

She remained motionless, smiling, squeezing my hand tighter. That had to be the signal. I leaned in until her warm lips pressed against mine. A shockwave coursed through me. My first real kiss and she wasn't pulling away or screaming in terror! She kissed me back, and it couldn't have been more perfect. For a moment, everything but us faded away.

On the drive home in the dark, we arrived on the outskirts of the residential areas, where unoccupied homes were spread out on larger properties.

Truly recounted what happened to her during her time of captivity, which she previously wasn't ready to share. I watched and listened to her intently as she described her experience.

This girl was impressive. Strong, capable and determined. She never backed down and always did what was right. I had so much to learn from her and didn't deserve her.

She paused, then changed the subject. "I've wanted to tell you something, Aiden. Something that I've never told anyone before."

"What is it?"

I watched her as she seemed to muster up the strength to continue.

"It's about my family," she said. "I sometimes dream about leaving because..."

She suddenly screamed, pointing at the road ahead. "Look out!"

I slammed on the brakes, only seeing the blur of something hitting the windshield, sending cracks spidering across the glass as the object went up and over the car.

"What was that?" I asked, out of breath.

Truly's voice trembled. "I don't know. An animal, maybe."

"That was a big animal. It wasn't a kid, was it?"

After grabbing a flashlight from the center console, I quickly exited the car and ran toward the unknown figure, praying it was a coyote, though I knew better. Truly followed cautiously behind.

It was curled up in a ball, motionless in the middle of the street. My heart stopped as my worst fears came true. This was no animal. A small amount of blood pooled next to it, and I knelt to begin my assessment. Truly stood next to me, nearly frozen from shock.

I rolled the motionless body onto its back, immediately jumping back and falling to the ground. Slowly, I shined the flashlight on its face, and could see it breathing, but unconscious.

Truly whispered, disbelief in her voice. "Is that..."

"I think so," I answered. "It's... an adult."

Acknowledgements

Thank you so much for reading my story. If you enjoyed it as much as I hoped you would, would you please take a moment to leave a review on Amazon or Goodreads. It helps more than you know. Thanks again!

I would like to thank my editor, Salima Alikhan, for her enthusiasm and dedication to helping my story come to life. You were so helpful throughout the entire process.

I also want to thank my cover designer, Felix Tindall, for creating something very special to me.

Finally, I want to thank my family. They supported and guided me through the very rough first drafts. My smokin' hot wife, Jelissa, thank you for supporting me during this new adventure of mine. I really like you! My kids for reading and giving me their feedback. My sisters and mom for constantly reading, critiquing and promoting.

And I especially want to thank my dad, who was always there, just as excited as I was to create this story. Thank you for always being willing to let me bounce ideas off you. I've had a blast navigating this journey with you and look forward to continuing to do so.

About the Author

Laric Tolleson is a firefighter with Las Vegas Fire & Rescue, where he has served since 2014 and was promoted to Captain in 2023. Over the years, he has witnessed the traumatic, the heroic, and the unexpectedly funny moments that come with the job—experiences that have deeply shaped the stories he tells.

He grew up in the tiny town of Beatty, Nevada, 100 miles north of Las Vegas, before eventually starting his career in Las Vegas. He married a gorgeous girl in 2009 who loves traveling and adventuring with him and is now the proud father of four children—two boys and two girls—who continually inspire him.

In his writing, Laric hopes to show both kids and adults that young people are often far more capable than we sometimes give them credit for. At the same time, he seeks to share pieces of the real world he's lived in as a firefighter, honoring both its weight and its humor.

The Fire We Inherit is his debut novel.

Follow Me For More

If you enjoyed this story, please follow me for more from
the "We Inherit" series.
The fire isn't extinguished yet!.

Laric Tolleson